POPULAR PUBLICATIONS — FACSIMILE EDITIONS

Dime Detective Magazine #12 (October 1932)

Dime Detective magazine was the flagship detective pulp in the Popular Publications stable, running for almost 300 issues over twenty years. The October 1932 issue contains stories by Carroll John Daly, J. Allan Dunn, and Frederick Nebel, and includes installments in the Cardigan and Vee Brown series.

Authors:

Carroll John Daly, Frederick Nebel,

J. Allan Dunn, John Lawrence

Illustrators:

William Reusswig, John Fleming Gould

1

EVERY STORY COMPLETE

EVERY STORY NEW

Vol. 3   CONTENTS for OCTOBER, 1932   No. 4

Watch for the November Issue   On the Newsstands October 20th

Published every month by Popular Publications, Inc., 2256 Grove Street, Chicago Illinois. Editorial and executive offices 205 East Forty-second Street, New York City. Harry Steeger, President and Secretary, Harold S. Goldsmith, Vice President and Treasurer. Entered as second class matter Feb. 26, 1932, at the Post Office at Chicago, Ill., under the Act of March 3, 1879. Title registration pending at U. S. Patent Office. Copyrited 1932 by Popular Publications, Inc. Single copy price 10c. Yearly subscriptions in U. S. A. $1.00. For advertising rates address Sam J. Perry, 205 E. 42nd St., New York, N. Y. When submitting manuscripts, kindly enclose sufficient postage for their return if found unavailable. The publishers cannot accept responsibility for return of unsolicited manuscripts, although all care will be exercised in handling them.

Larry Campbell
student of
GEORGE F. JOWETT
from drawing by
PRYOR

>>> I WILL ADD 3 INCHES TO YOUR CHEST

...or it won't cost you one cent!" SIGNED: GEORGE F. JOWETT

YES SIR! Three inches of muscle added to your chest and at least one inch to your biceps, or it won't cost you a penny. I know what I am talking about ... I wouldn't dare make this startling guarantee if I wasn't sure I could do it.

All I want is a chance to prove it! Those skinny fellows that are discouraged are the men I want to work with. I'll build a strong man's chest for them and do it quickly. And I don't mean cream puff muscles either—you will get real, genuine, invincible muscles that will make your men friends respect you and women admire you.

For the past ten years it has been my sole purpose in life to develop he-men and give them the strong, husky bodies that nature meant them to have. When I look over my records I find that in a great majority of cases I have added MORE than THREE INCHES to the chests of my pupils, so I now make it a part of my unqualified guarantee! Test my course —if it does not do all I say—it won't cost you one penny! *You are the judge!*

Complete Book on Chest Building

25c

In one inexpensive book you can get a complete course that will show you how to develop a Herculean chest. The greatest analysis of vital, vigorous chest development ever written—complete with illustrations.

3

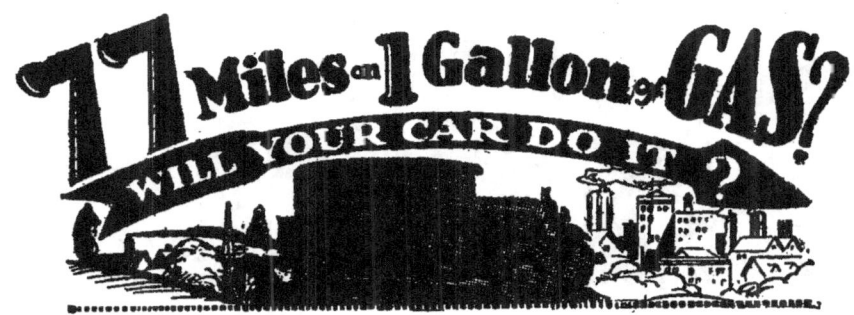

The head engineer of a great automobile research laboratory said in a recent public statement that it is possible to get 450 miles from one gallon of gas IF we can find some way to get ALL of the power from the gas!

Just imagine getting 77 miles from one gallon with a new gas saver like reported by G. W. Williams of Okla. Even one-half of that is more than most of us are getting.

Here Is Good News for Auto Owners Everywhere

An Illinois Inventor has patented a new idea gas saver and engine oiler that will perhaps prove the greatest MONEY-SAVER to car owners ever gotten out. It is a combination gas saver and inside engine oiler. It is entirely NEW. There is nothing else like it. It SAVES gas. It SAVES oil. It gives the engine MORE power and FASTER speed. It is low priced. It is easy to attach. It fits all autos. Also all trucks, tractors, motorcycles, taxis and aeroplanes. Also all stationary engines.

New Fords report up to 40 miles on one gallon, old Fords 77, Chevrolets 32, Plymouths 34. Other Makes up to 35. It SAVES more than the new tax.

It is guaranteed to save 10% to 50% every time you drive. The Inventor will allow you a 10 days trial on your own car with an unqualified money-back guarantee. No risk to you.

Agents, Salesmen, Dealers, Distributors Wanted

He also wants NEW Users, Boosters, Agents, Salesmen, Dealers, Distributors, General Agents everywhere to make $100.00 to $1,000.00 a month introducing it. 100% to 230% profits are allowed.

Send in your name and address today for full and complete particulars free. No obligation to you. Use coupon below and mail in 3c envelope. Or just send your name and address on a 1c postal card if you prefer. Either will do. He even offers to send one free to introduce. Hurry and write in today sure. Address

NEW GAS SAVER— ENGINE OILER PATENT
B-156 Street—Next to City Hall
WHEATON, ILLINOIS

USE THIS COUPON TO WRITE IN WITH IF YOU WISH

New Gas Saver—Engine Oiler Patent,
B-156 St.—Next To City Hall, Wheaton, Illinois.

Please send me full and complete particulars entirely free and your FREE Gas Saver—Engine Oiler offer. No obligation to me.

Name ....

Address... Car...............................

Town... State...............................

5

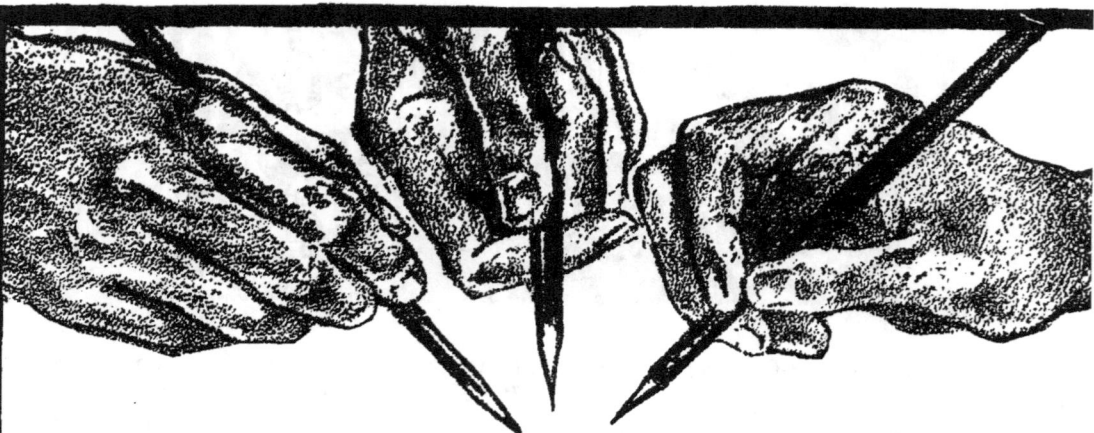

6

Follow this Man!

Secret Service Operator 38 Is on the Job

Follow him through all the excitement of his chase of the counterfeit gang. See how a crafty operator works. Telltale finger prints on the lamp stand in the murdered girl's room! The detective's cigarette case is handled by the unsuspecting gangster, and a great mystery is solved. Better than fiction. It's true, every word of it. No obligation. Just send the coupon.

FREE The Confidential Reports No. 38 Made to His Chief

And the best part of it all is this. It may open your eyes to the great future for YOU as a highly paid Finger Print Expert. More men are needed right now. This school has taken men just like you and trained them for high official positions. This is the kind of work you would like. Days full of excitement. Big salaries. Rewards.

Earn $3000 a Year and Up
You study at home in spare time

No advance education is needed. Any man who can read and write, and think can make good. A wonderful book tells all about what others have done. Shows pictures of real crimes and the men who solved them. We'll send you a FREE copy with the free reports. Get our low prices and easy terms. Mail the coupon.

INSTITUTE OF APPLIED SCIENCE
1920 Sunnyside Ave., Dept. 73-87, Chicago, Illinois

Hisdale reached his gun first and
his finger closed on the trigger.

*The surest shot—the quickest draw—
the greatest marksman in the world.
That was Major Hisdale. And Vee
Brown frankly admitted it, bowed
before the magic of this prince of
pistols. But—at the showdown—the
major lacked one thing. And its absence spelled death in the murder
marts of crimeland!*

A Vee Brown Story

AS MIDNIGHT STRIKES

by

Carroll John Daly

Author of "The Death Master," etc.

CHAPTER ONE

The Man in the Window

MORTIMER DORAN, the district attorney, moved his huge frame sideways in his chair, set his steady eyes on me for a moment, then turned back to Detective Vee Brown and began to speak.

"Things went wonderfully well for a time," he said and tossed some papers across the desk. "Now the Mandozza influence is back at work again. I had four of his men taken in, with real evidence to convict them—one, about to talk. Then the big blow! High-priced lawyers; alibis that will go a long way with juries; pressure being brought to bear, by political figures. I'm trying to fight it, Brown —but it's the same old racket. Mandozza's power is being felt in the city again. When he returns—"

"Mandozza won't be back!' Brown said sharply.

"Yes—I know, I know. You told me that, told me to go ahead. But I've got the feeling that he is back—back in the city now, picking up the strings just where he dropped them. Tell me how you drove Mandozza from the city, and why you think he isn't back."

"Mr. Doran," Brown was serious, "you wanted to be rid of the Mandozza influence. The less you know of the reason for his being out of the city—well— you've always let me work my own way."

"Yes, of course." Mortimer Doran seemed to expand in his chair. "You need not tell me anything officially; just something in friendly conversation."

"I can't," said Vee Brown. "Friendly or not, it would make your official hair stand on end."

Mortimer Doran frowned. "I've given you full swing, Brown—full swing. Now, there're many nasty stories going the rounds of the underworld." The district attorney looked at me.

"Dean Condon knows everything that I know." Brown nodded. "So shoot the official wrath."

"Not wrath; just curiosity, and perhaps a slight apprehension. The story is— mere gossip, perhaps—that you shot Mandozza's right-hand man to death, made no official report of the killing, and —well—in some way sent the body to Mandozza."

"I heard that, too," Brown said simply.

"Hm. So—" Mortimer Doran's left hand caressed his heavy jowls. "There is also the rumor that you had a gun fight with Mandozza and one of his men, and that you spared Mandozza's life because of a woman—a girl."

The corner of Brown's mouth curved slightly, in that slow, whimsical smile of his. "I have been accused of many things," he said. "Of course, when the Mandozza case is entirely cleared up I'll make a report to you. Why do you tell me this? Is it in way of criticism or— warning?"

"Warning," said Mortimer Doran. "That's Inspector Ramsey's story."

Brown nodded. "Ramsey always disliked me, envied and hated me. It was because of Ramsey that I was going to chuck the force—and then you took me over."

"And I've never regretted it,' the district attorney said quickly. "Your methods are peculiar, violent, and at times alarming. But you get surprising results —surprising and gratifying results. I believe, with you, that in this war on crime we must meet gunfire with gunfire, death by violence with death by violence." He leaned across the desk. "And, above everything else, I want Mandozza—and I'll let you get him in your own way. I admire you, Brown. Damn it! You've created a reign of terror in the underworld, just as the underworld has created a reign of terror in the city. You should have been a criminal."

Brown grinned, but he said seriously enough: "I have often thought of that—but decided against it. And surely, Mr. Doran, you didn't bring me here today to suggest such a thing."

"No. I brought you here to tell you that the influence of Mandozza is felt again. And I brought you here to tell you that Inspector Ramsey believes that story enough to hunt for the girl. He's bending every effort to find her."

Brown smiled crookedly, and his face showed no alarm. Yet his eyelids flickered slightly—which, to me, was the cue that he was disturbed.

"If Mandozza returns, I'll get him for you." Brown spoke as we both rose to leave. "Anything else?"

"Yes. I want you and Dean to dine with me tonight at the Sportsman's Club. There will be Inspector Ramsey and a guest. I want you to meet him. He's the world's greatest shot."

"Another one!" Brown turned to me and laughed. "Mr. Doran is always trying to find someone who can shoot straighter and quicker than I can. But he hasn't succeeded yet."

"Not yet," said the district attorney. "But the club's president saw this man perform and rang me up. He claims he's never seen anything to equal it. Fastest draw, quickest shot, and finest marksman he ever saw!"

"But the president of your club has never seen me. I think I can say, without conceit, that there is not a living man today who can draw faster and shoot straighter than I can." Brown said this as if simply stating a great universal truth, and when Mortimer Doran winked over at me, Brown added: "And my proof is—that I am still alive."

"Well, we'll see." Mortimer Doran shook hands with both of us. "I dare say he'll prove another fizz. That's why

I've invited Ramsey along again. This man's name is—is—" He looked toward the ceiling — "Major Hisdale — Major Robert Hisdale." And when Brown shook his head and we stood in the open door he said seriously: "About this other business. Watch out for Inspector Ramsey. Forewarned is forearmed."

The door closed and we were in the hall. I looked at Brown and he grinned back at me.

"That's what I like about Mortimer Doran," he said vigorously. "He knows or suspects or has been told that I pulled a fast one in the Mandozza case. Yet he doesn't criticize, advise or bellyache. If I'm in a jam he'll let me work my way out of it and trust me not to embarrass him. Certainly I spared Mandozza to save the girl, and certainly if it wasn't for the girl I wouldn't have been alive to spare Mandozza."

BUT I was thinking of Una Coles, of her slipping the gun into Brown's hand and saving our lives there in the basement of that deserted house. And Louie Mandozza! I shuddered slightly as I thought of him and of the grip he had on the girl. But then, Mandozza had left the city. Brown had let him go to save the girl from death. Brown had promised not to use the fraudulent income-tax evidence while Mandozza stayed away from the city. That evidence which Brown had obtained from Mandozza's crooked lawyer, Quinley—whom Mandozza had murdered.

Mandozza couldn't harm the girl, for I had seen Brown place that evidence in the small steel safe behind the bookcase in his music room. If Mandozza returned to the city, those statements in that envelope would send him up for many years. For with all Mandozza's great power, he could not influence the United States Government. But I got to wondering as the elevator shot down to the ground floor. Certainly Mandozza had lain down very quietly since that night a few weeks back. It didn't seem right, didn't seem like Louie Mandozza—the master racketeer.

What of Una Coles? She was afraid of the police; had somehow, against her will, been mixed up with crime. Inspector Ramsey might prove as great a danger as Mandozza. A pity, too; a catastrophe, I thought, if the police should get her now; uncover things about her now, when she was free of Mandozza and given the chance to go straight. But who was—

"I've often wondered," Brown voiced my thought aloud, "just who is Una Coles."

"I don't care who she is," I told him, "if she is safe. You see Mandozza is not stupid. He searched you well that night, knew you didn't have a gun. He must know, or have guessed by now, that she slipped you the gun that saved our lives; caused him to lose that evidence which you have, and also caused the death of his bodyguard. He'll want vengeance."

"Mandozza is out of the city. He wouldn't dare come back while I have the evidence. Besides, there have been no attempts on my life lately."

"But he couldn't have you killed while you have that evidence. You'd be more of a menace to him dead than alive. You promised not to use it while he stayed away. He wouldn't want you dead, so that's no proof that he's not back."

"There is other proof," said Vee. "Like most powerful men he has one weakness—a woman."

"Una Coles?"

"No. Entirely different. It's his sister. Mandozza's wild about that sister, Dean. He's spent a fortune on her voice—and although it's nothing to brag about he's financed her concert tours. I understand he's even trying to force her into opera. But this is the thing. He worships that girl, and if he were in the city he would

go to see her. I've had her shadowed every moment. He hasn't seen her."

I shook my head. I was thinking that we had not heard of Una Coles since that eventful night she saved us from Mandozza.

WE WALKED down a dirty side street. Many tenements; many children playing on the street; the homes of the poor. And yet, even in these squalid dwellings of poverty the depression had struck its blow. Many families of seven or eight, who had been living in a few rooms, had doubled up with other families. "To Let" signs hung in dirty windows, in many languages—Yiddish, Italian, English.

Vee Brown liked these side streets of the lower city. They brought him close to the people, he said. Stirred emotions within him for those sentimental song hits which, under the famous but still unidentified name of Vivian, paid him a bank president's income.

"You see—" for the moment, anyway, Brown had forgotten Una Coles and Mandozza as he pointed to a couple before a tenement—"that girl there, with the boy. She's unconscious of all this misery; unconscious that her clothes are shabby and worn; that the boy who holds her hand and sits so close has no job—perhaps no home, or maybe one where an invalid father and a broken mother need the help that he cannot give. They aren't even talking, Dean. They are planning though. And the picture is a pretty one. Of marriage and a glorious future that—"

I was knocked suddenly to one side as Brown's right elbow dug into my ribs. I saw the face of course, and heard the single shot as Brown jarred against me. There, in an open window below a "To Let" sign, was a ruddy, swarthy face. But it wasn't that which made me clutch quickly at my right hip pocket; try frantically to get my gun out. It was the thing that for a moment hung over the edge of the window sill. It was a Thompson sub-machine gun.

Why didn't it spit lead? Why— And I wondered if that single shot had been enough; if Brown's body against mine had been the result of the force of that single shot. And I knew it wasn't.

The mouth of the man in the window hung open; red flowed from it. Then the face was gone, but not before I had seen that the glaring eyes were now dull and lifeless. The man and the machine gun had disappeared from the window not ten feet from us. There was the soft thud of the body, then a louder crash as the machine gun followed it to the floor.

A few women had run screaming into the street, gathering up dirty tots. Someone shouted that there had been murder. And Brown had me by the wrist, forcing my now drawn gun back into my pocket.

"What happened, Brown? What happened?" I stammered. "The man in the window! He's dead. Someone shot him." Then a cop ran up, and Brown identified himself.

"Don't shout it to the whole neighborhood," he threw at me. Then to the policeman, "Keep these people out of it." And as another policeman came hurrying up, and curious—more than frightened women were gathering in little knots, "Have Moriarity telephone in for the wagon. Yes, yes—I just shot a man. I had to kill him, of course. I couldn't chance wounding him in the shoulder, with all those children on the street. He had a typewriter. Come along, Dean."

I GASPED, and looked at both Brown's empty hands as we entered the ill-smelling hallway of the tenement. "You killed that man! The one with the machine gun in the window!"

"Of course, of course." He nodded impatiently. "I saw the Tommy gun peek over the sill when I turned my head. Then I let him have it." He spoke authoritatively to a man and a woman who were coming down the stairs, ordering them back to their rooms. Then he swung open a door that was unlocked, and we were in that little front room—bare of everything. Bare of everything but the dead, crumpled body of a man and the ugly weapon with which he would have scattered death into the crowded city street.

Brown closed the door and walked over to the body that lay face downward. One arm was bent up beneath it, holding the body somewhat on an angle.

"The dirty rat!" Brown turned the body over with his foot. "He wanted to kill me, and he didn't care how many little children were maimed or killed so long as he got me. Not a mark on him, Dean. Rather neat at that. I shot him through his open mouth. I—" He looked long and earnestly at the dead face. "By God!" he said suddenly. "It's Charlie Pazzcato, Mandozza's gunner." He broke off—then snapped, "Let's get home, Dean. Quickly. Wong—"

Brown spoke hurriedly to the officer outside, and the plainclothesman who was pushing through the crowd of jabbering women. Then we were down the street; in a taxi—and Vee Brown was frantically urging the driver to hurry.

"A car is not much good in city traffic," he said to me, after waving away a motorcycle policeman and shouting something at a traffic cop as we shot by a red light.

"What's wrong, Brown?" I asked him. "You think Mandozza is back and that he'll try to steal the evidence out of your safe?"

"Try to steal the envelope in my safe!" Brown turned to me. "He's already got that envelope, else he wouldn't have tried to have me killed. No. I killed Curry and shipped him the body. It's Wong, now, I'm thinking of. Wong, who would gladly die for me. Mandozza would have him murdered—tortured maybe. As he once planned to kill you, my friend—he would plan now to kill Wong, my servant."

In front of our pretentious Park Avenue apartment houses, the lease of which was in my name, we dashed from the cab. Across the lobby, down the long hall, and to the elevators.

Brown pushed me into an automatic lift, slammed the door—and up we shot. When he spoke his lips were tightly compressed.

"He won't forget, Dean. Mandozza won't forget Curry's body. I know it. I am afraid we will find Wong dead. Killed in some horrible way."

I saw Brown slip a gun into his right hand as we reached the top floor. And we were at the door of our penthouse—the inside hall door. My fingers trembled but I got the key in the lock.

"Wong. Wong!" Brown called sharply as we ran across the entrance hall, through the open foyer into the huge living room, and straight to the music room.

CHAPTER TWO

Wong

I KNEW as soon as I entered that the place had been robbed. The bookcase was thrown aside; the door of the wall safe hung open. It was broken, and there was a great hole in the center of it where the combination dials had been. Brown looked around quickly, started back toward the living room, paused and looked at the highly polished floor between the rugs of the two rooms. There were thin scratches.

"No struggle!" Brown said. "No signs of a struggle. But a man was dragged from the living room into the music room. There, plainly, are the scratches of his

heels. Wong!" He paused and listened.

I heard it too—clearly—the falling of water. Brown and I turned together. There was a bathroom off the music room, and it was from that bathroom that there came the steady fall of water. Like a light rain upon a lake.

I was on Brown's heels when he threw open that bathroom door and rushed in. I bumped against his back, nearly knocking him over, when he stopped suddenly with a little gasp. Then he was across that room, bending over the tub as I stood transfixed with terror—horror—at what I saw.

Wong lay in that tub, gagged and bound hand and foot. His feet were roped to the handles of the water faucets at the foot of the tub. Around his neck was tightly drawn another rope, which was fastened to the pipes of the shower and securely knotted to the hot and cold water handles that controlled the shower. Cold water from the shower above poured steadily down.

The water was already above Wong's mouth, above his nose. I was sure he was dead as Brown leaned over the tub and lifted the body in his arms, supporting the head above the water.

"Quick, Dean—your knife." And when I stood there, petrified, "You fool! Cut the ropes and help me get him out of here."

Stunned or not, I cut the ropes and helped Brown as he worked over Wong there on the bathroom floor.

"He's going to live; he's got to live!" I heard Brown saying over and over. And then, "Get downstairs. Doctor Bellinger, on the first floor. Bring him up. Tell him—tell him—oh, tell him that there was an accident and that he has to come at once."

And then, as I reached the front door, Brown called after me: "No. Come back. He's alive! I need you here."

In physical exertion Brown was not

much good. I had to work over Wong until I was almost exhausted. Then I hung out the bathroom window, sucking in great gasps of fresh air. There, far below me, was the court. Along the ledge to my right and about ten feet beyond the window was our private terrace, and the stone steps from the little fountain, which led to the floor above.

Privacy here; safety here; a place apart from the criminal world, I had always thought. But even here, far above the city streets, Mandozza had struck. From now on there would be no peace. Fear would be every place.

WONG was fast coming around. Brown and I carried him to his own room. His eyes were no longer bulging. The lips that were purple—almost black —were now turning their natural color. But it was a good half hour longer before he could talk. And for some time there would be the ugly red welt across his neck where the rope had burnt the skin in his struggle for freedom.

"You see," Wong explained, "the house phone tells me there is a man with a package to come up. Then when the single footsteps come to the door, I open it—and men are there. There is a dull crash—many stars, and I find myself being dragged across the floor.

"They say many things concerning you, Mr. Brown, and the big man whose face I never see thinks it very funny. But, mostly it is talk of the horror that will follow you day and night, if you should live to find my humble body. That is all I know, except that I am—like a rat— to be drowned."

"It must have been terrible—horrible— waiting there, Wong," I gasped.

"Not horrible to die so, if I could accomplish anything for Mr. Brown—for to him my life is due many times. No. I know much of death, and to die by water is a death not unpleasant—if it is of

your own choosing. But I wish to live, and so very nearly strangle myself."

Brown squinted up his eyes and said to me: "What a way to kill a man, Dean! And, why? Because Mandozza hates me; because I killed his friend; because I drove him from the city; because— Do you know, Dean, the real reason for attempting to drown Wong in the tub?" And when I shook my head, "You know the gossip—that Mandozza never takes a bath. You remember how I taunted him with that when he visited us up here not so long ago. Well, it's little things, sometimes, that mean most in life. Yes, I believe he hates me mostly for that silly remark I made, and so he plans to kill my servant in a way that will remind me of my insult to him."

There was little to get from Wong. Indeed, now that the thing was over, he was the most composed of the three of us. Two of the men he thought he would know again. The big one, who arranged for his horrible death, he did not see, but thought he might recognize him by his voice. So we left Wong and went back to the music room.

"It was my fault," Brown said as he looked at the shattered face. "I should have warned Wong against admitting anyone. But, you see, I saw no danger in Mandozza."

"The envelope is gone—the evidence is gone." I stood up from the safe and turned to Brown. "You underestimated Mandozza. You once told me one of your rules was never to underestimate a crook's intelligence, and now—"

Brown shook his head. "Not underestimated, Dean. I overestimated Mandozza's intelligence." And after a pause, "Or perhaps Mandozza underestimated my intelligence."

"You should have placed *the envelope* in a safe-deposit box in some bank, and—"

Brown grinned. "Good, honest, respectable old Dean. Safe-deposit vaults are the last word in safety and secrecy to the common citizen; a place to hide things to the man who has nothing to hide. But court orders have opened the boxes of mayors and lawyers and senators, and Mandozza—with his influence—would have no trouble in starting a bona fide investigation into the activities of Vee Brown, first-grade detective who rides in a high-priced car and lives in such diggings as these on Park Avenue. Of course it wouldn't come through Mandozza. You see, Dean, all the crooks in our great city don't go around with guns in their hands and murder in their hearts. Some of them wear long robes and dispense justice."

"But leave it here, and—"

THE phone rang. Brown picked up the receiver. "Yes—yes." I saw him look over at the safe. "Well—I suspected he might be. . . . Just the same as usual; tag his sister, Rosa." He laid down the phone and turned to me. "That's the dick I have watching Mandozza's sister, Rosa Mando—she calls herself. He's a little late with the information that Mandozza's back in town. He doesn't appear to be hiding either."

"Mandozza has the evidence then?"

"No," said Brown, "but he's been informed that the evidence was taken. He feels safe and—"

The phone rang again. This time when Brown put it down he frowned. "That," he said, "was Mortimer Doran. Louie Mandozza has just stopped in to see him. Just a social call, to let the district attorney know that he's back on the job."

"And then—Una Coles," I said. "Mandozza will have nothing to fear from you now. No evidence to convict him! Look what he would have done to Wong, whose only offense was being your servant. Imagine his vengeance on Una, who saved your—"

"Una Coles is safe. Doran may think me a fool. Mandozza may think me a fool. But surely you—Dean, I'm not the detective of fiction who forgets his gun and locks valuable papers up in the obvious place to have them stolen. Here—" He walked to a corner of the room, slid back a section of wood in the thick top of a table and pulled out a long envelope.

"Proofs—affidavits—bank statements——cancelled checks!" He shook them at me before putting them back again. "The others were copies—no good to anyone. Fairly good copies, of course. But if Mandozza goes over them carefully he's bound to recognize his signatures as frauds. But he may be satisfied for a bit with a quick glance. We'll see how far he'll go with the bit of rope I've given him before he hangs himself with it. Damn it! Dean, I could turn these over to the government now. He's broken faith with me. But I'll wait a bit. I hate to see Mandozza do seven years for the government. I've never had a greater desire to see any man fry."

The door bell rang. Almost at once Wong appeared. A little unsteady upon his feet, but placid and calm as usual.

"You'd never think," said Brown, "that hate burns in Wong's heart against these men—against Mandozza. You'd think it was all in a day's work to him. But beneath that cold exterior, fires rage. I know Wong, and I know he'd give his life for me; take a life for me. Now, this will be someone else telling me that Mandozza is back in town."

But it wasn't.

Feet beat hurriedly down the little hall, across the foyer as we came into the living room. Our visitor was Una Coles.

"Lock the door—chain it." She stood looking at us wildly. "Someone saw me come in, I think, but I held my head down. He didn't recognize me."

"You're quite safe here." Brown led her to the long couch. "There—I haven't thanked you for what you did for me and Dean." He took both her hands and looked at her very seriously. "You can be sure, Miss Coles, no matter what your trouble—I will help you. No matter what you've done I will protect you. No matter—"

"It's Mandozza. He's back in town!"

"Mandozza can't harm you now."

The girl looked straight at him. "He has only to beckon me, and I must go to him. You—you must believe that."

"I do. But I have only to beckon him and he must return you. You must believe that."

"You have something—something over Mandozza! Yet, he's back."

"I can give him seven to ten years in the Atlanta penitentiary any time I wish. But I don't think he's fully aware of it. Now, Miss Coles, don't you think it might be wise to tell Dean and me—your friends —just why you fear Mandozza. Just why, when he beckons you, you must go to him?"

"But not who I am—not who I am!"

"Not who you are, but why you fear Mandozza."

SHE hesitated a long moment, looked half toward me—then avoiding my eyes, turned back to Brown, lowered her head and spoke. "I married a thief— and a murderer."

"Una!" I started toward her but Brown thrust me back.

"Yes." Una Coles raised her head now and looked straight at me. "I was very young. I didn't know, of course. He told me he was wrongfully accused of a crime. He was tall and handsome and 'wronged' —and I was a fool. My parents didn't know. And then, for him, I trapped a man to his death."

"Una—you couldn't!" The words shot from my mouth in spite of the glare in Brown's eyes.

"Oh—I didn't know. I thought I was

to get information from the man. But I saw him die; saw the man I had married shoot him down—and—I didn't see him again. I went away, sick; not wanting to live. But I did live, and later— much later—Mandozza met me. He knew, and threatened me. I—I'm a common criminal. First I wanted to kill myself— then I wanted to kill Mandozza. And Mandozza told me my husband was dead. Now—my husband is alive; is back in the city and has sent for me."

"Your husband! He's alive!" All my dreams seemed to go with those words. "But why didn't you tell the police in the beginning?"

"I should have. But I couldn't. I didn't. My people—my— I was frightened. And then it was too late."

"And your husband's name?" Brown urged.

"His name"—she hesitated a long moment—"was Thomas Craven. I can't— I can't go to him again. I'd be glad to go to jail. I'd want to go to jail. If it were only myself I would have faced it squarely long before. Now—it's my mother, my father. Don't you see? They'd die with the shame of it." And after a moment, "I thought he was dead. Mandozza told me that. It was Mandozza who straightened everything out about the shooting—the murder. At least, he told me he did."

"Thomas Craven wasn't his real name though, was it?" Brown asked.

"No. No—I don't think so."

"Craven—Thomas Craven." Brown seemed to think aloud.

"And you won't tell the district attorney. You— Oh, I feel better to have talked to someone who understands. You won't tell?"

"No. Dean and I will keep your secret and help you. You needn't fear Mandozza—and you needn't fear this husband, who is controlled by Mandozza. I'm glad you told me this."

"Dean had to know," she said, without looking at me. "And you, Mr. Brown. Well—you had to know, because I think Mandozza has brought my—this man here to kill you. He's a remarkable shot. In fact, he's a genius with a gun."

"Yes," said Brown. "Just what does he look like, and—"

The door bell rang.

"I knew someone saw me come in." The girl sprang to her feet.

Brown walked to the music-room door as Wong crossed the foyer and looked at us for instructions.

"All right, Wong." Brown nodded to him and motioned the girl to the music room. "It's probably Mortimer Doran. He's worried about Mandozza," he said as he closed the door on the girl.

CHAPTER THREE

The Closed Door

OUR visitor was not Mortimer Doran. It was Inspector Ramsey. Inspector Ramsey, like the district attorney, was a big man, but unlike the district attorney, he was not given to weight; that is, not excess weight. He was just past forty, stood six feet two, and probably carried a hundred and ninety pounds of hardened muscle. In his earlier days and up until its disbandment, he was a member of that famous "Strong Arm Squad" that so terrified the dives of the city.

"Hello!" said Brown, and he could not quite keep the surprise out of his voice. "This is a pleasant surprise."

"Is it?" There was nothing diplomatic about Inspector Ramsey. He didn't like Brown and he showed it.

"Sit down." Brown suddenly assumed a hostile attitude. "Dean and I are not particular."

"No—" Inspector Ramsey set his jaw slightly and his gray eyes were hard. "Well—I am. I haven't got a pretty way

with words, like you. I'm a plain-speaking man. I've come to get the girl who just came in here."

"Get the girl!" Brown stood leaning on the long table in the center of the room. As the inspector's eyes flashed around the room and settled on the closed music-room door I sauntered over—between him and that door.

I didn't need Brown's glance of warning to tell me that I'd made a mistake. The sudden gleam of satisfaction in Ramsey's cold gray orbs told me that he had guessed my purpose in guarding that door.

"Yes—get the girl," Ramsey said, setting his lips tightly and shoving his chin forward belligerently. "I haven't come here to make a deal with you. I haven't come here to ask you favors. You sold out to Mandozza for the woman—Mandozza's woman."

"That's a lie!" I cried out. "She's not—" I caught myself up quickly and Brown laughed.

"I don't need your wealthy friend here to give the show away to me," Inspector Ramsey sneered. "I saw her come in. I didn't get a good look at her face, but I will. And I think, when I get through with her, she'll talk. And I think, after she talks—or maybe, before, you'd better resign—for the good of the force."

"Certainly," said Brown, "you're a very efficient officer, and, I understand, a very honest one. I don't want to make trouble for you. But you're in a private apartment belonging to Mr. Dean Condon. You haven't a warrant. You have no law to stand on. Now—how, if there is a girl, do you expect to speak to her?"

"By walking over to that door there," Ramsey jerked his head toward the music room, "and by dragging her out and down to headquarters."

"No." Brown shook his head. "You can't do that. It's against the law to force your way into a home and search that home without a warrant. Now—get out!"

Inspector Ramsey laughed. "Against the law, eh? You and me, Brown, discussing the law! That's a hot one. I'm learning things about you. I want that girl and I'm going to get her. I want you and I'm going to get you, finally." He turned from Brown almost contemptuously. "You ain't big enough to stop a pickpocket. You can't work your famous gun racket on me."

Inspector Ramsey stepped forward suddenly, glared at me as I barred his way.

"I'm not fooling, Condon," he said. "I'm an inspector of police, and if you try to—" And as I held my ground he struck out suddenly, viciously—without any warning.

I DON'T say I could have won out in a fight with Inspector Ramsey, for he was a brute of a man. But I do say that, given a chance; having an idea of his intention, I could have given a very good account of myself. As it was, he took me completely off my guard. His blow caught me just under the ear, sent me reeling across the floor. I landed in a heap against the long couch.

Half dazed, I was getting to my feet when Inspector Ramsey reached that music-room door and put his hand upon the knob. But he didn't turn that knob. Brown spoke.

"Don't open that door, Ramsey—or I'll put a bullet in you." Brown's voice was very low; his words very calm and clear. There was nothing threatening, certainly nothing melodramatic about the order. But there was something very real about it; something real enough to make Inspector Ramsey hesitate, turn his head slowly and look straight at Brown—at the gun he held in his hand.

"You can't pull that stuff on me," Ramsey said. "Drop that gun, or I'll have you up on charges. I'm going in this room."

He half turned his head again, and I thought I saw his fingers tighten on the knob when Brown spoke again.

"So you're going to open that door," Brown said quietly. "That was a dirty blow you struck Dean, Ramsey. Do you know I half wish you would open it."

Ramsey's head turned back again. "You've hated me a long time, Brown," he said slowly, and there was a question in his voice.

"No more than at this moment," said Brown, and as Ramsey turned the knob slightly, "Better not!"

"You're bluffing." But though Ramsey's hand remained on the knob, he did not open the door.

"Maybe," said Brown. "Why don't you open the door and find out?"

For a long moment Inspector Ramsey looked at these steady black eyes, the outstretched right hand, and the nose of the gun that covered him—without the slightest movement.

"By God! I believe you want to do it. Guilty conscience, eh? But don't forget you'd have a hard time explaining it."

"Oh, I guess I'd think up something. I always do," Brown said indifferently. And suddenly, "Come on, Ramsey—get away from that door! You've had your warning. Now hop!"

And Ramsey did hop. At least, he stepped away from that door and moved back into the room.

"You'll hear from this later," Ramsey threatened, but the hardness had gone out of his voice. He was watching Brown's hand carefully. There was relief in his face when that hand dropped to Brown's side and the gun disappeared.

"I know my rights," Brown said as Ramsey backed toward the foyer. "I won't tell the story if you don't. It doesn't seem funny to you maybe, but to others—to the papers, if they get hold of it—"

"Then you didn't really intend to shoot?"

"Of course I did. If you had any sense you wouldn't have put yourself in such a position."

"You must think a lot of that girl," Inspector Ramsey snapped.

"Or very little of you," Brown snapped back.

"All right," said Ramsey. "I'll forget it if you do." And when he reached the door, "But I won't forget that you're supposed to have kept to yourself certain evidence against Mandozza."

And he was gone, stamping down the hall.

"So—" Brown stroked his chin. "He knows about that evidence, or suspects it. That lawyer, Quinley, must have had a couple of strings out. But Ramsey can't be sure. And now——" He went to the music room and threw the door open. The girl was gone.

THE large closet was empty, as was the bathroom, but the bathroom window was open and Brown stuck his head out. My heart missed a beat as I looked out too, far down into the court below. Then I looked to the right, along the ledge which ran ten feet, to the little terrace.

"She took a chance," said Brown, "though I've done it myself, just to be sure it could be a means of quick exit. Some day, I thought, it might come in handy. She went down the steps, to the door on the floor below. She had only to turn the knob to gain the hall. All that gunplay for nothing, though I liked the uncertain look on Ramsey's face a lot."

Though it all seemed simple enough, I kept staring down into the court at the flagging far below. The ledge from the bathroom window was wide enough of course, but I shuddered just the same as I looked down. If Una Coles had lost her nerve! But she hadn't. Yet, somehow the fear of Mandozza was getting me. I spoke about it to Brown.

"You are worrying about Una Coles of course." He looked at me, raised his hand when I would have cut in. "Yes, yes, I know. Mandozza's hot blood calls out for vengeance. But above everything, he wants my life. Any time that is necessary, I'll give it gladly for Una Coles. There are not many people who can claim the—the distinction of saving Vee Brown's life. Una Coles has that distinction. She's in a tough spot. This husband business and her family complicate things. Craven—Thomas Craven. Yes, he had a way with women. But I don't believe he married the other one." He started pacing the room.

"What other one? You know this Craven?"

Brown ignored my question. "You stay here, Dean, in case Una Coles telephones. Doran always dines at seven; that leaves me time enough. I want to see Irving Small."

Irving Small! I knew him, of course. The little pawn broker. The fence who sold Brown so much information about criminals.

"But don't you think Una may need us? Can't we put off this dinner? Anyway, Inspector Ramsey will be there, and—"

"Social obligations." Brown grinned at me as he took his top-coat and hat and walked toward the door. "Besides, I want very much to meet this Major Hisdale— the crack shot. Just pride, Dean. I want to see how good—or perhaps, how bad he is."

I was dressed before Brown returned. He was humming softly to himself when he stepped into the living room scarcely ten minutes before seven.

"I've got it," he said, when I followed him to the bedroom and he tossed off his clothes.

"Something that helps Una?"

"Una—Una." He looked at me blankly as Wong told him his bath was ready.

"No—it's a song. Those two—the boy and the girl sitting at the tenement entrance gave me the idea." He was talking from the shower now. "Listen to this." And he began to sing—to bellow almost, against the pouring shower.

I couldn't get the words, and certainly couldn't get the tune. But when he jumped from the shower and was rubbing himself down vigorously, I did get a word in.

I said: "I'm worried about Una Coles. Mandozza, this husband of hers, and—"

"Hell!" Brown slid his arms into his dress shirt and let Wong button it in the back. "I've already attended to that husband of hers, or at least I think I have."

And I couldn't get him to explain that statement. I watched him hook his gun harness carefully below his left armpit and slip the heavy gun into the holster. He grinned when I shook my head.

"It's a matter of habit, Dean," he told me. "I'd as soon go without my tie as my gun, and the gun is quite as comfortable and a damn sight more useful. Try the shoulder holster for a year. Don't load the gun if it bothers you. Remember though—it's a good half second's difference between a shoulder and a hip draw, even with the ordinary gunman. And a half second in my business is very often—eternity."

CHAPTER FOUR

The Three of Spades

MAJOR ROBERT HISDALE was a big, broad-shouldered man, with a scar across his cheek. He explained that scar almost before his stiff bow of greeting was over. He had received it from a saber while in the German army.

"We've been telling the major about you, Brown." Mortimer finished his cocktail. "And he's going to show us a few tricks with a gun before dinner. Says

he shoots better on an empty stomach. You both know Inspector Ramsey, of course." Mortimer Doran noticed the coldness on Ramsey's part.

Down in the basement, in the huge shooting gallery, Major Hisdale did his stuff. And it was some stuff! I just watched, spellbound, while the major performed. I saw him start off with the small targets, and place six shots in succession smack in the bull's eye. I saw him turn his back to the range, stretch both his empty hands straight out before him—and turning suddenly, blaze away with two heavy sixguns, and snuff out twelve candles. I saw the attendant toss a card in the air, but I never saw the major's right hand move. Yet, the hand that had been empty suddenly held a spitting gun. Three times the gun barked; three shots that seemed to merge as one. And when Ramsey picked up the card, it proved to be the three of spades, with each of its black spots neatly shot out of it.

I looked at Brown in amazement, but he sat there smiling and nodding approval. Was there something of condescension in his approval, as if he were a master who watched a pupil? Yet, I had seen everything that Brown could do with a gun—everything that I thought possible for a human being to do. And I knew—knew beyond a doubt—that Major Hisdale could shoot quicker, draw faster, and place bullets that Brown could never place.

Major Hisdale looked at Brown from time to time, and his frown deepened as Brown nodded his approval and grinned pleasantly. Finally Hisdale turned to him. "I've heard about you, Mr. Vee Brown. Won't you show me something with a gun? I'm always willing to learn." There was a sneer on his lips and triumph in his voice.

"That three-of-spades shot." Brown waved a hand toward the long gallery.

"You use a sixgun, major. Surely you do the same trick with the six of spades."

"No—I don't," the major snapped. "Not at that distance. No man living does."

"No?" Brown's eyes went wide as he came to his feet slowly. "I was under the impression that it could be done."

"Without having the gun in your hand; drawing the gun after the card is already in the air!" The major fairly gasped the words.

"Certainly." Brown nodded vigorously. "To have a gun ready in your hand! Well—" Brown shrugged his thin shoulders. "To me that comes under the heading of parlor tricks, and would be of no use in my business. You know my business of course, major?"

"Certainly." Major Hisdale hesitated, and then, "It is the business of killing men."

"Exactly!" Brown had to raise his head to look into the major's cold steady brown eyes. "The business of killing men." And suddenly twirling the gun that he held in his hand and putting it back slowly into its holster, "I think that I will stick to that business."

MORTIMER DORAN had Brown by the shoulder. "Oh, come now. If it's the major's day, let him enjoy it. Let us see you duplicate that three-of-spades trick—or better still the six, you suggested."

Brown hesitated and Inspector Ramsey cut in. "He can't do it, and he can't duplicate the three. The major has done shooting of which I never saw the like before."

"Well," said the major, "do you shoot or do we eat?"

"Oh, come on—" Mortimer Doran started again, but Brown broke in.

"We eat, Mr. Doran. As you say, it's the major's day. Certainly the major is a most remarkable shot, and it would be

most ungracious to—" Brown hesitated, then didn't go on.

"I didn't think you'd lie down, or quit like that." Ramsey's tone was slightly jubilant.

Brown's thin lips drew together, and then he laughed. "Why," he said, "it isn't quitting to bow to such a marksman." But the tone of his voice belied his words.

The major bowed slightly, from the waist. "It's lucky then—lucky that I'm a law-abiding citizen and that we don't meet in this business of yours—the killing of men."

"Right'o!" Brown was smiling. "Very lucky. Very lucky, major."

Mortimer Doran didn't like the turn things were taking. The good-natured raillery he had hoped to hurl at Brown was forgotten. He didn't fully understand the sarcasm in Brown's voice, but he did recognize a certain antagonism which, aggravated further, would spoil the little dinner he had arranged. Now he took the major by one arm and turned from the gallery, calling to us to follow.

"The chef always makes a special effort for me," he said. "We're late now, and I tell you André is not a man with whom to play fast and loose. He'd poison our food in a minute if he thought we'd spoil his dinner." And his laugh rang back to us as he and the major started up the stairs, crowded by Inspector Ramsey, who tried to make a threesome on steps that were built only for two.

"Vee—" I said. "You— It's true? He's the better shot?"

"Shooting like that!" Brown looked at me. "You have an eye for such things, Dean. You've seen my best draw and my best shot. Why ask me?"

"Then it is true; you couldn't shoot with him. Why did you try to laugh it off? They all guessed it of course."

"Sure!" Brown nodded. "I wouldn't have believed such shooting possible if I hadn't seen it. You know he's quicker and keener than I am. I know it. Mortimer Doran and Ramsey have seen me shoot, and probably believe it. But the major! He can only guess at it, Dean. Only guess—he can't be sure. At least, he can't be positive. There was no reason to let him know."

"There was no reason not to." I felt badly about the whole thing. Brown was my friend. Now—well—like a kid, I felt that he had let me down. That he had not proved himself a good sportsman.

"No reason not to." Brown repeated my words. "Well, perhaps you're right. And if you are I'll bring Major Hisdale down here and let him shoot rings around me all Saturday afternoon." He grinned up at me. "And Inspector Ramsey can be his audience, too."

SO we entered the dining room. And though Brown and Hisdale laughed and chatted as they walked to the reserved table by the window that looked out on Fifth Avenue, I knew there was a feeling of hostility. I couldn't explain it but it was there. Something between these two men that I could not understand; that—

Brown was talking as he stood behind the chair that Mortimer Doran pointed out to him, close by the window. "You haven't enemies that might suddenly take your life, eh, major?" he asked.

"Not now." The major laughed. "There were many enemies when I was in the German secret service but," he coughed, and finished, "they are all dead now."

"Fine!" said Brown. "Then, of course you won't mind taking my seat by the window. I have many enemies."

Mortimer Doran looked slightly annoyed, Inspector Ramsey rather pleased, and I—just perplexed. But Major Hisdale took the seat by the window.

I watched Brown closely as we dined and listened to Major Hisdale. If all he

told us were true he had led an adventurous life, but as he explained with a laugh, "It all happened abroad or in South America." Then Mortimer Doran asked him about the saber cut on his cheek.

It was a long story, and nothing to the major's discredit, as he told it. He had received it behind the German lines, against the best swordsman in all Europe.

"The man died of course," he finished, caressing the scar.

"Saber, eh?" Brown looked at the scar. "It looks to me more as if it were made by a butcher's cleaver." Brown half raised the little table light, as if looking at the scar—and I noticed, too, that in leaning in front of the major to reach the light he pushed back the heavy drapes before the window.

The major turned and glared at Brown. His cheeks flushed quickly but he did not speak.

"I say, now—" Mortimer Doran was really annoyed and showed it plainly, this time. "You'll take the major's appetite away, Brown, with your ill-timed jokes, that—"

"No—" the major cut in quickly. "It has always been said that nothing ever interferes with my trigger finger or my appetite."

"That's a pretty broad statement; especially with regard to the appetite." Brown seemed to be set on heckling the major. "There's Fifth Avenue just below the window. The street of wealth! Many pass beneath this window, to dine at some club as pretentious as the Sportsman's Club. But others pause beneath the window—stare up with hungry eyes. There!" he leaned over and pulled back the curtain again. "For instance, major, look at the woman just below. The one with the shabby dress and threadbare coat. There's hunger in her eyes; envy—and certainly a hatred. Maybe not so long ago she too sat at such a table; such luxurious surroundings. Why—what's the matter, major?"

And there was something the matter. The major had suddenly jerked the curtain back across the window, pushing Brown's hand roughly from it. His face was ghastly and his eyes bulged. The scar on his cheek turned a livid red. He ran long strong fingers beneath his collar. Then turning quickly, he jerked the curtain aside again. I guess we all looked out the window this time. Many people hurried by; none loitered on the sidewalk. There was no woman.

MAJOR HISDALE recovered slowly. The color rushed into and receded quickly from his cheeks before they took on their former healthy hue.

"It gets you of course," Brown said easily, avoiding the district attorney's eyes. But for the rest of the dinner Major Hisdale was strangely silent, and though he did eat, it was plainly evident that he was forcing himself.

It was Brown who carried the conversation from then on.

"If you'll excuse me I'll make a telephone call." The major consulted his watch and rose from the table. "Things have been so interesting that I forgot the time. I'm afraid I may have to leave you. We'll see." And with a bow and a showing of his teeth, which I think was meant for a smile, he departed.

"Well—" Mortimer Doran could restrain himself no longer. "He showed you up, Brown, and you didn't like it. You took it well enough on other occasions, when you could shoot all around the adversary I selected in these little gatherings. Now, when the major returns I hope that—"

"The major," said Brown slowly, "is not coming back." And as Ramsey started to horn in, Brown continued, "To save you both embarrassment, it is my belief

that the major is both a thief and a murderer."

"What!" Mortimer Doran half rose to his feet, to slip back in his chair again. "You—you must be mistaken. He had the best of references."

"Yes?" Brown raised his eyebrows. "Just what were his references?"

"The president of the club— But there's the president now—Mr. Chidwick. I'll have a talk with him."

It was five minutes before Mortimer Doran returned to the table. His lips were rather tight and the pouches under his eyes were drawn into thick ridges.

"The president doesn't exactly—know the major. But he saw him shoot, and—well—he was introduced by Chauncey F. Raymond, the—the criminal lawyer."

"You might as well say it." Brown smiled cheerfully. "Both you and Ramsey know that Chauncey Raymond is Mandozza's lawyer."

"But that doesn't make the man a criminal. Raymond has many respectable clients and acquaintances."

Brown laughed.

"I think," he said, "Mr. Louie Mandozza sent the major, to throw the fear of death into me."

"But he tried to have you killed this afternoon. If you were dead, what would be the use of this—" I started.

"Nonsense, Dean!" Brown cut in. Mandozza couldn't be sure I'd go down the street I went down. He only knew that I did, on occasions. He couldn't be sure, either, that I'd use that side of the street." And with that crooked twist to his lips, "He couldn't be sure that I wouldn't shoot first. Mandozza is a man of many lines—many guns, but all leading to a single end—my death."

"But who is Major Hisdale?" This from Inspector Ramsey as a page boy brought Mortimer Doran a note.

Mortimer Doran tore open the envelope. "Major Hisdale," he said slowly, "has been called away. Now, Brown—"

But Brown was on his feet. "I'm not sure," he said, "that the law has anything on Major Hisdale. And if I were sure, I'd work it out myself and not let Inspector Ramsey mix— But come, Dean! Like Major Hisdale, we, too, are called suddenly away. No, no, Mr. Doran. you've often said yourself that suspicion, and even knowledge, is not evidence. I am going now to get evidence."

AS I followed Brown across the dining room I saw Inspector Ramsey come to his feet, and Mortimer Doran take him by the shoulder and restrain him from following us. Then we had gotten our things from the cloak room; were out on the avenue and in a taxi.

Brown talked, after assuring himself that we were not followed.

"More girls than Una Coles are forced into a life of crime by clever scoundrels," he said. "Six years ago there was such a case. Margaret Dresden came from Atlanta, Georgia. Her family was a good one, but in this case the man did not marry her. Margaret Dresden was deserted by this man, whom the police thought they wanted for murder. The man was missing, but she was willing to testify. Then came the word that he was dead, the word that sealed the girl's lips. You see—dead, she believed in him; living, she would have betrayed him. I thought of that tonight, when I got information from Irving Small where the Dresden girl was—broken in health and mind. She still held to her love for her 'dead' lover and I could not convice her he was alive. But I did know if she once saw him alive, that love would turn to hate. She would believe he had left her in poverty and shame, and—well—I got her to stand beneath the window tonight. From Major Hisdale's face, he recognized her of course—and recognized that

this woman was the only living person who could put him on the spot for the murder of Oscar Fineburg—a butcher, Dean."

"Oh—" I said. "That's what you meant —that the scar looked as if it were made by a meat axe!"

"Exactly." Brown nodded. "Now we are going to see Margaret Dresden; get her identification. The major is wanted for more than one murder."

"But if you knew this, why did you let him leave the club?"

"A scene there would embarrass Mortimer Doran." And when I looked at Brown in surprise. "Come, come, Dean! His arrest might embarrass someone else. Haven't you guessed who Major Hisdale is?"

"No," I said. "Who is he?"

"Well," said Brown, "I'm not sure, exactly, who he is. But I feel certain that at one time he passed under the name of Thomas Craven."

"Craven—Thomas Craven!" Then it struck me. "Una Coles' husband!"

"Exactly. I can't be positive, for I didn't get a description from her. But his marksmanship—and his face when he saw the woman. Well, we'll get this Margaret Dresden to speak out. It'll be a shock to her to find that he's still alive, apparently well supplied with funds and leading a life of luxury, while she suffers and believes in him."

"And Una—Una Coles?"

"She's his wife, and—" Brown's eyes knitted— "I have killed many men, Dean. It would be nice if I could—did kill one more."

CHAPTER FIVE

Room and Bath

NOW, as we drew up before a dirty tenement far across town, Brown's jaw set grimly. He talked as we entered the tenement and climbed the three flights of dirty stairs.

"The girl—or rather, the woman—will be expecting me, Dean. She was once a very beautiful girl. It was a shock to Major Hisdale to see the life he had wrecked. Not a shock to his conscience, but a shock to his stomach. He read the sudden hate in her eyes, I guess, and understood . . . But this will be her room . . . Hello!"

Brown stopped dead in the narrow, dim-lit hall before a door. His gun shot suddenly into his right hand; his flashlight into his left. I saw the beam of light play along the door, close to the knob; center on the lock and run quickly up the door.

"The wood's splintered," Brown whispered as the flash went out.

"But the whole place is dilapidated, and—"

"I was here this afternoon." Brown's hand went onto the knob. "If the door was splintered like that I would have— Damn it, Dean—stand back. The lock is broken."

Brown stepped to one side quickly as he turned the knob and thrust the door inward. It swung back against the wall with a thud. Rusty hinges creaked for a moment—then silence—a dead silence from within that room.

Although he warned me again to stand back, I followed him, my own gun drawn, as he stepped quickly into the room, covering the small dirty interior with his flash.

A moment later he had closed the door and turned on the single electric light bulb that hung from the ceiling on frayed wire. It didn't take long to search that small room. A couple of chairs, a rusty oil heater, a curtained corner that served as a closet—and the bed.

The bed! I gasped as I looked at it. A blanket was stretched over the entire length of that bed. A blanket that, by its peculiar contours, covered—could cover but one thing. A human body. A dead body! I knew that before Brown walked to the bed.

"This time, Dean," Brown said, somewhat grimly, as he grasped the blanket, "I think I underestimated the intelligence of Major Hisdale. Oh, I knew that Irving Small had kept track of the girl, but I didn't know that Hisdale or Mandozza had. Now—" He threw back the blanket, jumped back a step and shook his head a moment. Then peered down at the body.

I SAW the dead woman, of course. It will be a long time before I forget that sight. Her face was lined and her skin rough, her sunken eyes wide open. I turned my head quickly away. The woman's throat had been cut. It was horrible—nauseating.

Brown stood for some time at that bed, and I know that his face was very white when he turned away.

"Write me down as a failure here." His voice was very low and very husky. "It was Hisdale who cut her throat of course, but we'll never prove that. There will be a good alibi for him from the moment he left the club." He set his teeth. "It's better for the girl. She had nothing to live for. Drugs and disease had taken their toll. But it's tough on you and me—and Una Coles. If this woman had put the finger on the major, he'd never have bothered Una Coles again."

"Poor girl!" I turned toward the door. "Poor Una!" And suddenly, "What of that evidence against Mandozza, Brown? What use are you going to make of it?"

He stood in the center of that room.

"I don't know," he said finally. "Even the death of Mandozza will not free Una Coles. There will be this Major Hisdale now to bother her. She's in a tough spot.

Mandozza was bad enough. This other is worse." He tapped his pocket suggestively. "I wonder if this evidence won't influence Mandozza to influence Major Hisdale?"

"The evidence! You've got it with you—in your pocket?"

"Certainly." Brown nodded vigorously. "Mandozza will find out his error before long and may make another raid on the penthouse. Then—there's Inspector Ramsey, who suspects I have this evidence. Ramsey has worked several investigations and knows where to look for secret drawers—hidden—" He broke off and looked at the dead girl, then tossed the blanket back over the body. "Come on, Dean! Let's get out of here."

IN FRONT of the tenement Brown said: "You go back home at once. If Una Coles phones, have her come directly to the penthouse. If she should come there, keep her until I return."

"And you?" I asked.

"This murder will have to be reported of course."

As we walked down to the corner, Brown hailed a taxi and shoved me inside.

"You think Una is in danger, immediate danger?" I said.

Brown laughed harshly. "What do you think?" was all he said as he closed the door and the cab slipped from the curb.

Through the rear window I saw him cross the street, flag a passing taxi and disappear within it.

Wong met me at the door as I entered the apartment.

"It is a telephone message, Mr. Dean," he told me. "A woman's voice, which says it is Miss Una Coles. Twice she tried to get you, and the second time leaves a message. She wants you to meet her." Wong handed me a slip of paper. "She said that after ten o'clock it might be too late."

I looked at the paper. Una wanted me to meet her at Fifth Avenue and Twenty-first Street.

"Did it sound like Miss Coles' voice?" I asked Wong. I looked at the clock and saw that it was twenty minutes of ten.

"It was the voice of a woman, a very frightened or excited woman. More I cannot say. It was just a woman."

Was it a trap of Mandozza's? But why would he trap me? And how could he trap me at Twenty-first Street and Fifth Avenue at ten o'clock at night? Mandozza would certainly arrange things better than that. Wild thoughts went through my head. Mandozza had sent for her. She was afraid. She needed me—and I was hesitating.

"Wong—" I called to him at the door. "If Mr. Vee calls, tell him where I went, and that I will do everything to bring Miss Coles back with me." But before I left I slipped my gun from my hip to my coat pocket.

Finding I had ten minutes leeway I left the taxi at Twenty-fourth Street, cut along the edge of the park, crossed Twenty-third Street and passed quickly from the activity of a great city. It's surprising how dark and deserted Fifth Avenue is below Twenty-third Street, even that early in the evening. Few cars passed along the broad street; few people walked on the sidewalk.

At last I came to Twenty-second Street, Crossed it and went slowly down toward Twenty-first. A man and a girl were walking toward me; another man hurried in the same direction. Then a single man, following the pair, approached me, My hand tightly gripping my gun, I watched that single man.

The man and the girl passed me; the single man behind them was very close. He was a big man. His hat was pulled far down. His coat collar turned well up. I watched him closely and edged nearer the building, for he was close to the curb.

I was almost at Twenty-first Street when the big man slowed down and changed his direction, as if he would come toward me. Both his hands were at his sides, and both his hands were empty. I could see the whiteness of them as he drew closer.

I gripped my weapon tighter, half drawing it from my pocket. I can't do the things with a gun that Brown can. But I can draw a gun and I can shoot a gun, and I can hit a man if he's only a few feet from me.

Yes, I was ready. Ready—though reason told me that this man would simply ask the time, request a match or seek direction. I smiled, and—

Something hard dug into my back and a voice spoke close to my ear. "Drop that gun back in your pocket. Follow instructions to the letter, or I'll lay a row of lead buttons up and down your spine."

I hadn't heard the owner of that gun slip up behind me but I knew he must have come from a doorway. I didn't even sense his presence until the gun bore into my back and the voice whispered harshly in my ear.

Then things happened quickly. A big high-powered sedan turned the corner, coming toward me; drew up at the curb, and the door opened.

Stunned? Yes, I was stunned. I didn't even move when the man ordered me to climb into the car. It wasn't courage; it wasn't even obstinacy that kept me there. It was just stupefaction, I guess. I was frozen to the spot. The spot! I sucked in a deep gasping breath. That was it. I was on the spot.

I was being taken for a ride; kidnaped right off one of the most famous streets in the world. Yes, in full view of the blue-coated policeman I could plainly see two blocks away.

"Hop in that cab, brother!" The voice behind me spoke again. "Unless, of course, you'd prefer to lie here on the sidewalk. Come on! Nothing will happen to you if you're nice. Mandozza wants to see you."

What could I do? What should I do? What I did was to step into that car; feel rather than see the two men get in behind me. The one who had faced me and attracted my attention, and the one who had taken advantage of that attention and stuck the gun in my back.

The door of the car closed, my gun was lifted easily from my pocket and the car moved slowly from the curb and started leisurely uptown. I just sat between two men, felt the presence of two guns—one in my right side and one in my left. It was not a pleasant sensation.

Had I made a mistake in obeying the order to climb into that car? I was still alive, and I knew that Mandozza did not fool; that his agents would obey his orders to the letter, and that I had but one choice. To climb into that car, alive, or lie on the sidewalk, dead.

We were up at Fiftieth Street when the man on my right spoke.

"Watch him," he said to his companion, "while I take off my coat and throw it over his head."

After that I rode in blackness. Was I going to my death?

The car pulled to a stop; the door creaked open. I was hustled from the car between the two men; half pushed, half dragged up stone steps—and into a house.

THE coat was jerked off my head—and I faced Louie Mandozza. His big head bobbed up and down as if it were controlled by a wire, as he stood looking at me. Although his thick, cruel lips parted and he laughed, his eyes were cold black points. Then the eyes softened and the queer pink that made them resemble a cat's eyes shot into them, and he extended his left hand and shook my right one.

"You'll excuse my left hand, I know," he said apologetically. "My right one, as you see, is still bandaged. I had an accident to my wrist." The pink went from his eyes and the points of black flashed again for a moment. "But then, you no doubt remember the occasion. Mr. Vee Brown put a bullet through this wrist." He held the bandaged right hand up, shaking it in my face.

"But—there." He directed me to a flight of stairs. "I must remember that I am the host, that you entertained me once, entertained a friend of mine—Frankie Curry. Remember what I told you and Brown then?"

And I did remember, though I did not answer as I preceded him up that flight of stairs. Frankie Curry, the man Brown had killed! Mandozza's right-hand man, whom Vee had returned to him—dead.

"I said," Mandozza went on, "that I would never be under obligation to any man; that I always paid my debts."

I didn't speak. Perhaps, after all, I wasn't going to my death. I'd wait and see what Mandozza intended to do. I had a trump card to play.

"Just a moment." Mandozza pushed his huge broad body, with those long apelike arms, by me as the two men paused and waited. "Look there!" He stretched out a hand and threw open a door, then switched on a light. I turned my head and looked into the room.

It was a bathroom, as old as the house itself. A wooden tub, lined with well-worn zinc, took up a good part of the room. I just gazed at it at first, not understanding; then I did understand, and the horror of it struck me even be-

fore Mandozza started to speak. He intended to kill me, then; kill me horribly, as he or his men had intended to kill Wong. For from the tub faucets and from the shower above the tub were hung coils of rope.

"I always said, Mr. Condon," Mandozza squeezed my arm, "that your face was far more expressive and human than Brown's. 'Emotional' perhaps is the word. But I wonder if Brown wouldn't betray his feelings at such a sight. You remember, of course, that crude jest of Brown's—that I never took a bath. But he will not be able to say that I do not provide accommodations for my guests."

"You're mad." I turned to him suddenly, speaking for the first time since I entered the house. "If you did dare do this thing, Brown would find you. But you won't dare. Those documents, that evidence which you think you have, is false. The real evidence Brown still has."

Mandozza nodded slowly. My trump card had proved a flop.

"I was quite aware of that within five minutes after I examined the documents. And I saw the danger, too. There were only two courses left open to me. One, to gather together all my resources and flee the country, a wealthy man. The other, to hold Brown's friend in exchange for that evidence." He started walking me down the hall, toward an open door at the end of it.

"He'll find you and kill you," I told him.

"Will he?" Mandozza said thoughtfully. "You have great faith in Brown, but not as great a faith as someone else. A little lady. She tells me that Brown will come to her no matter where she is, and—" He thrust me suddenly through the door at the end of the hall and into a lighted room. "And there she is!" He could not keep the triumph out of his voice.

CHAPTER SIX

Death Duel

MY mouth hung open. Seated across the room in an easy chair was Una Coles. Her face was white; her thin lips set tightly, but her eyes were bright and defiant. She tried to come to her feet when she saw me—then fell back in the chair again, for her arms were bound tightly to either arm of the chair.

"I'm free. I'm to go! I'm—" And Una stopped suddenly as she saw the truth in my face. Her eyes flashed fearfully toward the tall man who leaned against the mantelpiece before the open fire.

The man turned as I looked at him. It was Major Hisdale.

"Good evening." Hisdale bowed mockingly. "I understand that you fancy my wife. Divorce evidence there, but Mandozza assures me there is an easier way of getting rid of matrimonial ties—and perhaps even collecting insurance."

I looked at Una, looked at Mandozza; then looked at Major Hisdale, the man who less than two hours before had brutally slashed a woman's throat. And things went red, or black, or—I don't know—but I sprang across that room and had him by the throat.

Mandozza gave quick, calm orders. Someone tore at my arms, but my fingers sank the deeper into that throat. They couldn't tear me free. They might shoot me, but my fingers would grip that throat until— A dull thud, a sudden pain in the head and blackness.

When I regained consciousness Mandozza was talking, and there was a threat in his words. "You are talking like a maniac, Hisdale," he was saying. "You marry my sister! You must be joking! Do you think I'm killing your wife for that? No. Una double-crossed me, sold

me out. You're just getting a lucky break in getting rid of her."

"It would cement our friendship," Major Hisdale said stiffly. "I come from a good family, and—"

"Rosa marry a crook and a murderer! You, a—"

"She should have no objection to that, since her brother is—"

"Stop!" I opened my eyes in time to see Mandozza slowly cross the room and stand before Major Hisdale. He spoke very plainly. "Listen, Hisdale. My sister, Rosa is to have a great career, men of wealth and position at her feet. I can use you. Your front, your gun hand, your quick eye and your lack of conscience. And you can use my money and influence. Very well! So much as try to see my sister; so much as couple her name with yours, and I'll wipe you out like a dirty mark. Remember that!"

The major scowled. His lips parted but he did not speak. Then the phone on the table by the long couch rang.

"That," said Mandozza, "will be Vee Brown. Don't look alarmed, Hisdale. Brown can't trace the call. I am calling from a house far down the block; there is an extension wire to the phone here. I am going to promise him the freedom of Condon and the double-crossing woman for that evidence against me."

"But the girl! She's got to die. You said—"

"Sure—sure!" Mandozza waved a finger at Hisdale. "I simply said that I was going to promise him their freedom." He winked, then looked at me as he picked up the receiver. "Chuck some water on Dean Condon. Brown may want to hear his voice as proof that he's here." And into the phone. "Hello—hello there. It's Mandozza talking."

I sputtered and sat up, and tried to hear Mandozza's conversation as one of the gunmen who had brought me there tossed water in my face.

Mandozza was saying: "Condon and the girl are both here. You must meet the car at Sixtieth Street and Fifth Avenue. You must be alone and you must bring the evidence. It means their lives. What!" Mandozza listened a minute, and then very seriously, "You have my solemn word of honor. You bring me that evidence and they both can leave the house with you. Yes—I swear it."

A few minutes of silence while Mandozza listened. Then, "Yes, yes. I know all that. But if you don't come I will simply dispose of the two of them by means of the bath, from which, I understand, Wong escaped. Then I have made arrangements to leave the country. For months I have been gathering money for just such an emergency. You'll come! But why not at once? Very well! The car will be there for you at—" Mandozza consulted his watch— "at twelve o'clock exactly. You're sure you can get the envelope with the income-tax evidence by that time?"

NOW what did he mean by that? Brown had the evidence on him when I left him earlier in the evening. Had he put it away some place? But Mandozza was talking, turning to Hisdale. He said: "Drag that tough guy, Condon, to the phone." And to me, as Hisdale jerked me to my feet and half supported my staggering body across the room, "Just let Brown know you're here."

"Hello, Vee—" I gasped into the phone, while Mandozza held the receiver between his ear and mine.

"So they got you." Brown's voice came back to me. If it wasn't cheerful, at least there was determination in it. "Is Una there too?"

"Yes," I said, "she is." And then, almost shouting the words, "You're coming to your death. Don't come. Mandozza's going to—" Hisdale's hand clasped over my mouth, shutting off my

words. But I heard Brown's answer before I was dragged away.

"Even so, Dean, I'm coming."

Then Mandozza, soft and persuasive. "Condon has little faith in my word of honor, or perhaps he didn't hear it, or—well—to be perfectly frank, Condon played the fool and had to be subdued, rather forcibly subdued. You're coming, Brown. You can trust to my word of honor absolutely. Of course I have yours about the police? Good!"

The receiver clicked on the hook. Mandozza's eyes shone brightly. "The fool," he said, "he's coming." And looking over at Una, "She was right. He's giving his life to her—but not for her."

"Watch out, boss." One of the gunmen at the door spoke. "This Vee Brown, he's walked into more traps and come out again without—"

"Not traps that I laid." Mandozza went to pacing the room, but he made no objection when I staggered over to Una and sat down on the floor beside her. He simply looked at Una and said, "This time there will be no girl to slip a gun into Brown's hand. No rat to sell me out."

I was whispering to Una. Words of comfort that I did not myself believe. Did Brown actually trust in the word of Mandozza? Mandozza— But to Una I said: "Don't worry—don't worry. Vee will do something to save us."

She looked at me for a long moment, waiting, I suppose, for me to tell her what that something was. But I said nothing. There was nothing to say. What would Brown do? What could he do?

It seemed hours and hours until twelve o'clock came. And I was not to spend that time in talking to Una. Mandozza paced the room for a while, then he motioned toward me.

"Tie his hands behind his back." He spoke to the men in the doorway. "And sit him over in that chair. If he gets frisky again, cave his head in with a black-jack."

But I didn't get "frisky" again. I just sat there in the chair thinking of that huge tub and the ropes that hung there, and wondering if Una was to die like that, too.

Mandozza grew nervous as time passed. He frequently consulted his watch, and twice sent one of the men below. Each time the man returned and shook his head. Mandozza cursed. Once he turned to me, and the black points in his eyes flashed.

"He isn't coming." He shook his fist in my face. "And it was you, with your damn warning shout, that—"

Mandozza paused. Footsteps pounded on the stairs outside the room, along the hall. A swarthy face appeared in the doorway. Excited eyes flashed. The man spoke, and his voice trembled in his eagerness.

"He's come! They just brought him in. It's the dick, Brown, all right. We searched him, too—not a thing on him now. But the boys lifted a couple of wicked-looking rods. He never made a kick."

"His cigarette case, his fountain pen. Nothing tricky! You're absolutely sure?" The black points went out of Mandozza's eyes and the queer pink color crept in.

"He ain't got a toothpick even. Nothing left but the envelope. We didn't open that, but it feels like papers only. If you want us to go through it, and—"

"No!" snapped Mandozza. "Bring him up." His thick lips parted; white teeth flashed. He rubbed his great hairy hands together as the man left the room.

VEE BROWN stood in the doorway between the two men wilth drawn guns who stood slightly behind him.

Mandozza smacked his lips, but I think Brown was the most composed man in that room. At least, he spoke first and his voice did not waver.

"So we meet again, Mandozza." And to me, "You always were one for getting into trouble, Dean. But there's Miss Coles, and we'd have gone through with it anyway." And suddenly raising his head and seeing the major, "If it isn't Major Hisdale! All spruced up, too—after slashing a woman's throat."

Hisdale took a step forward and stopped.

Mandozza knitted his brow and rubbed a hand across his mouth before he spoke. It was plain that he didn't understand Brown's attitude of ease, and that it bothered him.

"You've kept your word?" he asked Brown. "Didn't notify the police, didn't try to have the car tailed—nothing that would endanger me?"

"I kept my word," said Brown, "just as you are going to keep yours. Here is the evidence you want. After tonight, we start even. But," he looked over at Hisdale, "that doesn't prevent me from putting the finger on the major for murder."

"No, no." Mandozza grabbed the envelope, tore open the flap and sat down behind the table. But before he went carefully over each separate document, he nodded to his men in warning. Two men in that room, two men in that doorway, and at least one other in the house. Even so, Mandozza cautioned them to watch Brown. Certainly Mortimer Doran had been right. Brown had created a reign of fear in the underworld.

"You have nothing to worry about— at least, not tonight." Vee spoke to Una Coles. "And don't shake your head like that. You misjudge Mandozza. He wouldn't break his word to me. I'm sure of that."

"Wouldn't he?" Major Hisdale laughed. "A word to a dick doesn't mean much."

Mandozza got up from the table, walked over to the fireplace and tossed the papers he had gone over so carefully into the flames. Brown half stretched out his hand as if to stop him, and I thought he was going to speak. But his hand fell to his side and he said nothing. Mandozza was smiling when he turned from the fire.

"All there—everyone of them. So you and the major know each other. He was telling me about your being a bit yellow; about your refusing to shoot with him."

"With him." Brown's lips twisted slightly. "But not refusing to shoot at him."

"At him—at him!" Mandozza held the sides of his lower lip between his index finger and thumb and pulled at it thoughtfully. Then he suddenly burst out laughing.

"At him, eh? There's an idea in that." He swung suddenly to Hisdale and clapped him good naturedly on the back. "How would you like to kill this man—this Vee Brown, that I was going to pay you fifty grand to kill?"

Major Hisdale shrugged his shoulders. "I thought you had other plans," he said. "But whatever you say."

"You don't understand." Mandozza seemed bursting with good humor. "He wouldn't shoot with you, but maybe he'll shoot 'at you.' By God! Hisdale, it's a natural; make you strong with the boys. You and Brown can shoot it out over the billiard table downstairs."

Brown's eyes shot up. Major Hisdale cursed. "I'd be a fool," he said, "to put a gun in a rat's hand when he's slated for the bump anyway."

"But you could do it." Mandozza seemed insistent now, once the idea came into his head. "And besides, there would be the fifty grand. Yes—I'd be glad to pay the fifty grand to see you snuff him out. To see Vee Brown, killer of men, take a bullet in the head."

"You'd put a gun in his hand and—"

"Just one bullet in his gun." Mandozza was eager now. "And fifty grand is a lot of money. Why, a day or two ago you didn't want to wait. You wanted to go straight for him and—"

"Gentlemen—" Brown broke into the conversation now— "you're reckoning without me. This man is wanted by the State for murder. I can't simply kill him, you know."

"You see!" said Major Hisdale. "He's yellow."

Mandozza raised his hand and said: "You've been quite a gun on the Avenue, Brown. You have killed many men. You are lauded in the newspapers for your courage. But was it courage? Didn't you know that they didn't have a chance? Now comes a man who can shoot quicker. You've always been willing to give it, but you can't take it."

And Brown laughed. "Mandozza," he said quietly, "I have seen this man shoot and he hasn't seen me shoot. To give me a gun and give him a gun, and give us an even break would be—well—just plain murder. I'd kill him like that." Brown snapped his fingers contemptuously. "When I leave here tonight, you and I start even. I'll have nothing on you. I'll keep my word about forgetting the kidnaping of Dean and Una Coles. So—sic this Hisdale, or Thomas Craven, or whatever his name is, on me then. Put a gun in his hand, and if I have to protect myself—why—I'll—I'll—" Brown paused. He looked at Una, but whether that had anything to do with his sudden decision or whether it was the determination in Mandozza's face or the sneer on Hisdale's lips, I don't know. But I do know that Brown said suddenly: "All right. Have it your way, Mandozza. Give me one of my own guns and I'll shoot this man to death for you."

EVERYTHING seemed confusion after that. Laughter from those gunmen in the room and at the door. A satisfied look on Major Hisdale's face.

I know that Brown wanted assurance from Mandozza that he wouldn't hold it against us if he killed Hisdale. I know that Hisdale wanted assurance that he would get the fifty thousand dollars if he killed Brown. I know that Mandozza laughed and talked loudly. And I knew, and I knew that Brown knew, that Hisdale could shoot quicker and surer than he could. Now, why was Brown going deliberately to his death? Why— But Mandozza was talking. He took Brown by the arm and walked to the door.

"Everybody's in on the show," he said. "Bring the girl and Condon along. Keep the ropes on Condon's wrists but untie the girl." This to two men who waited to take charge of Una Coles and myself.

A man was going to die. A man was going to be shot down. I shuddered. A holiday spirit prevailed.

It seemed some time before Una and I were marched down those stairs. Then we were in the basement, by the furnace, through a door and into a recreation room that was lined with imitation logs, that gave it the appearance of a rustic cabin.

There was one light only in that room, and that from a single green shade that hung above a billiard table, splashing a brilliant arc down upon it and leaving the rest of the room in semidarkness.

Brown came over to me and slipped a piece of paper into the breast pocket of my jacket.

"Mandozza has been kind enough to let me write this little note." He pinched my shoulder and grinned. "It's a message for you and for him if—if anything should happen to me." And in a louder voice, "Don't look so serious, Dean. You'll be laughing over it all in half an hour. It's not the first man you've seen me kill. Remember," and this plenty loud enough for Hisdale to hear as Mandozza called him to take his place at the table, "Hisdale brutally murdered a woman tonight."

I looked over at Hisdale as Brown finished speaking and turned slowly from me. If he had hoped to get Hisdale's nerve, he had failed, I thought. The major stood at one end of the billiard table, his arms folded across his chest, a sneer on his lips.

I looked around that room, trying to peer into the shadows as Brown took his place at the other end of that billiard table. It seemed as if ten or twelve dim figures stood in the darkness. The whiteness of their faces, the whiteness of their hands was plainly visible. Or were their hands white—wasn't there something black in each hand; something that looked like a gun—that was a gun?

Mandozza stood by the center of the table now, addressing Brown and the major. "You will stand so—one at either end of the table. When Zelli, here, claps his hands that will be the signal for action. I should like to give the signal myself but—" he indicated his bandaged wrist and sneered at Brown. Then continuing, "Just the single clap, and everything goes. Your guns will be in the center of the table. Yours, Brown, with the butt toward you. Yours, major, with the butt toward you. You may—"

"But I say," Brown cut in, "that's giving the major quite an advantage in reach. He's got a good several inches on me, and—" Then, with a shrug of his shoulders, "All right. I've seen him shoot and guess I can spot him that much."

And Brown scored. At least, I think that he scored, for the sneer left the major's lips. His jaws set tightly—grimly.

"One further warning," Mandozza said to Brown. "There are several men in this room, all armed. There is only one shot in your gun. If you make one false move, lean so much as an inch over the edge of the table, before the signal, I'll put a bullet through your head."

"And if the major tries to beat the signal, does he get the same dose?" asked Brown. Certainly he seemed to face death with indifference.

"If the major makes a false move he loses that fifty grand. I might add that he's hard up and very fond of money."

"All right," said Brown, and half swinging his body around to the figures in the shadows, "You boys are all witnesses to the fairness of the arrangement, and that I'm forced, in self-defense, to kill this man."

"Get to it," said Hisdale, and his voice shook. But I think it was with anger.

Mandozza leaned forward, placing two guns upon the table, the butt of one toward Brown; the butt of the other toward the major, with nearly the width of that full-size billiard table between them.

"Any questions?" Mandozza said, and there was an eagerness in his voice. Mandozza, who had thought his thrills in life were over, was experiencing a new one, I guess.

"Yes—" said Brown. "Zelli claps—and then any kind of shooting—any kind of death? No restrictions—no rules after the signal?"

"No rules, no restrictions." Mandozza's voice was shrill as he backed from the table, pushed close to Una Coles and myself. "Just grab your guns and fire. Are you ready?"

Fear left me then, I think. Just a wild pounding in my heart, perspiration on my face, and my eyes darting to each of those two erect figures in turn.

There was nothing of indifference in Brown's face now. There was no whimsical twist to his lips. His black eyes flashed brilliantly. He was not the Master of Melody proclaimed by Tin-Pan Alley. There was a hard, perhaps even cruel determination in his face. He did not look like a man going to his death. He was the deadly, cold, calculating detective. Vee Brown—Killer of Men.

"Ready!" said Mandozza.

And both men acted the same in the hushed silence of the room. Each set his eyes on the other's hand for a moment, then set those eyes steadily upon their guns. Set them there and kept them there, riveted to those stub-nosed black objects which in another second would spit death.

CHAPTER SEVEN

Killer of Men

THE clap came. Two bodies hurtled suddenly forward. White, drawn faces flashed beneath the light. Hands stood vividly out above the green baize of the billiard table. Grasping fingers sought those guns.

My eyes were fixed on those two guns—on the hands that darted for them.

Hisdale reached his gun first. There was no doubt of that. Plainly I saw those strong white fingers close over the blue steel. He had only to bend forward from the hips, while Brown had to half fling himself onto the table.

Surely this was the end. Death for Vee Brown! For even as Brown's slender, long fingers reached his gun, Hisdale had already gripped his tightly; had even lifted it from the table. He was straightening his body, swinging his arm—his hand—his gun toward Vee.

My eyes were on Hisdale's face then. I couldn't—couldn't see Brown die, and I couldn't take my eyes off the man who was to kill him. There was triumph in Hisdale's face; that evil lust to kill that I had seen in men's faces before. Then, something else in Hisdale's face. Uncertainty, surprise, a touch of fear—and, by God! I knew. There was horror, abject terror in his face as his gun roared—as two guns roared.

I gasped, and my eyes bulged. There was a hole in the major's forehead, a black hole that was ever widening and turning red. The look of horror was still on the man's face. And I knew the truth, knew it before Hisdale sank slowly upon the table, turned his head slightly so that glaring glassy eyes stared unseeingly at me. Then his knees must have given, for the upper part of his body slid slowly along the table, twisted oddly and disappeared—to fall with a thud upon the floor.

Yes—I knew the truth. Major Hisdale was dead, and Brown had fired without jerking his body back from the table; fired the moment his hand reached that gun and his finger caressed the trigger. Just a sudden upturn of his wrist and he had chanced it. Chanced that single shot —or had he chanced it? Wasn't he just as sure of himself when his finger closed upon the trigger as he always was? And I looked at Brown.

He still half lay upon the table, his wrist twisted up, his gun in his hand. Was he— And he wasn't. For even as I looked at him in the dead quiet of that room he straightened and rubbed a hand across his forehead, wiping away a tiny trickle of blood. Then his eyes sought the shadows where Una Coles and I stood. His lips parted and twisted slightly at one corner, and he winked at me.

"She makes a charming widow, Dean." His voice sounded loud and clear in the silence.

The tension broke, and men cursed. Guns flashed, and one man stepped into the light and thumped a gun against Brown's ribs.

"Will I give it to him, boss? He's done for Craven; done for Tom."

Brown stood with his back against the table now, trying to pick out Mandozza, I think. That twisted, crooked smile was still on his lips when he spoke.

"Call off your dogs, Mandozza," he said calmly. "What else did you expect when you put a gun in my hand?"

"I thought," said Mandozza, in a husky awed voice, "that he could shoot faster and straighter than any man living." His voice changed suddenly and he spoke to his men. "No gunplay now. I have other things in store for Mr. Vee Brown. Out of the room, all of you but Joe and Marato. Take that empty gun from Brown first; I don't like the looks of it in his hand. Yes—yes," he went on, somewhat irritably, when some of the gang muttered, "I'm going to kill him, of course. Craven shall have his vengeance. Take the body out!"

OTHER lights flashed on, illuminating the entire room. All but the two men to whom Mandozza had spoken had left the room, and the body of Major Hisdale had gone with them. Those two stood by the door, guns in their hands. Mandozza walked over to Brown. His voice was low but I caught his words.

"It is better this way," he said. "I am half glad you killed him. Ideas were forming in his head that were not good for him. Besides, you saved me money. And now, Mr. Vee Brown, do you know what I am going to do with you?"

"Yes—" said Brown, as he still leaned easily against the billiard table. "You are going to keep your word. You are going to let me and Miss Coles and Dean Condon go."

Mandozza's laugh was like a shovel on dry pavement. "I am going to let you sit and watch Una Coles and Dean Condon drown slowly. Drown in my bath, the bath which you said I do not use myself. Then—" Mandozza paused and looked at Brown.

"Then—" Vee encouraged.

"Then it will be your turn to try the bath. Do you think I'd let you kill my best man, Frankie Curry; kill him and return his dead body to me? Do you think I'd let this female rat, who turned stoolie and slipped a gun into your hand, go free? Do you think I'd let your friend live after you killed mine? No. You're going to watch them die, slowly—horribly. Then I shall watch you die the same way. What do you say to that?" Mandozza stuck his face close to Brown's. Hate was there now.

"I say there's been enough of play-acting," Brown said sharply. "I insist that you let us all loose, take care of your own dead, and forget the incident as you passed your word you would. I came for Dean—and because of my promise to Una Coles."

"You must think a lot of that girl." Mandozza looked, half indifferently, toward Una.

"Yes." Brown said quietly. "But not so much as you think of your sister, Rosa."

"What do you mean?" Mandozza swung on him suddenly. Maybe there was alarm in his voice, maybe just surprise.

"I mean this," said Brown. "I'm not a fool, and only a fool would trust your word. I made preparations to safeguard my return and the safe return of Una and Dean. In plain words, Louie Mandozza, your sister's life is the price you will pay for not letting us go free."

"That's a lie—a lie," Mandozza screamed suddenly, and a knife flashed into his hand.

"That won't help you," said Brown, and the very coolness of his voice, I think, stayed Mandozza's hand. "I am telling you the truth. When you called me on the phone I had the evidence you sought in my pocket. I told you it would take me an hour to get it. In that hour I found your sister, made a pretense of arresting her for questioning, and turned her over to a friend; a friend who will kill her at three o'clock unless I stop him. You see, it is all very simple."

"You, a city detective, would have her killed!" I think there was doubt more than fear in Mandozza's voice. But certainly he was stunned.

"Why not?" Brown shrugged his shoulders. "You know me. Know that I meet violence with violence, death with death. Why not crime with crime?"

"But who could you get—possibly get —to do this thing? No—it's bluff. No one would dare harm her. Not Rosa, not Louie Mandozza's sister."

"You don't think so?" Brown put those black eyes on Mandozza. "Well, perhaps you are right and I am wrong. But Wong is the name of the man who waits for three o'clock. Wong, the man you tried to kill by drowning, in the bath tub. And I explained to him very carefully that you were the man, Mandozza; and I explained to him very carefully, also, that the woman he was to kill was your sister."

But Mandozza was rushing from the room. "You lie—you lie!" he shrieked over his shoulder. "But I'll find out." And he was gone, hurling some orders back at our two guards.

I WHISPERED hoarsely, looking at the two men at the door. "You— you didn't—didn't do that!"

"Of course I did," Brown snapped. "That's why I shoved the note in your pocket. I wanted Mandozza to see it if I—if Major Hisdale, with his parlor magic, happened to get me. The note would have saved you and Una."

"But—but he could shoot faster," I stammered. "How did it happen that you killed him? Those candles and the three of spades"—

"I am not," said Brown, "the spots on a playing card. Spots on a playing card do not shoot back. When a man shoots to kill, he needs more than a keen eye and a quick finger. That is, when a man shoots to kill me. He needs one thing more. That one thing the major lacked in the final moment. I saw it in his face, Dean, just as our guns spoke. Yes, I had something that he lacked and needed very much at that moment. It's a common word, Dean; perhaps even a vulgar word. But it's a very expressive word, and in this case it meant the difference between life and death. The word is 'guts!'" And suddenly, "But we're forgetting our young widow, and— There! I didn't mean that."

Brown put an arm about her shoulders as she burst into tears suddenly. The two men at the door were watching us, but they didn't interfere as we talked.

"It was terrible—terrible," Una sobbed over and over. "I didn't want to look, but I had to—I had to. I hated him; he had no right to live. But to see him die like that!"

"It's hard, Una, I know." Brown spoke very low. "I feel the same way about death very often. But tonight, when my finger closed upon the trigger, I thought of the woman whose throat he had slashed; of her life and her death," and hardly above a whisper, "and wondered if some day it mightn't be you, Una—if I missed. Then, it was very easy to kill him."

Five—ten—fifteen minutes—a half hour we must have stood there before other men came and we were taken upstairs to the room where we had been before. Mandozza was pacing the floor and watching the phone. He spoke to Brown without looking at him.

"Rosa is gone from her apartment, but I don't think you have beaten me. I have sent three men to your apartment to bring her back, if they have to blast their way in."

"You waste time," Brown cut in. "Wong has a brother downtown, and your sister is there. You didn't think I'd be fool enough to keep her at my apartment!"

Mandozza turned and faced us. His face was deeply lined. He was about to speak when the phone rang. He snapped up the receiver quickly and said: "Man-

dozza speaking. Let me have it. Quick!"

After that the conversation was one-sided, but of course I knew that it was one of the men he had sent to our penthouse who was talking to him. Then Mandozza was saying: "The door was open, eh? No woman—just a man— Was it a Chink? It wasn't? No— I don't care what you did then."

Mandozza slammed up the receiver and turned to Brown. There was a hurt tone in his voice.

"A representative of the law!" he said. "I didn't believe it of you, Brown. It's hard even now to believe it. Rosa—little Rosa, there with a Chink. A Chink who—" And suddenly, threateningly, "By God! if anything happens to her I'll tear you limb from limb. How do I know you'll return her safely?"

"You'll have to take my word for it." And then Brown laughed. "You're quite a character, Mandozza. I'll miss you when you're gone."

"What do you mean by that?"

"Oh, it's inevitable that I'll kill you." Brown shrugged his shoulders. "But don't worry about Rosa. I'll have no use for her after we're out of here and safely home."

THERE was more of course. Mandozza threatened and blustered. But it was over at last. My hands were free and Mandozza was making a final threat as we left his house.

Brown's guns, his cigarette case, and all his other little possessions were returned. He stood in the doorway, lit a cigarette and accepted the car which Mandozza offered to drive us home.

He said to Mandozza at parting: "You see how easy it is for even the innocent to be dragged into our crime wars." He snapped out his watch. "Don't worry about Rosa. If you had read the note in Dean's pocket you would understand that Wong will ring up the penthouse at three o'clock for instructions, before—But good night. Your sister will be safely back at her own apartment shortly after three. It's an even start from now on, Mandozza." And to me, as we descended the steps and I helped Una into the car,

"You will back me up, Dean, when I advise Mortimer Doran that I'm still the best shot in the world. The best living shot, of course."

I held Una close to me there in the car, trying to comfort her. But I did ask Brown: "Wong wouldn't really have killed her?" And when he didn't answer, "Would he?"

Brown turned toward me in the darkness, but I saw his black eyes shine as he said: "You expect too much of me, Dean. Wong is a Chinese—and who can tell what an Oriental will do. Certainly I can't. But there was a man in our apartment. Who could it be?"

Standing before our Park Avenue apartment we watched the car speed away. Then Una insisted upon leaving. She smiled when I expressed fear at her being on the streets that time of the morning.

"Let her go her way." Brown agreed with her. "When Miss Coles is ready to tell us just who she is, we will be ready to listen. As to her safety. She was

never more safe than now—between this hour and three o'clock. She can telephone us and let us know she's all right, before Rosa is sent back."

And Una Coles was gone, slipping into the night.

The door of our apartment was unlocked. Brown opened it cautiously and we entered. The lights were burning in the hall, the foyer—the living room beyond. And I drew back with a start.

There—on the floor beside the low, soft couch was the body of a man. He was tied tightly with heavy rope that was wound around and around him.

I followed Brown to the trussed-up figure, heard his short laugh as I looked down at the gagged man—the flashing gray eyes. I recognized him as Brown spoke.

"Someone has sent us a present, Dean." And then suddenly, as if in great surprise, "Bless my soul! If it isn't the famous sleuth, Inspector Ramsey himself. Now what possessed him to tie himself up like this?"

But I didn't need Brown's wink to tell me that Inspector Ramsey had come to our apartment to hunt for the evidence against Mandozza. The evidence that a few hours before had gone up in smoke.

"Carry her inside," Cardigan said. "It'll keep your arms occupied."

THE DEAD DON'T DIE

A Cardigan Story

by

Frederick Nebel

Author of "Lead Pearls," etc.

Giles Jacland lay stabbed in Room 904 weltering in a pool of crimson. And only Cardigan had sense enough to spot the single clue to murder. Had gall enough to lift that paper from under the very noses of the cops and read between the lines.

CHAPTER ONE

Curtain Column

THE hotel grapevine vibrated with the news. The telephone operator going off duty at 8:00 A. M. gave it to the red-head coming on. The page-boy, on his way through overheard it and, scooting out of the little office, he passed the word on to the bell captain. The bell captain slipped it sotto voce to his favorite hop, and the hop, headed downstairs to get a pressed suit for 900, gave it to the valet, the head porter and the engineer. The head porter passed it on to the housekeeper, but she'd already heard. The red-head who had relieved the night operator plugged in a surreptitious call to a newshawk friend on the daily tab.

Her voice was a dramatic whisper. "Listen, Hank. Get this on the nose and don't ever tell me I'm not your pal. Giles Jacland is dead in his apartment here. . . . Go on now, ask me a lot of dumb questions! Ain't I told you enough?" She plugged out, plugged in, lilting, "Good-morning-sir-Hotel-Saxony!"

M. Brouée, the Swiss managing director, got it from the fourth assistant manager at breakfast and dropped his half-eaten croissant into the coffee. "But no!" he exclaimed.

"The police," said the fourth assistant manager, "are here."

"And Strout, the house officer?"

"He is there representing the management."

"The press?"

"No one knows of this but you, the housekeeper, Strout, myself, and the police."

Downstairs, at that moment, the second porter was giving it to the head car washer in the hotel garage.

SO Giles Jacland, the dramatic critic, aged fifty-two, was dead in a welter of blood that was darker than the red blocks of the Bokhara upon which he lay in the great living room of Suite 904. There was a moment of inactivity while the police photographer set his lenses.

"Them pajamas are the nuts," he remarked.

"Get that picture," Lieutenant Bone said.

"No kidding. If I busted out in a rash of nightdress like that the wife'd leave me flat."

Bone said, toneless, "Get done and scram." He had a dour, slab-cheeked face with high cheekbones and a chin like a doorknob. He stood paring his fingernails with a penknife.

Sergeant Raush was stocky and still worrying about the fifty bucks he'd lost on Schmelling. Strout, the house dick, stood near the windows, short and fat and white in dark clothes. The photographer got his picture, hummed, said, "O. K., Abe," to Bone and strode light-heartedly out of the apartment.

Strout said, "Did he begin life in a slaughter house?"

"No," Raush said seriously. "He used to be a barber upstate. He had political pull in the county and he used to get all the jobs shaving dead men."

Bone suddenly went across to the telephone and made a call to headquarters. "I think maybe I ought to have a fingerprint man up here. . . . This is Abe Bone, on the Jacland kill, at the Saxony."

When he hung up, Raush said, "It must have been somebody Jacland knew."

"Maybe Cardigan'll know."

In Jacland's checkbook there was a stub showing that a check for $300 had been made out to the Cosmos Agency on the day before.

Bone said, sourly, "How about this guy's women, Strout?"

"Well, you know Jacland."

"If I knew him, I wouldn't be asking."

Strout shrugged. "He had the pick, I guess. He was a gay old bird and his women were usually young. No woman carved that throat, though."

"No. Some woman's boy friend, maybe."

The door opened and Cardigan loomed through, his battered felt in hand and his mop of black hair shaggier than ever.

Bone said, "Hello, Cardigan." He jerked his doorknob chin toward the body and added, "Get a load of it."

Cardigan looked. He came in, closed the door and leaned back against it. After a moment he looked back at Bone.

"That's tough," he said.

"What's the dope, Cardigan?"

"Dope on what?"

"This."

"Search me, Abe."

Bone sighed, strolled across the room and picked up the checkbook. "This guy was a client of yours. It began yesterday. Why was he a client?"

"It was his idea, not ours. He walked into our office yesterday morning, sat down and drew out his checkbook. He wrote a check for three hundred berries and said, 'There's a retainer. I may telephone at any time for a bodyguard, or for advice.' Like that—see?"

"Yeah. Now go on."

Cardigan shrugged, said, "That's all there was, Abe," and went across to the body.

"You mean to tell me," Bone dug in, "that this guy just planked down three hundred bucks and didn't give any details?"

Cardigan took his time in examining the body, then rose and said, absently, "Yes. We knew of him. A perfectly respectable citizen."

Bone chopped off, "I don't believe it!"

"Me, neither," agreed Raush.

"It does," Strout said, "sound crappy."

MEANWHILE Cardigan rolled across the room, disappeared into regions beyond—the bedroom, the bathroom, the dinette, the pantry. He reappeared in the living room plucking grapes from a bunch in his left hand and eating them. He blew the seeds into his right palm and deposited them in a tray on the desk. There were two newspapers on the desk. One was folded; the other lay flat. They were, otherwise, identical issues of the same newspaper— The Press-Call. On the desk, also, there were half a dozen pictures of as many beautiful women.

Cardigan pointed. "He was a good picker."

"Listen, you!" Bone snapped. "Why did Jacland hire you guys down at the agency?"

Cardigan disappeared again but returned in a moment with another bunch of grapes. "I told you, Abe," he said, unruffled. "I don't know. In times like these, when a guy walks in and signs his name to three hundred berries' worth of negotiable paper, what are we supposed to do, call him a dirty name?"

"You're lying, Cardigan!"

Cardigan indicated the body. "I'm lying, huh, when our client's been knifed to death? I'd give you a waltz-me-around, huh? Why, Abe? Why the hell should I? That looks like a head on your shoulders, boy—use it."

"I still don't believe you, Cardigan. I don't believe a guy would engage you birds, and pay for it, before he gave you a sound steer. It ain't being done. There's something crummy about it, and you know there is."

Cardigan ate grapes.

Raush said, "That's him, Abe; that's him all the time. Funny. Funny as hell. Maybe he knows who did it and maybe he figures on raking in a couple of grand from the right party for keeping his mouth shut."

"Hey, Abe," Cardigan said, "what's this crackpot's name?"

"Who—Raush?"

"Maybe that's what you call him."

Raush got up. "I don't like that, bozo."

Cardigan walked to the desk, dumped a handful of seeds, picked up the folded paper and pointed it at Raush. "That dirty crack you made, copper, is going to cost you a pinch. I told you guys the God's honest. Jacland came in and did just what I said. There was no explanation. He left the check because he knew it would bring prompt action when he needed us."

Bone broke in with, "Then you do know something."

"Who said so?"

"You just said Raush's crack would cost him a pinch."

"It will, honeybunch, if I land on the killer's tail."

He swung across the room, yanked open the door.

"Nuts, Cardigan," Raush said. "Lots of nuts."

Cardigan went right on out, slamming the door. A few minutes later the telephone rang and Bone answered it. "What?" he growled; and then, angrily, "Forget it!" He slammed the receiver into the hook.

"What's up?" Raush said.

"Room service," Bone growled, "said an order was just left for nuts for you. They wanted to know what kind."

SO Giles Jacland was dead. . . . Dramatic critic extraordinary, raconteur, bachelor. Some said acid dripped from his pen and that he could make or break an actor. Merciless in his criticism, he was rarely satisfied with a performance. And once on the trail of an actor he considered bad, that actor thenceforth had little peace of mind.

But all that was done. Giles Jacland was dead and the crime lacked an exotic note. No woman's handkerchief left behind, no scarf, no scent of perfume. A knife had done it. A knife wielded, apparently, by a strong man's hand. Jacland had dabbled much in women; at fifty-two he had been a gay blade, lean, handsome, conceited, seen here and there at night clubs with a beautiful woman, but never the same one.

When Cardigan rolled into the agency office Pat Seaward was fixing her mouth

with a lipstick and regarding the process in the mirror of a compact vanity case. She looked small, neat, trim in a summer dress of dark blue.

"Where's George?" Cardigan said.

"He just stepped out. For a drink. Every time Lieutenant Bone calls up, the boss has to go out an' get a drink." The vanity case snapped shut. "Bone was sore. So the boss is sore at you."

"Why me?"

"Said that since you won two hundred on that Sharkey-Schmelling adagio, there's no holding you. You walk up on the street and smack perfect strangers. You call nice little police officers names and things. In short, you're an old meany."

He gave her one of his dark, malignant looks—that really meant nothing—and swung across to the iced water cooler. He drew and drank two tall glasses. He said, "You're another one who's joined the razzberry bandwagon."

She turned and was suddenly sincere. "Gosh, chief, why don't you cut out riding people? Why get Bone mad?"

"Listen, duchess, I went into that apartment feeling swell. They asked me some questions. I answered truthfully. Then Abe started getting sarcastic and his busboy, Raush, pulled a crack I didn't stomach. So—" he slashed his hand down— "to hell with them. I—me—I, Pat, am going to find out who killed our late client. There's three hundred dollars' worth of finding out to be done, and this little choir boy is going to do it. Did Bone say I took anything out of that apartment?"

"No. Now you're not going to stand there and tell me you walked off with something right under their proboscides!"

He made a face. "You've been going in for deep books again." He drew a copy of The Press-Call from his pocket. "This, little bluestocking—this."

"A newspaper."

"Don't knock me over with those fast

come-backs." He sat on the desk, unfolded the paper, which had been folded four times, and held it up. "Understand," he said, "when I found this paper, on the desk in Jacland's living room, it was folded just as I showed it to you. Before who ever had it, folded it, he'd been reading, as you see now, the dramatic page."

"Wouldn't Jacland read it?"

"There was another paper, just like this one, on his desk. Same issue, same everything—except that it had on it a little yellow slip saying: 'Good Morning! Compliments of the Hotel Saxony.' The hotel supplies one every morning to its guests. So why should Jacland order another sent up? He didn't. Even if he had, he wouldn't have folded it like this. You fold a paper this way only if you're carrying it on the street, either in your pocket or in your hand. Am I screwy?"

"No. It reasons."

"The guy that killed Jacland came in with this paper. You see this short column here?"

"Yes."

"What do you see? Don't read it, nosy; just tell me what first draws your attention."

"The paper's wrinkled right there, cracked a bit as if—as if—"

"As if," he took up, "some guy, while talking heatedly, kept jabbing it right there with his finger."

She looked at him. "Yes, chief."

HE gushed a great sigh of satisfaction through his teeth. "I'm glad to see I'm not entirely ga-ga. We are going to, in time, make a call on Rosalie Wayne."

"Rosalie Way—"

"Read that column," he cut in. "The last from the pen of Giles Jacland—aged fifty-two, a town rounder, an intellectual snob, a bum and, to borrow a crack you pull on me sometimes, a cad. Read it—and weep and I'll bop you."

Pat read it aloud.

"Last night these weary eyes beheld, this tired brain sought to absorb, the warp and woof of a play entitled *Sacrilege*. Why it was entitled *Sacrilege*, I do not know; unless perhaps the author, unwittingly, named it appropriately in its relation to the drama and what we like to believe the drama stands for. It was, indeed, a sacrilege—to make myself clearer—to thrust so infantile a potpourri into the laps of a much abused public.

"Yet more of a sacrilege to the Art of the Drama was the performance of Rosalie Wayne. Garbling her lines, throwing her arms about like a tree in a fall gale, but with less grace, she helped to make ludicrous a play that was already woebegone. Apparently devoid of talent, obviously lacking in subtlety, she tramped, wept, stumbled and clawed her way through three ungainly acts with the questionable agility of an elephant. She—"

"You get it?" Cardigan broke in.

Pat looked up and there was color in her face. "It's cruel!" she cried. "It's too personal, too unutterably bitter. It's malicious and horribly uncalled for!"

"You've got the language, kid."

"But," she hastened to say, "this would have no connection with Jacland's death."

He grinned. "No?"

"Of course not! People—people like Rosalie Wayne—don't do that sort of thing."

He still grinned. "No?"

"It's unreasonable. It's not sense."

"Suppose," he said, "you hang around so you can be on hand to give me the horse laugh when I'm wrong."

He took the paper from her, folded it and thrust it into his coat pocket. He said, "I'll probably need you along—since there's a jane in it. I called her apartment but she's not in. The maid said she motored to Greenwich this morning—left at a quarter to nine; about three quarters of an hour after Jacland was bumped off. She'll be back in time for tonight's performance at the Rosemont. Afterwards, she sings one song at the Club Cordova—a kind of torch song. Wear the ice-blue rag that makes you look like a million."

She made a mock curtsey. "Yes, O Master."

The phone rang and Cardigan made a lazy sweep at it. "Hello. . . This is Cardigan talking." He listened; then his eyes darkened, his mouth crowded the mouthpiece. "Oh, yeah? . . . Well, listen to me, mister— Hello, hello!" He juggled the hook. "Hello—" He whanged the receiver down. He stood holding the instrument and staring hard into space. Then he rasped out a short, contemptuous laugh and planked the phone down.

"Bone?" Pat dared to inquire.

"No. Some guy said, 'Cardigan, stay off the Jacland murder or you'll regret it.' And hung up."

She said, "Maybe Bone or Raush got somebody to call up and scare you. You know they hate like the devil to see you reach a case first."

He looked at her. "Maybe." He looked away and added, "Maybe not. Maybe it's the other side. If it is, there's only one way they'd know I'm on it. The maid. The maid in Rosalie Wayne's apartment." He smacked the paper in his pocket. "This rag is going to cause somebody a headache."

Pat sighed. "Heartache, maybe." And she didn't sound happy.

He said sharply, "Listen. You go up to Rosalie Wayne's apartment. Pass yourself off as a sob-sister from a daily tab. Get a load of the apartment and the maid. Especially the maid."

She said, "I've a feeling I'm not going to like this."

He was lighting a cigarette. "Don't be a sap. You work here, don't you? Scram."

CHAPTER TWO

Nice Knife Work

THE Petremont Plaza was an apartment house, tall, thin, white, off Park Avenue. Pat entered the dim, deftly lit lobby and was aware of quiet elegance. A black-and-chrome elevator lifted her noiselessly to the twelfth floor and she walked down a wide corridor on soft, plum-colored carpet. There was an ebony knocker on the door marked 1212. She used it.

A little plump woman in a black dress and an Eton collar opened the door. She wore old-fashioned spectacles and had a small, quaint face, a friendly but hesitant smile. Pat's heart sank, but she had a job to do.

"I'm Ann Walters from The Daily Flash. Could I have a few words with you?"

"Come right in, miss; come right in."

Friendly, Pat was sure; gray and dainty in an old halftone way.

"You're Miss Wayne's maid?"

"Yes, kind of."

The door was shut and the maid was indicating a chair. Pat sat down and the old woman took a chair nearby and let her hands lie in her lap.

"Well, Mrs.—"

"It's 'Miss,' please; Miss Leadley."

"How long have you been Miss Wayne's maid?"

"Many years."

It was tough going, but Pat went on. "Miss Wayne's a good actress, don't you think?"

"Yes." Her chin went up. "One of the best. And a good girl, miss. A very good girl."

"I like her myself. Some don't."

A shadow fell across the quaint old face. "Yes—some don't."

"Who, for instance?"

Miss Leadley looked up, startled. Then

she said, "Oh, it doesn't matter, does it?"

Pat was quick: "I understand our great dramatic critic Giles Jacland—"

A hostile light shone in the old eyes. "Yes! But he will not—" She stopped short, flushed; went on, flustered. "He will not get anywhere with his bitterness."

"Why do you suppose he's so bitter?"

Miss Leadley sat back. "Miss, what is it you want to know?"

"I want to get an inside slant on Miss Wayne's life. I want to write a piece about her—from a human angle." She felt her face was going to flush any minute. "The human, heart-to-heart angle. I want to—"

A sharp sound, as if something had been knocked over, stopped her short. She swung around but there was no one else in the room. When she turned back, Miss Leadley had risen and was staring across the room. Pat followed her gaze toward a closed door. She stood up.

"There's someone in your apartment," she said.

"No—no, I think not."

"I heard something—in that room."

"It couldn't be."

Pat said, "You'd better call the superintendent. There have been apartment robberies in this neighborhood lately—"

"I—it must have been our imagination."

A door closed.

Pat went across the room swiftly, opened the connecting door and looked into a bedroom. On the farther side was a door, parallel with the one through which she had entered the apartment. She heard a sharp intake of breath behind her; turned and saw the maid, white-faced, with hands clenched. She looked into the bedroom again, then entered, stopped after she had taken a few steps and looked around.

The maid's exhaled breath was accompanied by "See, we must have imagined it."

THE room was empty. The maid was peaceful, smiling again, but the white look ebbed slowly from her face. Pat felt she had played the fool. She shrugged and was turning away when she caught sight of a small, brocaded footstool—overturned. Her glance darted from it to the closed door. She sniffed. She smelled, she was sure, the odor of smoke—heavy, strong, the kind that a cigar leaves behind.

But she said nothing. She laughed. "I guess I was mistaken. You see, I'm used to living alone—and I'm kind of scary of prowlers."

The old woman beamed. "Yes, I know how it is. . . . Perhaps, Miss Walters, you'd better call again—when Miss Wayne is at home. Walters is the name, isn't it?"

Was there sly mockery in her tone as she said that name?

Pat felt uncomfortable. "I'd hoped," she said, "I would find her home. Thank you, Miss Leadley."

Red color did not flood her face until she was in the corridor. She waited a full minute before ringing for the elevator. In the lobby, she got beneath one of the lights and resorted to her vanity case. Snapping it shut, she went out into the street and walked west. She did not see a man step down from a doorway opposite and stare after her. She boarded a bus at Fifth Avenue and rode downtown as far as Forty-second Street. She got off, crossed the curb and spotted Cardigan in front of one of the library lions. He was always big in a crowd—big and a little shaggy.

"Well, Pat?" He searched her face with a dark scowl.

When she held her head level her eyes always rested on the knot of his tie. "I didn't find much, chief. The maid's an old woman—a dear, sweet old thing—"

"Did I send you up there to bring *me* a sob-story?"

Her eyes flashed up at him. He passed a hand across his mouth and made a face. "Sorry, kitten." But he didn't smile. "Well?" he said.

"She's been with Rosalie Wayne for many years."

"That means she's a good maid. Go on."

It came hard. "I think she suspected me."

"Why?"

"Well—I heard a noise in the other room behind a closed door and . . ." She related it briefly, ending with, "I guess I kind of fumbled it."

He stared west at a southbound elevated train. "The maid, then—she knows Jacland's dead. It's not in the papers yet, but she knows it. That's swell. See any pictures of Jacland?"

"No."

He caught hold of her arm. "Come on, cid. You did well. Could you stand an Old Fashion?"

She blew her nose quietly. "To be frank, I think I need one. Maybe two."

"You're going soft on me."

"I know," she said. "I'm a wash-out."

He chided roughly. "Yeah. Yes, you are."

THE Club Cordova was in East Fifty-seventh Street. You entered straight from the sidewalk beneath a dark-green marquee and a flunky in dark-green livery opened the big door and didn't bow as you passed in. The checkroom girl was small, dark, and she could smile, throw backchat, without looking you in the eye. Antonio, a Brooklyn dago with a marcel, met you in the foyer and did the gladhanding. He was a nice fellow who had found waiting on tables in a chop house beneath his ability. White, happy-faced, he treated names and nobodies alike.

"I have not seen you since—when, Mr. Cardigan?"

"Riddle me right away," Cardigan chaffed, and hooked his black fedora on the checkroom girl's hand. No matter how evening clothes smoothed down his bulk, his hair remained loose, shaggy, untamed, and the whiteness of his shirt front made his face look browner, bigger, in its rough masculine way. "This is Miss Seaward, Tony. . . . Pat, this is Antonio. A table for two, Tony, on the edge of the dance floor. We'll be in later. . . . Before me, Pat."

"Ah," said Antonio, "I will give you the royal box."

"Yeah. I heard that crack in Paris once. Look out for the copyright law, kid."

He piloted Pat into the bar. It was small, intimate, with few mirrors and lots of shiny woodwork, dark and impressive and paneled. There were high stools in front of the bar and the bartender, in a white jacket, vestlike but for the sleeves, was quiet, efficient and, carrying out the mode of the new era, properly self-effacing. It was exactly 11:00 P. M. and few people had come in.

Pat climbed onto a stool and Cardigan stood and said, "Name your weakness."

"You know it."

"Two Old Fashions," he told the bartender; and to Pat, sotto voce, "With the dress, Patrick, I myself could fall for you."

"Pouf!"

"Think—think of all the women who are mad about me?"

"That wouldn't call for much extended thought."

He sighed. "O. K. Maybe we'd better drink instead. Here's to you, duchess."

"Is it true that you once pulled stroke for Princeton?"

"What have you got against Princeton?"

She said, suddenly, "Oh-oh."

"Huh?"

"Father Bone, entering."

Abe Bone came up to the bar. "That

cab you were in, Cardigan, should have been pinched for speeding."

"Hello, Abe. Have a drink. Did you tie Raush outside?"

"I'm on the wagon." He was dour, wrinkle-browed. "We got no fingerprints. There was a dead end. Whoever bumped off Jacland knew him, because nobody asked the desk for him; they knew his apartment number. I checked up on phone calls this morning. though. He got a phone call—early."

"Swell! You get a break then."

"Yeah. I get a break. I find out you been two-timing on me."

Cardigan turned to Pat. "You better turn the other way, chicken. The Bone and I are headed for words."

Bone said under his breath, "You stay right here, Miss Seaward."

Cardigan faced him. "Spill it, Abe."

"What I want to know is, how did you find out Rosalie Wayne phoned Jacland a half hour before he got bumped off?"

"I didn't. Me—find out? You're crazy."

"That's a rumor you been tossing around town a long time. If you didn't know about the phone call, why did you send Miss Seaward to Rosalie Wayne's apartment this morning?"

Cardigan blinked. That was a fast one and he stalled, saying, "Who said she went there?"

"I got it from the maid there. She said a girl from The Flash dropped in. I called The Flash. No girl from their office went there. I asked the maid to describe her. She did it perfect. I got a hunch and I went to the taxi stand near your office. A guy remembered taking her from in front of your office right to the Petremont Plaza."

Cardigan said, "O. K. She did. Now what? You damned well know I'd have a hell of a time trying to get any dope out of the telephone exchange."

"That's just what I know. And now what I want to know is, how'd you find out about Rosalie Wayne? What did you pick up when you prowled through Jacland's apartment eating grapes?"

"Nothing."

Bone narrowed an eye. "I'm a tough baby, Cardigan. When a private dick bursts into an apartment I'm covering and walks off with some info, I'm tough. What did you find?"

"Nothing."

"Then how the hell did you get onto the Rosalie Wayne steer? Answer me that!"

Cardigan leaned back, looked down his nose. His face was not pleasant. "If I got onto that steer, Abe, I didn't find anything. And how did I get onto it? I use," he said softly, "a Ouija board."

"You can't pull that crap!" Bone muttered, grabbing Cardigan's arm.

"Take your hand off, Abe," Cardigan snapped. "You're not tough; you're just nasty. Take it off!" He wrenched free and a sullen look swept into his eyes. "If you found the Wayne steer, land on her—not me."

"I did," Bone said, slowly. "I quizzed her over at the theatre. She admitted calling Jacland, but she said she called him in a fit of temper—about something he wrote. I asked her if she was ever in his apartment. She said no. And that's why I tailed you here. What, Cardigan, what the hell did you lift out of that apartment?"

"I told you."

"The truth, I mean. You found some evidence there, damn you! You found something—a card, a case, something— that made you send Miss Seaward to the Wayne apartment!"

Cardigan patted Bone on the shoulder. "There, there, Abe. It's probably been your diet. You need a rest."

Bone flung the hand down. "I'm not kidding, bozo!"

"Neither am I!" Cardigan shot back at him, darkening. "If you want me to answer questions, get a subpoena, but for God's sake stop tailing me around town like a pup!" He turned. "Come on, Pat. We dine."

"You wait, Cardigan!" Bone cut in.

CARDIGAN ignored him. He handed Pat down from the stool, guided her across the bar and on into the dining room. A few people were at table and the orchestra was tuning up. Antonio led them to a table at the edge of the dance floor and a minute later Ken Strange, the owner, came over and bent over the table. "What's the matter with Bone, Cardigan?"

"He's got an idea, Ken; that's all."

"Listen, Cardigan. If he starts clowning around here I'm going to get in touch with Inspector Gross. I'm paying enough for peace in this scatter and I'm not going to have any dick raising a howl. I'll have him bounced out."

Cardigan laughed. "You don't hurt my feelings, boy. On second thought, Ken, I wouldn't do that. Abe's a nasty guy to cross. Especially in your business."

"I just ain't going to have him raise a disturbance!"

Cardigan shrugged and Strange turned on his heel and walked off.

Pat wasn't at ease. "Why didn't you try to humor Bone?"

"You ever try humoring a guy that's naturally bad-humored? Abe's a grifter. He's up a blind alley and for the sake of his face he's trying to shake me down for some dope."

The crowd began coming in. The jazz band began playing and couples swung out onto the floor. Cardigan danced with Pat, he could handle himself for a big man; and from time to time he caught sight of Bone beyond the entrance. There was consommé waiting when they re-turned to the table and Cardigan ordered some Chablis for the fish course. At 11:30 Rosalie Wayne came in with a tall, broad-shouldered young fellow and neither of them looked gay. They went to a table in a corner.

"She's lovely," Pat said.

"There's one thing about you I like, kid; you're no cat." He dropped his voice. "I think she's headed for the dressing room. Run along and get a close-up of her. See how she looks—how she feels. Hop!"

Pat left and Cardigan beckoned Antonio over. "Who's the guy just came in with Rosalie Wayne?"

Antonio leaned close. "Robert Drummond."

"That's a name. What's he do?"

"You haven't seen him in the play *The Backlands!*"

"No."

"Say, he's great. Leading man! And you know, he's come up. Yes, sure! And this play—I tell you, Mr. Cardigan, is the berries, like. Strong! For men! It is in the jungle, maybe Africa, I think. And in the last act—ah! In the last act, there is the jungle, dim and sinister, and the villain leaning in the girl's hut—the doorway, you understand. He laughs. The girl inside cries out. Mr. Drummond appears from the wings. He makes one grand leap and with a knife kills the villain. I understand he studied for two months the use of the knife. Grand! Swell!"

"Thanks," said Cardigan. "See about that wine, will you?"

He got up and drifted into the bar, whence Robert Drummond had gone a moment before. He leaned on the bar beside Drummond and said, offhand, "I like your work in that play, Mr. Drummond."

Drummond turned. "Thanks. Thanks a lot."

"The knife work was swell. The way

you leap across the stage and use that knife— You know how to use a knife, I'll tell you!"

"I—studied for the part."

Cardigan nodded, his eyes wandering. "It's a dangerous asset."

Drummond started. "I don't quite get you."

"Oh, nothing." Cardigan laughed. "I was just thinking of the Jacland case. Well—good luck!"

He turned away, taking with him an impression of the sudden white look that his words had brought to Drummond's face. He returned to his table, cocked an eye at the lemon-yellow Chablis. In a few minutes Rosalie Wayne returned to the table accompanied by Drummond. Cardigan began to get impatient when, with the lapse of five minutes, Pat did not put in an appearance. At the end of ten minutes he called Antonio.

"Send someone up to ask the maid in the dressing room if anything is wrong with Miss Seaward."

In three minutes Antonio was back, palms spread upward. "But she left the dressing room ten minutes ago—"

Cardigan was on his feet, a wicked look in his eyes.

CHAPTER THREE

If the Cap Fits

KEN STRANGE met Cardigan in a private room off the bar. "Look here, Cardigan, what the hell do you think—"

"Cut it, Ken!" His voice was low, thick, his eyes lowering. "I want to speak to that maid."

"But she said Miss Seaward—"

"Are you going to get the maid out of that dressing room or am I going to crash it and start a lot of female shrieks?"

Strange took a breath. "O. K. Come on."

They went up to the second floor, into a small, private dining room.

"Wait here," Strange said.

He went out, reentered a moment later with a young woman dressed in black with a small white apron. She looked frightened.

Cardigan said, "Did any word pass between Miss Seaward and any other woman in there?"

"There was only one other woman— Rosalie Wayne."

"Well?"

"N-no. They didn't say anything—not to each other. Miss Wayne, I thought, at one time was crying. I can't be sure. I just thought so."

"Who went out first?"

"Miss Wayne. Miss Seaward left a moment later."

"O. K. You can go."

She went.

Cardigan turned to Strange. "Is there a back way down and out from this floor?"

"Yes."

"Where does it go?"

"A courtyard in the back. There's a through alley to the next street south."

"Where'd you last see Abe Bone?"

"In the bar. About fifteen minutes before you sent Antonio up here."

Cardigan turned, pulled open the door and went downstairs. Strange was at his heels saying, "Now for God's sake, Cardigan, don't start a rough-house!"

Cardigan strode into the bar, stopped short and turned on Strange. "Ask the bartender when he last saw Abe?"

Strange shrugged and went to the bar, spoke for a minute or so, returned. "He said he saw Rosalie Wayne go through here to the back hall. Then the girl you came in with. He said Bone saw them too and went into the hall also. The men's room is at the back of the lower hall."

Cardigan went down the lower hall, took a look and returned. "The nigger in there said Bone wasn't in. Did anybody see Bone after he went into the hall?"

"He didn't come back here."

Cardigan jerked a thumb. "Go in and ask Rosalie Wayne if she saw a man hanging around the hall upstairs when she came out of the dressing room."

"Look here now, Cardigan—"

"If you don't, I will!"

Strange touched a handkerchief to his forehead and walked away. He returned in a moment shaking his head.

Cardigan said, "Now come with me, Ken, and show me every room in this place."

"Cardigan, I'm not going to have my place—"

"And me, Ken, I'm not going to have Pat Seaward drop out of sight in your joint. Get going."

"Hell, what a guy—what a guy! Come on."

They searched every room in the three-storied house, found nothing.

"There's no monkey-business goes on in my place," Strange said.

Cardigan grouched, "Hell, I've nothing against you, Ken. But I wanted to see. Listen. Get Pat's wrap from the chair and leave it in the checkroom, will you?"

"This kind of knocks me over, Cardigan."

"You should be knocked over!" Cardigan laughed grimly. "What about me?" He wheeled away. "I'll probably be back."

HE got his hat from the checkroom and rolled out the front door. He hailed a cruising cab and gave an address. He sat on the edge of the seat, the heel of his right hand grinding on his knee. He was too upset, too angry, to attempt to find solace in a smoke.

He snapped at the driver. "Listen, you! I've seen Broadway too many times. Get out of the traffic. Get over on the West Side."

"Geez, chief, I'm doin' me best!"

"For that meter of yours, yes. Hike west."

Ten minutes later the cab pulled up in front of a station-house's green lights. Cardigan heaved out and said, "Wait here."

He swung across the sidewalk, climbed steps and barged into the central room. A fat lieutenant at the desk was unimpressed by the noisy entrance.

Cardigan said, "Hey, Bromfield, where's Bone?"

"Bone?"

"Bone."

"He ain't called in lately. I don't know. Say, Cardigan, you think that Sharkey-Schmelling thing was fixed?"

"Where's Bone?"

"My, my, you got to take the roof off the house?"

Cardigan cursed and sailed on into the back room. Three plainclothesmen were sitting around, smoking.

One said, "Ask Cardigan, now. Go ahead. Hey, Cardigan, don't you think Sharkey beat hell out of—"

"Where's Abe Bone?"

"I mean, take it now like this: Sharkey boxed—he boxed, I say, and in the last round, why in the last round—"

"Where's Bone?"

The man gave it up in disgust. "I don't know," he growled.

Cardigan turned and went out of the room with slow, lagging steps. In the central room, he stood looking sourly at Broomfield, who was complacently eating an apple. He muttered and strode to the door, reached the curb by the taxi and stood there tapping his foot.

The driver stirred. "I see a lot of guys ain't satisfied with that there Sharkey-Schmelling decision. I—"

"You," bit off Cardigan, "start back for the Club Cordova."

He paid up in front of the green marquee. The flunky opened the door and Cardigan went into the foyer. The check-room girl reached for his hat. It was in his hand, but he didn't see her. He ran into Ken Strange in the bar and he could tell by the look on Strange's face that something was up. Strange stopped him with a palm.

"Take it easy, Cardigan."

"What's on your mind?"

"Bone—"

"Where the hell is that bum?"

"Easy, Cardigan! For God's sake, easy! I may be in a jam, but so help me, it's not my fault! This way."

He led the way into the room off the bar. Bone was sitting in an easy chair, foggy-eyed. There was a welt on his fore-head and his hair was tangled. He didn't seem to notice anything.

Strange was whispering. "We found him under the stair well in the hall up-stairs. He was beaned—and out cold. For cripes' sake, look at the jam I'm in!"

Then Bone, seeing things, suddenly cried hoarsely, "You, Cardigan! You, damn you, you cracked me!"

Cardigan said to Strange, "Imagine!"

"You, Cardigan—" Bone heaved to his feet and clawed at his hip pocket. But he was sluggish.

Cardigan leaped, man-handled Bone back into the chair and took his gun away from him.

Strange rasped, "Damn it, Cardigan, don't do that!"

"You think I'm going to let him play cops and robbers with this rod?" He flung it on a table, spun on Bone. "Listen, Abe. I didn't crack you. I'm looking for the guy that did."

He wheeled about and with Bone's abuse still ringing in his ears he crossed the bar and was stopped by Antonio at the entrance to the dining room.

Cardigan said, "Get Miss Wayne—and her boy friend."

"But they left, Cardigan."

"Left! When?"

"Maybe half an hour ago. Miss Wayne, I think, did not feel well."

"Maybe," Cardigan said, pivoting, "she'll feel worse."

HE went upstairs, found the rear staircase and followed it down to a rear door. The door opened into a dark courtyard. He used a flashlight the size and shape of a fountain pen. Going round and round the courtyard, he covered every inch of brick with the small but thorough beam of light. Then he took the alley that cut between two stone buildings. The alley was a narrow strip of cement and he followed it with his flashlight. Half-way through, he picked up a crumpled handkerchief. Pat's initial was in the cor-ner. She'd dropped it purposely, he guessed, to point the line of flight out to him.

Reaching the street, he caught a taxi and gave an address. In five minutes he alighted before the Petremont Plaza and strode long-legged through the lobby. The elevator whisked him upward and he went down the twelfth floor corridor look-ing very dark and malignant. He used the knocker of 1212.

Rosalie Wayne opened the door and Cardigan, dispensing with overtures, walked right in past her. She made a little startled outcry and Drummond, rising from a chair, rapped out: "Look here!"

Cardigan went toward him, patting down air with an open palm. "I am, Drummond. Right here."

Drummond looked awestricken. "What in the name of thunder do you think you are doing?"

Cardigan swung around, shaggy-headed, brutal-eyed, and pointed at Rosalie Wayne. "Why did you phone Giles Jacland this morning?"

Drummond got between them. "Now look here, whoever you are—"

"My name's Cardigan, of the Cosmos Detective Agency."

"Oh!" quietly; and Drummond stepped back. "I see." Then he flared up again. "That still gives you no right to blunder in here and—"

"Blunder, is it?" Cardigan snapped.

"Please, please!" Rosalie Wayne cried.

Cardigan was hard at it. "Listen to me, you two! The girl I was with to-night disappeared from the Cordova. She was the same girl that came to this apartment this morning and spoke with your maid." He stopped short. "Where's that maid?"

"It's her night off," Rosalie Wayne said.

"Disappeared!" Drummond was echoing.

Cardigan turned on him savagely. "You heard me! Disappeared!" Then he was back at Rosalie Wayne, ripping out, "Why did you phone Giles Jacland just before his murder?"

She held hands to her face. "I—oh, it was nothing—nothing! It was stupid of me but—but I was angry, so—"

"Was Drummond here at the time? Did he go, then, directly to Jacland's apartment?"

"No! No!"

Drummond's voice shook with anger. "What the devil are you implying?"

"If the cap fits, wear it."

"Why, you dirty—"

"Wait!" Cardigan broke in, his voice low, held back. "Let that slide for the moment. All I'm interested in now is the disappearance of Miss Seaward. You two left the Cordova directly after she was kidnaped. She was up here this morning. There's got to be a connection. Now I don't want any dramatics or wise-cracking repartee or third-act heroics or any other kind of bushwah. I want Miss

Seaward. Get that. *I want Miss Seaward!*"

Rosalie Wayne drew herself erect. "I know nothing about her. I don't even know the girl. I'm sure Mr. Drummond doesn't."

"You?" Cardigan shot at Drummond. "I know nothing."

CARDIGAN walked across to the telephone, picked it up and turned to face them. "I hate to do this, but I'm getting a couple of precinct detectives over."

Rosalie Wayne started. "But why?"

"They can get rough," he said, eyeing Drummond, "and they have the law to back them up. I haven't."

Drummond came across the room. "Please, Mr. Cardigan, wait, let us get this thing straight."

"Straight? This thing is about as straight as a roller-coaster. I tell you, I never run to the cops. I usually can settle my own troubles. But this time—my side-kick is in trouble and my hands are tied and nothing else matters and you're either going to come clean or play house with the precinct dicks. I'm not—"

The ringing of the phone cut him short. Rosalie started across the room but Cardigan answered it, said, "Hello." Then he looked up, pressed the mouthpiece against his chest. "This is your maid calling, Miss Wayne. I want you to tell her to come right home—as quick as she can. Understand?"

"Yes," she said, breathless.

"I want you to ask her where she is. I want the address."

"Yes."

He gave her the phone and she said, "Hello, Janie. . . I know, I know; I thought you were out rather late. . . But listen, Janie. I want you to come right home. It's imperative. . . I'll explain later. And, Janie. Where are you? . . .

You must tell me. . . You must, Janie!
. . . Oh. Oh, I see."

She hung up, said, "She said—a drug-store."

Cardigan laughed shortly, unpleasantly. Then he said, "I'll be seeing you two later. The best way to get yourself into a pot of trouble is try leaving the city. You get that, Drummond?" he whipped off.

"I had no intention—"

But Cardigan was on his way to the door. He went out.

Standing in the doorway at the entrance to the Petremont Plaza, he was deep in shadows. The doorman had retired. Lights were low in the lobby behind and the street out front was dark, quiet. When he had been standing there for half an hour, a cab drew up to the curb. A woman got out, paid the driver and the cab shoved off. The woman hurried toward the entrance.

Cardigan took hold of her arm. "Miss Leadley?"

"Yes— But see here."

She was small, quaint-looking in a quaint bonnet that sat high on her gray head.

"Mother," he said, "you and I are going places."

"Let me go! Let—"

"Yelling will bring only the police."

She stopped short, breathing hard. "But—but—"

"You don't really want to see the police: that's right. Come along with me."

"But I have to—"

He had no scruples. He showed her a gun. "I mean it! You're going to take me to the place you just came from!"

"I— No! No!"

"Madam, it's that or—" he moved the gun—"this." He lifted his head, called, "Taxi!"

CHAPTER FOUR

Guido

SHE huddled in one corner of the rear seat, her hands tensely locked, her eyes wide behind her little old spectacles. She stared straight ahead. It was as if she dared not look at the man beside her. She had given an address.

"You know," Cardigan said, "you're a pretty old woman to get mixed up in a thing like this."

She bit her lips to keep words from issuing forth.

"Murder," he said, "and kidnaping are dangerous pastimes."

She muttered, "I murdered no one! I kidnaped no one!"

She began crying. The cab rolled on, heading west, its tires swishing through the dark, empty streets. The sound of her crying was hardly audible. Presently the cab stopped in front of a shabby brownstone house.

Cardigan said, "This it?"

"Yes," she sobbed.

He backed out, reached in and handed her to the curb. He paid the driver and the cab ground into gear, rolled off. He held the little woman's arm. She hung back. He tugged at the arm with his left hand. In his right was his gun—inside his pocket.

"Oh, please," she gasped weakly.

He lifted her bodily, under the arm-pits, and carried her up the brownstone stoop. He set her down in front of the vestibule and moved to one side.

He said, "Ring that bell."

She put her hand on the bell, her head on the hand, sobbing. He was touched by the hopelessness of her small, quaint figure, but he was also determined. He said nothing. Waiting, his hand was hard on the gun in his tuxedo pocket. He used his left hand to turn up the collar and drew together, as much as he could, the lapels. He regretted the low waistcoat, the expanse of boiled shirt.

The inner door clicked. Cardigan pressed close against the stone to one side of the vestibule. There was a pause, and then the vestibule door opened. The little woman swayed. Suddenly she let out a faint cry and collapsed.

A man pushed out of the vestibule and Cardigan said, "Up you!" quietly.

The man almost stumbled. In the darkness he looked tall, burly, had a bald head and what looked like white hair above the ears.

"Oh, yeah?" he said.

"Pick her up," Cardigan said. "It'll keep your arms occupied. Pick her up and carry her. I'll be behind you."

The burly man said, "I guess you got me," cheerfully, and lifted the old woman. She made a small package in his arms. Cardigan got behind him and they entered, Cardigan closing both doors.

The hall was lighted and at the head of the stairs stood the figure of a woman. She did not look young. She was plump and tall. The burly man carried the old woman up the stairway and Cardigan went behind him. The woman at the top could not see the gun in Cardigan's hand.

"What's the matter, Matt?"

The burly man's answer was in the nature of a short, guttural laugh. Brass strips on the steps clicked beneath his heels.

"It's Janie," the woman said.

"Yeah," the burly man said, hard humor still in his tone.

"Who's the man—" They were at the top and the woman caught sight of the gun. "Oh," she said, quietly.

She had a dowager look about her. Gray-white hair, piled high, and a black ribbon around her full throat. There were lines in her face, a double chin, growing hardness in eyes that were a queer shade of green. Majesty was in the straightness with which she held herself.

Matt said, "She fainted outside and this mug was there, waitin' with a rod."

"She fainted and— Oh, I see."

There was the sound of a piano, casually, softly played, in a room beyond. A door was part way open.

"Get going," Cardigan said.

THE woman turned and walked majestically toward the door and Matt followed. Cardigan crowded close behind them, entered the room with them. He remembered the drab outside of the house and was instantly struck by the splendor of a large living room containing scattered floor lamps. At a grand piano, a small, dark man was rippling his fingers over the keys. He seemed unaware that they had entered. Then he looked up— and stopped playing. Leaped to his feet and shot a hand toward his hip.

But Cardigan had him covered. "No you don't!" And to Matt: "Keep holding her, you!" He swung his voice back to the dark man: "Keep your hands up and come over here." The man came over. "Turn around." Cardigan removed a small automatic from the rear pocket.

There was in this room, about these people, a strange air that was oddly sinister. Cardigan sensed it vaguely but could not lay his finger on anything. The tall woman stood like a Tussaud figure, motionless; Matt stood holding the old woman and smiling with hard amusement; the dark man stood stonelike and stared fiercely, his eyes never blinking, at the floor. Cardigan moved until he could tap Matt's pockets. He withdrew a gun and stuffed it into the pocket where he had put the dark man's.

"Put her down," he said.

Matt laid Miss Leadley on a large divan. She muttered something and moved from side to side. Matt straightened and stared at Cardigan. The tall woman stared at him. The dark man stared fiercely at the floor. No one said anything.

Until Cardigan said, "I'm looking for Miss Seaward."

Matt and the tall woman looked at each other. Their glances showed nothing. They returned their stares to Cardigan and after a moment's silence the tall woman turned, walked leisurely to a straight-backed chair and sat down. She lit a cigarette, unhurried. Matt shrugged, took another chair and looked fixedly at his fingernails.

"Miss Seaward?" the tall woman said.

Suddenly the small dark man began crying. His shoulders shook and tears ran down his face. He returned to the piano stool, sat down, drew out a handkerchief and continued crying into it.

Cardigan looked exasperated. "Am I in a nut-house?"

The woman got up, crossed the room and patted the dark man on the shoulder. "There, there, Guido," she said. "There, there."

She returned to the high-backed chair and sat down. "So you want Miss Seaward, Mr. Cardigan."

"I'm glad you know my name."

She regarded her cigarette. "You are a very able detective. You are well known in the city and you wield a certain amount of power. So do I," she finished, sharply. "Do you know who I am?"

He shook his head. "I don't care. I told you what I want."

"You may as well put the gun aside, because it won't help you get Miss Seaward."

"I'll hold the gun while I can."

The little dark man was weeping into his handkerchief and rocking from side to side. Matt got up and rocked over and bent down. "Snap out of it, Guido. You got to snap out of it. Come on,

be a pal and snap out of it." He rubbed Guido affectionately on the shoulder with an immense hand.

Cardigan said, "You, Matt, get over to that chair!"

"Me?" Matt chuckled hoarsely. "Sure."

Miss Leadley, only half conscious, was moaning. "O God, protect Rosalie! O God . . ." She trailed off into muttering.

The tall woman looked at her, then looked at Cardigan. She stood up and her head went back arrogantly, green flame moved in her eyes. "I will bargain with you, Mr. Cardigan! I have Miss Seaward in my possession and—"

"Get her," Cardigan chopped in.

TEETH, still fine and regular, shone between lips curving open in a smile of challenge. "The bargain, you remember." She went on swiftly. "I have her. I had her kidnaped right from under your nose in the Club Cordova tonight. I had to do it, you understand! And now—now, we shall bargain. Her life—against the thing I want."

"Spill it."

"You are to forget this address. You are to forget all and everything connected with the Jacland murder case. That is all."

He said roughly, "If you have her, what the hell can I do but say yes?"

"You can, afterwards," she reminded him, "double-cross me."

"Naturally, I could do that. I may have to. I'm not the only one mixed up in it. The cops are after me for what I already know. They're after Miss Seaward too. I can take it; I could talk them out of anything. But if they corner her, there's no telling."

"You're frank, at least."

"I'm frank even with killers. I'm telling you that so far as I'm concerned, so far as things stand now, it's a bargain.

It's tough to swallow, but it's a bargain. I'd be crummy to walk out on her." He was scowling, his face was dark and unpleasant and he was impatient. He growled, "Get her. Get her."

"First, put down that gun."

He gripped it hard. "I've got to see her first. I'll not put this rod down— not with that crying hyena there and this roughneck here. Get her! Get her in here and, so help me, I'll do nothing more than walk out with her!"

The tall woman folded her arms. "I, Mr. Cardigan, am making the terms of the bargain. You forget that."

Cardigan's eyes blazed. "Why, damn it, another crack like that and I'll get the police here! I'll phone them!"

"You will put your hands up, Mr. Cardigan."

Startled, he twisted his head around. Miss Leadley was sitting up, holding a gun in her hand. "Put them up, please. You forgot about me."

Matt heaved out of the chair and started toward Cardigan.

"You all forgot about me," another voice said. "Steady!"

Matt stopped in his tracks. Miss Leadley ducked her head. Pat came through a curtained doorway—small, trim, white-faced. There was a big gun in her hand.

She said, "Never bind a woman with plain rope. And never leave loaded guns around in bureau drawers. . . . O. K., chief. I guess that does it. The little dark gentlemen there did it. He carries a knife in his right sock. I felt it in the cab with my ankle. You'd better get it."

Cardigan turned on Guido. "Shell out, you."

Guido wept again and, bending, drew a knife from his trousers leg. He laid it on the piano, sat down, put his face in his hands and began weeping hard.

Cardigan said to Pat, "You're telling

me the Rosalie Wayne lead is all wrong? There's her maid."

Pat started. "I didn't recognize her!"

Matt's fists were clenched. "Listen, Cardigan," he growled passionately. "You can't drag Rosalie Wayne into this. You can't, you hear!"

"She's just as guilty—"

"She's not!" cried the tall woman, her eyes wide. "I tell you, she knows nothing about this! Nothing! She doesn't know me! Not even me! She doesn't know I'm alive! So help me God, she had no hand in this!" Suddenly she was out of breath, her face enflamed. "You can't ruin her, her career! You can't do what Giles Jacland tried to do! You can't!"

Cardigan was puzzled. He growled. "What do you know about Giles Jacland?"

"You ask me what I know? You don't know who I am. Well, Mr. Cardigan, I am Rose O'Day. I was—was Rose O'Day."

He said, "Rose O'Day was an actress who died—was drowned—when I was a kid. Fifteen years ago. I—" He stopped short. "You do," he said, his voice dropping, "resemble Rose O'Day."

She shook with emotion. "I am! I'm Rosalie Wayne's mother. Do you know who ruined me? Do you know who drove me to drink and then dope and who drove me from the boards?"

Matt was uneasy. He went to her. "Rosie—calm, Rosie."

BUT no one could have stopped her. She cried, "Giles Jacland ruined me! With his bitter criticism—his cruel, heartless satire. He ruined me! He made me lose faith in myself until I believed I was a rotten actress. And I went down. But going down—I thought of Rosalie. And I vanished. She was left with Janie Leadley. Janie knew everything.

"And Giles Jacland was ruining Rosalie. He hated me—hated me always because I was one actress who never came to him. And he suspected I never died. And he somehow kept track of Rosalie through the years—even though her name was changed. And he tried to do with her what he never was able to do with me. But he didn't tell her he knew. He had a better way. His pen."

She spun around. "Just as he ruined Guido. Because one night, years ago, Guido got up in a restaurant and called him a fakir, a cad and a bounder. He ruined Guido—made him lose faith in himself just as I did. Matt caught me on the toboggan. Cured me of dope. Matt married me. Thank God for that!"

She dropped to the chair, wringing with perspiration, shaking all over. Matt stood behind her, his hands on her shoulders. There was a long moment of silence.

Then Guido snarled. "I killed him! Me! With my knife! No one told me to! But I—I went and killed him! For Rosalie's sake—but for mine also!"

Pat sighed. Her gun drooped. She said, "I felt, chief, it was something like this. Jacland was that way. A cad."

Cardigan was saying, with difficulty, "I know, I know, but Bone is on this. Bone is after you and me. Somebody has to take the rap for it. I'm not. I'm not going to let you."

She threw the gun on the divan. "I don't care, chief. I'm walking out of this. I hate murder, but there are times when you can't call it murder. I'm not a cop. I'm walking out."

She turned and went to the door.

He said, "Pat, wait!"

"Chief, you heard me. If you've any sense of decency in you, you'll come with me, you won't be a heel."

He felt his neck redden. His jaw hardened. "O. K., wisegirl. The cops'll come after us for a shake-down. I hope you can take it." He backed across the room. He said, "You, Rose O'Day—and the rest of you—take a heel's advice. Scram out of here—now, this minute. Pack like hell and lam. You hear me?"

"I got you," Matt said.

Cardigan said, "Because that operative of mine is only a woman. And cops are cops. And if they get rough with her—I tell everything—the whole works. Me they can rough-house and make me like it, when I get used to it. But—" he shook his head—"not her."

He backed swiftly to the door, backed out into the hall and closed it. Pat was waiting.

He clipped, "So I'm a heel, eh?"

She gripped his arm. "Chief, I didn't mean that. I know you were thinking of me. But, hell, if we turned them over, if we raked up Rosalie Wayne—I'd feel rotten for the rest of my days."

T HEY reached the lower hall, opened the door and passed into the vestibule. Cardigan pulled the door shut. They went out of the vestibule, down the stairs.

A figure moved from the shadow of the stoop. "I've been waiting for you, Cardigan."

Pat's hand tightened on Cardigan's arm.

"Hello, Abe," Cardigan said. "I notice you waited outside—not in."

"Never mind that. I tailed you from the Cordova. I saw you get in a cab with a woman off Park Avenue and you come right here. So I've been waiting. It wasn't this jane you got on your arm now. What's in that house?"

"Rooms. Roomers, I suppose."

Bone made a jaw. "I'm not kidding, Cardigan!"

"The woman," Cardigan said, feeling his way, "was a stoolie of mine. I had her on this case. I had her planted out back of the Cordova. She saw Pat and the guy come through the alley and get in a cab. She wasn't sure, but she followed the cab. She followed it to here. When I left the Cordova I called up the office and told them I was going to Rosalie Wayne's apartment. The stoolie phoned the office to find out where I was. They said I'd gone to the Wayne apartment. The stoolie called me there and I told her to meet me downstairs. A little woman, Abe? That's the one. She brought me here and rang the bell and a guy opened the door when he saw it was only a woman. I crashed in, taking the woman with me, but I sent her out the back way. I held the guy up, had my gun on him. I told him I'd kill him if he didn't turn over Pat. We went into a room and there was a lot of talk. He wouldn't turn over Patrick unless I let him go. What could I do, Abe?"

"You let him go?"

"I had to," Cardigan said. "He lit out the back way."

Bone said, "I don't believe you, Cardigan! You're a dirty Irish two-faced liar! You know what I'm going to do? I'm going to pinch this jane! Why? For socking me in the Cordova. All right, you say she didn't. I say she did. I'm going to get some straight talk out of this if I have to break somebody's back!"

Cardigan was grave. "I told you the truth, Abe. You're not going to pinch Pat."

Her fingers dug into his arm. Was there a window open upstairs? She imagined she had caught a glimpse of a vague face. She gritted her teeth to keep them from chattering.

She cried, "I'll go, chief! He won't get anything! You must let me go!"

"No! Damn it, no!"

Suddenly the front door opened and a man started down the steps. Halfway down, he stopped. Pat let out a little cry. Cardigan, unable to figure this move out, stood rooted to the pavement. Bone whipped his gun out and leveled it at the man on the steps.

"Stick 'em up, you!"

The man walked down the steps, started to stop, then turned and began running. Bone fired. The sound of his gun banged in the silent street. The man pitched headlong and Bone prowled toward him, his gun raised.

The man turned over on his back and said. "All right, you shot me. It was a poor shot, though."

"I like 'em alive, guy."

"Not this one." Steel glinted in his hand. "You see this? It reached the throat of Giles Jacland, my mortal enemy, this morning. And so—"

"Stop that!"

But the blade was quick. It sank into Guido's chest and he gasped out and lay quietly on the pavement.

Pat was shaking. "Chief," she whispered, "he knew—he knew it couldn't be done! He heard Bone! He came down, giving the others time to get away by the rear! He— Poor Guido!"

Cardigan grimaced. Bitter-faced, he walked down the sidewalk, knelt, picked up the lifeless hand. He shook it and laid it down.

"What's the idea?" Bone crabbed.

"Just," Cardigan said, rising, "an idea."

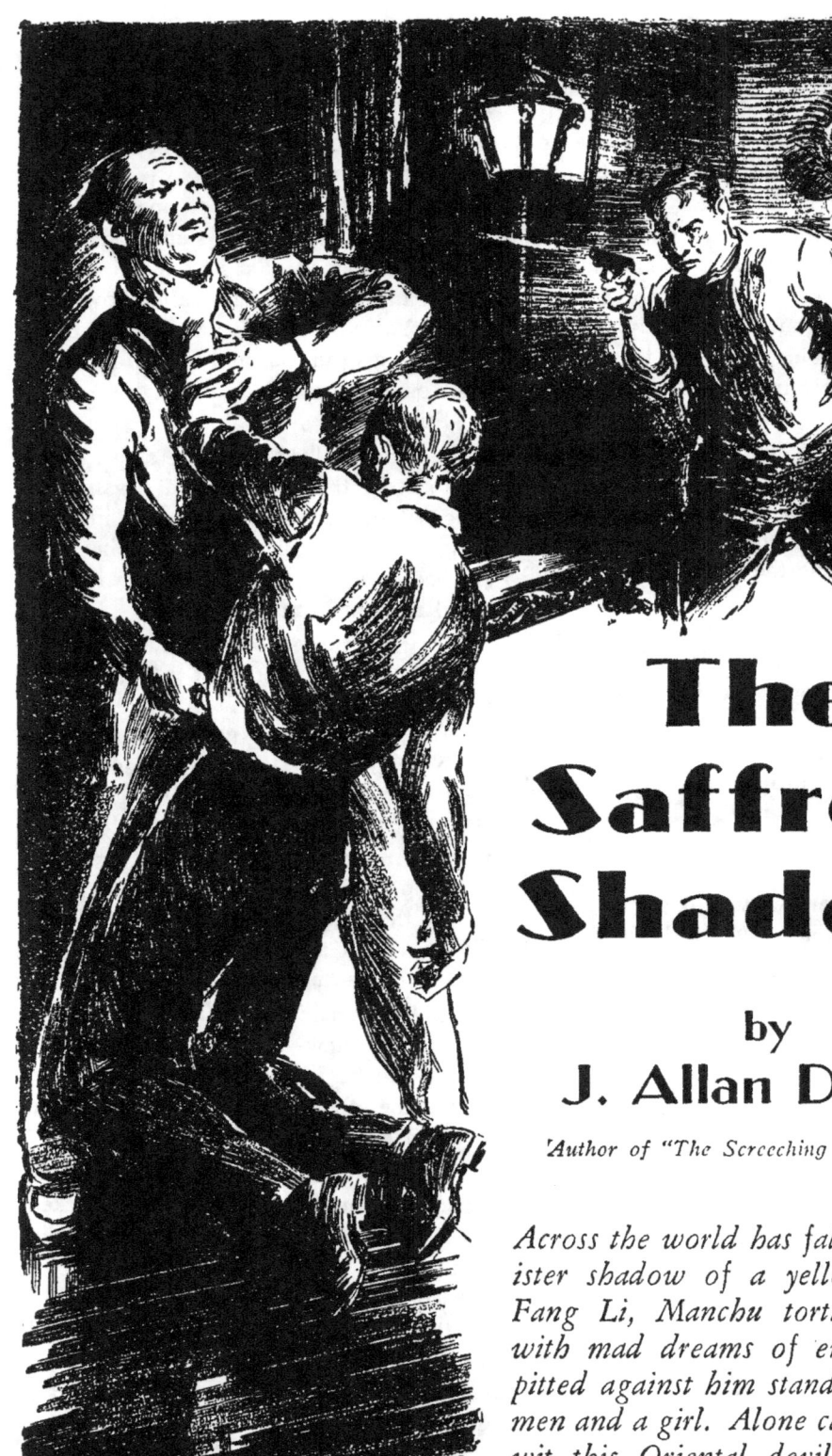

The Saffron Shadow

by
J. Allan Dunn

Author of "The Screeching Skull," etc.

Across the world has fallen the sinister shadow of a yellow fiend— Fang Li, Manchu torture master, with mad dreams of empire. But pitted against him stand two white men and a girl. Alone can they outwit this Oriental devil incarnate? Escape the hideous terror trap he has set beneath the sea?

As Foster fired he saw a knife
rise and fall.

CHAPTER ONE

Warning

THE sense of menace came to Paul
Foster as suddenly and strangely
as when the rider on some lonely
and remote desert trail scents the cool
savor of a wind that bears an utterly
alien odor.

It was born, perhaps, out of the memo-
ries he had summoned from the past,
recollections of the host to whom he was
traveling in the latter's magnificent car.
In front, separated from him by glass,
sat the Chinese chauffeur and footman of
Fang Li who had met him at the country
depot with kowtows and service that
amounted almost to reverence.

They glided over the road in the
splendidly appointed, custom-built sedan
with the driver an expert, the footman
changed to a robot, immobile as an idling
automaton.

Foster sank back among the cushions,
amid the solid silver fittings, and con-
jured up impressions of ten years ago
when he had been at college with Fang

Li, the only one to have any acquaintance with that imperious and inscrutable student with the manners of a prince, the fortune of a nabob and the reservations of a mystic.

He had seen nothing sinister then. They were both youths of barely twenty. There was an Oriental mystery attached to Fang Li, a proud aloofness and the impression of a profound and resolute ambition lending a look that seemed to lack humanity; a callousness that ignored the ordinary ills or welfare of other mortals; but surely there had been nothing evil.

Just then they turned off into a side road. It was fairly smooth but it was unpaved. The blinds were drawn down to within an inch or so of their bottoms on the side windows and Foster had thought nothing of it. Now it suddenly occurred to him that, for so comparatively short a distance from New York, there should have been a railroad station nearer to their destination. They had been traveling at a rapid rate for quite a while. He glanced at his watch. The train had been on time. Allowing for the brief transport of his bags from train to car, they must have been driving for almost twenty minutes at not less than sixty miles an hour. He had only a vague idea of the direction. Now the dirt road was curving. They turned again, into a side road.

Foster leaned forward and looked out of the door glass. He saw only tall banks, hedged, high trees back of them, the merest glimpse of starry sky.

And that feeling of evil spread, grew denser, almost tangible. It beat upon him suddenly and fiercely before he could fight it off and convince himself it was ridiculous, because it was beyond reason.

He was Fang Li's friend. There had been a sort of ceremony, a pledge of fealty between them. Fang Li revealed gratitude for what had happened in the laboratory where some careless student had misplaced bottles, and Fang Li, absorbed in his analysis, automatically reached for one that would have caused an explosion, marred and maimed him, surely blinded and perhaps killed him.

Foster, star student of chemistry, saw the danger and averted it. Fang Li a brilliant if erratic student, usually aloof and impersonal, had asked Foster to his rooms that evening, after the laboratory incident. He did not mention the event itself. Foster got the impression, which he shook off, in his Americanism, that he was being highly honored. The rooms with their hangings, rugs and furniture, the two deft, silent valets, might have been part of a summer palace up the Yangtze-Kiang, rather than in Connecticut. A violet cordial was poured from a crystal goblet into two small gold ceremonial goblets.

They touched these together. Fang Li bowed profoundly and spoke some words in his own tongue which he translated later as "a desire-prayer that his 'friend' might accomplish all his honorable ambitions and that the gods would bring him wealth and health and happiness."

BUT the friendship was never really intimate. They were too far apart. Foster was the student, bent already upon certain lines of scientific research that showed promise. Fang Li took his education imperially, as one might who expected to be served in all things, yet wished to acquire knowledge so he might be served intelligently.

His body, as Foster saw it under the gymnasium shower, was a beautiful thing. Its skin was golden; its symmetry was that of an exquisite vase. It held the poise of a fencer, and it was superbly muscled, curiously foreign.

His eyes were blue and they lacked the prominent eyefold of the Mongol or Manchu, though they were slanting. His hair was dark brown rather than blue-black, wavey rather than straight. There are blue-eyed, fair-skinned, wavey-haired men in plenty in China, ever invaded with countless raids from the north. But Fang Li was essentially a thoroughbred, not a mongrel. He possessed infinite pride of ancestry and he revealed it physically.

Then he left college suddenly. Four months later, Foster was called before the faculty and informed of the foundation offered the university. Its donor was Fang Li, the gift "an appreciation of the delight and wisdom he had attained at that honorable seat of learning, and an expression of gratitude for the timely energy of one of its distinguished students in saving him from grave misfortune."

Some explaining came in there and Foster mentioned, for the first time, the happening in the laboratory. Fang Li, it appeared, through his American lawyers, wished to donate ten million dollars for the establishment of laboratory equipment, with certain annuities to be bestowed upon distinguished students. There was a proviso that Foster was to be the first so honored. The situation was not too complicated. Foster was already honor-scholar. He was not well off. If he refused the allowance the college lost a ten-million-dollar endowment.

Without the annuity, he would be forced to accept employment and practically shut off his private research. Therefore he took it and, with its aid, he went far.

He had seen nothing, heard nothing more of Fang Li. It had been intimated by the lawyers and, to Foster, by the faculty, that the ten millions was mere kumshaw money to Fang Li, who was full master of his immense fortune. No more than the largesse scattered by a generous noble, who was also grateful. Foster sometimes wondered how Fang Li had fared in the upheavals and invasions of his country and then, suddenly, last week, he had learned that his one-time classmate was in the United States and "prayed he might be honored with a renewal of friendship."

That was by letter. It had been delivered at Foster's rooms while he was absent by a Chinese servant who had much impressed Foster's own man, who was a Filipino.

"Number One boy, *tuan*," was Felipe's verdict. It would not have been fitting to Fang Li to send a personal communication to a friend any other way. There had been a felicitous phrase or two that suggested that Fang Li had kept in touch with Foster's achievements though these were not generally matters of public knowledge or interest.

Foster wired, somewhat impulsively, his acceptance. The endowment annuity had bridged lean years for him. He had resigned it when one of his discoveries brought commercial reward. But he was grateful for it.

So he came to Rosewood Station and was met, and his natural review of Fang Li, as he had been ten years ago, seemed to evoke something malignant.

Some inner warning to order the car back to the station, urged itself so strongly and so startlingly that he almost obeyed it. It was not a matter of the will so much, as of the spirit. His soul was fearful, it cringed beneath this baleful influence.

But now the car slowed; it swung through iron gates that opened without visible agency and they were driving between high hedges of close-set, close-clipped cypress, or yew.

The warning, if it was that, vanished. A sane and healthy revulsion warmed him, as a vigorous body reacts to a cold-water plunge.

The headlights snapped out. He caught barely a glimpse of stone steps, a doorway discreetly lighted, a building of dark red bricks almost covered with ivy.

CHAPTER TWO

Fang Li

ALMOST the only modern, the only Occidental feature of the chamber into which Foster was ushered, was its fireplaces. Here were two rooms that merged into one, reception parlors in the hundred-year-old mansion.

Now rugs, tapestries, divans, furniture, embroideries, were all entirely Oriental. There were Chinese wall-scrolls, painted by masters who had their schools of art when Christ was born at Bethlehem. There were lacquered footstools, and stands with big-bellied gods upon them. Lotuses, pink and golden, were in a great bowl of bronze. There was the subtle smell of incense and the blue haze of its vapor. Wood fires were burning, for it was yet early summer.

Fang Li rose from his cross-legged seat on a low divan to greet his guest. He was clad in trousers and long tunic of brocade in the imperial, and otherwise forbidden, yellow—though the new young republicanism had smashed such reservations. He wore a black skull cap with a button formed of a ruby, red as pigeon's blood, large as a pigeon's egg. The frogs on his tunic fastened with topazes; a diamond gleamed on one finger with sudden, miniature rainbows.

He seemed unchanged. His face was serene as that of a Buddha yet it lacked the god's utter placidity. His lips were well curved but they were thin. It was a mouth that was never loose and could be adamant in purpose. Purpose emanated from him and, to Foster, in his first glimpse of him, he gave out something of the attributes of a god, albeit a cruel and relentless one. There was

force that was tinctured with geniality in his greeting.

Two servants were there, Chinese both, in garments of dark blue, felt-shoed, silent, submissive. On their backs were big ideographs in dull red, the crest of their master.

The same violet cordial was served in golden goblets, giving out an aromatic fragrance, warming in its pungency, tasting faintly of apricots.

"You are welcome," said Fang Li as he waited ceremoniously for Foster to seat himself in a capacious chair, its arms ending in tigers' heads, its legs those of a griffon, the cushions deep and enticing.

Trays were offered that held Chinese pipes and tobacco, cigarettes and cigars. Foster chose one of the latter. Its smoke vaguely suggested some tincture of opium or bhang and its aroma was delightful.

"Friendship," said Fang Li, "is first the blossom, and then the fruit, upon the tree of manhood. The friendship of women is but the fragrance of the flowers and the flavor of the fruit. Enjoyable but fleeting."

To Foster, sensitized, perhaps, by the manifestation he had lately experienced, there seemed to be something superficial in this sentiment. It held the philosophy of the Orient but he found it shallow. He found his mind singularly alert from the action of the cordial and for a moment, he wondered with what purpose Fang Li had renewed this friendship after so many years. It was not a deep amity. There was the gulf of many centuries of Eastern and Western trends of thought and custom between them. Then there succeeded as he smoked, a feeling of deep comfort and complacence.

They talked of the old days, then Fang Li spoke of Foster's achievements, lamenting his own lack of concentrated effort with an apologium that seemed to Foster, even in his congenial mood, to be hypocritical, or condescending, both phases a trifle irritating to his Americanism.

A LIGHT repast was served, a dainty dish of mushrooms, water chestnuts, young bamboo sprouts, pineapple and tender shrimp, chafed in a silver dish over burning alcohol. With it came golden tea in cups more fragile than eggshells, transparent, weightless. The tea was made from the young buds of the shrub, almost priceless, and it was tinctured with a few drops from a crystal vase.

Fang Li shared it with him. Under the comforting influence Foster felt himself warming toward his host, felt his will pliant while, with it, there came a slight recurrence of inner warning. It stiffened him slightly. It suggested that this meeting had deeper significance than a mere reunion. He wondered if he had been drugged. Fang Li might be immune from personal use and by heredity.

He sat relaxed but his will was alert. He felt Fang Li studying him. He fancied that Fang Li's narrowed eyes were blazing like the great jewel on his finger. He experienced a vague hypnosis.

"My friend," said Fang Li, "you know little of me but you may have speculated. I am going to be frank with you. I am of the old dynasty of Ming. My ancestors were the rulers of Cathay. That kingdom has passed, they say. The old order changeth, giving place to new; yet it was a mighty and a potent realm that gave to the world its truest philosophies, its science, its earliest fundamental inventions. Nowadays they try to make equal all men. You might as well style the ruby equal with the pebbles of the beach, or jade the same as any dull flake of mica'd rock. Men were not so created. Without leaders in thought or action the world would be a dull orb. It is foolish to demolish true aristocracies. It is true that genius flames at random, like comets blazing the heavens without regard for the ordinary courses of the firmament. To the dull peasant the fire of genius is something misunderstood, supernatural, awesome. The wise one understands it as the flash of divine revelation and uses it accordingly. You, my friend, are a genius."

This might be praise but Foster inwardly resented it. He felt that Fang Li again condescended here as if, by some freak, a gem had been found in common dirt, meant for the adornment and enjoyment of the aristocrat. Fang Li beneath all his show of friendliness, his hospitality, regarded him as a heathen, a primitive, a foreign devil. The jewel of genius was born for the princes, to take as their just tribute.

Then bitterness entered into Fang Li's suave phrases.

"I am not all Manchu," he said. "There is in me the spirit of my father, and his fathers' fathers, but I am not true Chinese. Even as there is no more united China. But *my* ancestors are *me*. Woman is but the matrix. My father, I have told you, was a Ming. My mother was of your blood though not of your country. There was a mission that was destroyed by rebellious bandits. The head of this British Mission had a wife who died, and a daughter who was carried off. My father's troops, pursuing them, found the wife dead, the daughter still unharmed. He took her into his household. He had many daughters but she was the first to bear him a son. I am he.

"If, perchance, the old orders could be reinstated, I might be deemed lesser than those of pure Chinese birth though there are none of my rank. My father saw the beginning of the end, he saw the chaos of China which must be recrystallized. He saw in me, he thought, his own spirit and the spirit of those who formed our House. He left me all his wealth and he handed down to me his own ambitions. But, to the world at large, I am Eurasian, a mixed-blood, a biological hodge-podge. I have been derided by the dwarfmen, the Japanese, by the Korean impotents.

"I will show them all! I, Fang Li! Son of the Mings! Son of the Sun! The matrix does not count. I come from the womb of a woman as a pearl comes from the flesh of an oyster, serene and of the gods!"

NOW his eyes were indeed blue diamonds. He seemed to tower. The effect on Foster was partly that of the things he had drunk or eaten, he fancied, partly of Fang Li's inherent madness, a sort of egomania or grandiose dementia. The man evidently believed himself a superman. He had a quick brain, imagination, pride, all stung by his taint of origin—as he regarded it—backed by great wealth and overwhelming ambition. His suggestion concerning his mother's racial humility was a slur that Foster did not overlook though he was conscious of a growing lack of resistance.

"You, Foster, a genius, have discovered the cosmic ray that can split the atom. You call it the Omega Ray. You claim, and you have proved, that you can use it to fulminate stored explosives, magazines of war, at a distance of as much as fifty miles, projected from land or sea or air. You have offered this to your government and your pork-barrel legislators, seeking to balance budgets, reducing your forces of offense and defense, have refused to accept it. I have seen a record—no matter how—since you know of it, that states you will not offer this discovery to other nations but will reserve it for the use of your own in case of necessity. That is correct?"

"That is true," replied Foster. He saw what was coming now, summoned his efforts to combat it. He could feel the will of Fang Li striving to compel him.

"Foster, I want that secret. I will give you a million for it, five millions."

"You want it to kill men, I wish to protect men from being killed," said Foster. Fang Li waved his hand impatiently.

"Ten millions, then. I, Fang Li, will bring about a new era. It is my destiny. I will restore the arts and sciences, I will reestablish the old order, slay the dragon of communism before its vomit poisons all mankind. Is a coolie my equal, is a serf the equal of a teacher of philosophy? Let fools imagine it. But let their vaporings be ruled with a firm hand, so that all may be content according to the measure of their true rating, may be advanced according to their real merit and achievement. It shall come to pass despite all obstacles but you, Foster, may hasten the true millennium."

"And see my own country destroyed first, perhaps?"

"No people shall be destroyed unless they are utterly unworthy. I, who am of no one nation, shall make all nations one. There shall be no ridiculous tariffs, no greedy holding of precious oil or gold or rubber. All shall be held for the great common weal and dispensed wisely. We shall not feed honey to nits, mark you, nor caviare to the mob. True art shall be restored and the tricksters who play upon primitive emotions for the lining of their own pockets abolished. We shall not dispense great learning to those with the minds of babes. To each according to his worth. One world, one kingdom, one law, one language—and one king!"

It sounded grandiloquent but Foster knew it to be nothing more nor less than the self-aggrandizement of a madman, trying to be a new and greater Genghis Khan in a modern world.

He shook his head. His formula could not be stolen. It was set down nowhere but in his own brain. There was one elemental factor in its success that he had himself only vaguely glimpsed in the path he had been following. He had almost stumbled upon it. It was so seemingly at variance with accepted theory and practice that he had little fear of anyone else duplicating his discovery. His tests had been made with himself as the chief operator.

FANG LI stood up. The firelight and the incense, the fumes of the liqueurs and the cigar, perhaps the last magical drops in the tea made Foster feel as if his physical self were dissolving. Like those who drink kawa, his head was clear but his body would not function. His will was still within its citadel but he could no longer feel the carving of the chair in which he sat; his sight was distorted so that Fang Li looked like an enormous djhin evoked by Arabian magic. His eyes were lamps. He held up his hand and the great jewel flared in concentric prisms of dazzling light.

"You see this gem?" he heard Fang Li utter though he was growing deaf. "It is a talisman. Sheba gave it to Solomon. It came from the tomb of the first ruler of Egypt. Gaze on it."

The voice died away, or seemed to. All Foster's senses now centered in his sight. It seemed as if his shrunken will were all that was left of his individuality and he strove to preserve it, knowing he was being auto-hypnotized. The cordial, the incense, the cigar, the food and tea, the drops from the vase all combined to bring about this trance, in which he felt his will might be chained but was still selective. As for the visions that slowly but definitely materialized, he considered them at first the figments of a type of dream evoked by the same sort of process with which the devotees of hemp conjure up the houris they hope to find in the Mohammedan Paradise.

There was a girl, supple, exquisite beneath the veils that served both to suggest and reveal the charms of her grace-

ful figure. Her head was clothed in silver net; there were bracelets, armlets, necklets and wristlets, heavily begemmed. She prostrated herself before Fang Li, reseated now, cross-legged and imperial. His two henchmen stood on either side of him, impassive as images. The girl danced, entrancingly, seductively, as a slave craving to obtain favor in the eyes of her lord.

But the rugs did not wrinkle beneath the paces and postures of her henna-tinted toes, and *through* her, Foster saw the play of flames in the fireplace, saw the figure of Fang Li as if through a glass, darkly.

He felt that he had known her before, in some previous life, in this one, or in a life yet to come.

The vision faded. It wisped away, losing color, until it could not be distinguished from the trailing incense that writhed as if an unseen, unfelt breeze were wafting it into a magic pattern.

That broke, reformed, and again the girl was there. Now she was stripped almost bare, held in the grasp of two yellow-skinned giants, bald and hideous—Chinese eunuchs with the faces of demons. Her jewelry was gone. She flung herself on the floor before Fang Li, pleading for mercy. While Foster gazed, striving to summon up some memory that would tell him who and what she was, they twined a pliant metallic serpent about the whiteness of her flesh. They brought a steaming vase and poured its boiling contents into the wide jaws of the serpent.

The girl writhed in frightful agony as the brazen tubing seared and scalded her tender flesh.

Through her, Foster could see the cruel, enjoying smile of Fang Li.

It was only a simulacrum, a phantasy, but he strove to burst the spell that bound him as she turned her head and he saw it was the face of the girl he loved—of Mary Callader.

That vision vanished and Fang Li's smile was clearer. Foster's mind seemed to function more normally.

"Now, will you let me have the formula?" he heard Fang Li ask. And he heard his own will—it could not have been his heart—answer: "I will not."

Fang Li clapped his hands. Two more servants brought in a metal coffer and set it on two low supports. This was real. Foster could not see through this tableau. They fetched white powder in a sack, which was quicklime. It soon proved itself. A man brought a black cat, stroking it. The brute purred though its legs were lightly hobbled. Its eyes shone like the topazes on Fang Li's tunic. Another poured water on the lime that half filled the coffer. The mixture seethed and bubbled and gave off vapor. They flung the partly fettered cat into it.

Foster could not close his eyes. He saw the frightful contortions of the beast as the lime bit into it, blinded it, stripped it of fur and ate into its vitals. He heard its hideous howls and saw the cruel, contemptuous and confident smile of the maniac he had once thought his friend.

The whole room appeared to swim. It was like a bubble that gathered, a pattern in a kaleidoscope that broke into shattering fragments. Foster's head swam with aching dizziness. Again he was nothing. He felt himself sinking into a dreadful abyss.

CHAPTER THREE

"Remember the Cat!"

FOSTER lay stiff and awkward upon a bare floor, staring upward to a plastered ceiling. Sunshine slanted in through drawn venetian blinds and made gratings of shadow, like bars that held him down.

His head was clear but he felt very weak as he essayed to move his limbs and found them free enough but tardy to obey his will.

Something seemed clutching him by the throat, from beneath. He groped and found a leather collar, rounded like the show-collars of large dogs, was about his neck. Its ends came close together and disappeared through two holes in the floor. Doubtless they were buckled beneath the planking.

It was an ingenious and diabolical method of captivity. He had little leeway. He could not lift his head, barely shift it sideways to survey partially the empty room. He saw a fireplace with ashes in it and recognized the design of its marble mantelling, ivy and oak in low relief.

This was part of the chamber where Fang Li had received him, where he had seen the visions, the terrible reality of the tortured cat, had refused Fang Li's demand for the formula of the Omega Ray.

The place had been stripped. The elaborate furnishings had vanished, like the palaces built overnight in the Arabian Nights' Entertainments. And he was there, alone, shackled by the neck, to perish of thrist and hunger unless, by some miracle, a neighbor or a passerby should hear him before he succumbed. He did not doubt that Fang Li had chosen the place wisely. He remembered the long ride from the depot.

He strained, but he was as firmly held down as a snake in the fork of a venom-gatherer's stick. His tongue had swollen slightly and he craved a drink, also food. It occurred to him that he might have been here for a day or more.

There was a tiny pattering on the boards. He moved and saw a rat scuttling to the baseboard. It darted through a hole, reversed, and sat watching him. He saw the play of its whiskers on its lean nose. Doubtless the rat was hungry also, and had companions.

Foster set his teeth into his lower lip not to scream as he fought off the wave of hysteria that threatened to swamp him. This was the aftermath of the drugs with which Fang Li had cunningly plied him. Every moment of the eventful night, whenever it had been, came to him.

But Fang Li, the egomaniac, clever as he was, had not got the secret of the formula. It was not to be lightly told in lay language, for one thing; and the hypnosis had been imposed. Unless Foster were willing he could only pervert his brain; not loot its secrets.

The vision of Mary Callader had been evolved from Foster's drugged cortex, to blend with the devilish suggestions of Fang Li's own inflamed cerebellum. But how had he known; how much did he know of Mary's whereabouts? He had kidnaped Foster. Had he abducted Mary, woven a web into which she had wandered? Did he now hold her in his power, hostage against the rendering of the formula with which he might indeed shake the world, if not reshape it.

Foster's reason trembled in the balance for a while as he thrashed about. He had been stripped naked, he had no weapon but his nails against the stout leather. He bruised his throat in vain, bruised his body, scraped the flesh from his elbows and subsided, choking and exhausted.

There was a distant chuckle. It came from below him. At the same moment he felt the collar relax. He plucked at it and it came loose.

Someone had freed him, someone in the cellar. But the laugh had been mocking. It was not mercy that had freed him. He had been taught a lesson. Fang Li still wanted the formula and meant to have it. Without doubt Fang Li had Mary in his power. He had suggested the visions to torment Foster. He had killed the black cat as a hideous, infernal threat.

Foster got to his feet, sweating, forcing his muscles to hold him erect, to give him movement. Whoever had freed him was gone. It was indeed the same chamber. He tilted the blinds and saw the overgrown wilderness of garden. The house had been long uninhabited. He might find out something about its temporary leasing but that did not matter. His one thought was to get in touch with Mary Callader.

THEY had taken his clothes along with the temporary furnishings. He was left naked to feel his helplessness against Fang Li's plans. The other floors were dusty, webbed with spider-snares. He doubted whether there were another house close by. If he wandered nude along the lanes, found a public thoroughfare, he would be taken for a lunatic. That did not matter so much but his tale would be laughed at; he would be detained before he could free himself. He wanted to avoid the certain ignominy of the press, the cruel limelight of the tabloids. Fang Li would have counted on all those things also.

He wandered between the high, unkempt hedges on sodden paths of weed-grown dirt and found what he had hoped for. A toolhouse in the latticed foundation of an arbor that overlooked a tangled rose garden. There were tools and the rotting, mouldy, utterly disreputable overalls of a gardener long since discharged. A tramp would have scorned them but they were covering.

He fingered his chin and cheeks and knew by his beard that at least a full day had passed. There was nothing else, neither hat nor shoes, only the one clammy and barely decent garment.

Foster went to the gates and found them locked. Weakly he climbed a tree and so scaled a brick wall with a stone coping, dropping feebly into the dusty road. South was his general direction but the immediate way ran east and west.

He chose west, at random, and went slowly on, making up his tale. His speech should count for something, if he could keep it coherent. And they had left, overlooked perhaps, or found they could not remove, the gold signet ring that fitted his third left-hand finger very tightly.

It seemed a mile before he heard a sound that proved to be the voice of a power lawnmower, handled by an elderly man who shut off the motor at the sight of Foster, erupting from the hedge. He took out a wrench from his hip pocket and bade the intruder halt.

"Git out of here!" he said, with emphasis.

Foster told his story. As he had expected, his accents were convincing. He had, he said, been kidnaped and he described the house where he had been held. He did not talk of Chinamen or Fang Li.

"That would be the Lawson house," said the gardener. "Been shut up two years. Our folks ain't opened up yet but I'm still holding down my job, despite the depression. What do you want me to do for you?"

"I've got this ring," said Foster. "It's tight but you can file it off and there's gold enough in it. I want to get to a telephone, that's all, though I could stand something to eat. What day is it?"

"Thursday."

Foster groaned. It had been Tuesday evening when he arrived.

"I'm batching it in the lodge," said the man. "I can give you something, mister, while you get your connection. There's a phone there and it's working. I don't want your ring. You can pay for the call when your friends come."

Foster put in two calls while the friendly gardener and caretaker warmed some food. His first call was to Mary Callader. He reached her mother who wondered where he had been.

Mary, she told him, was with friends in Massachusetts. She had tried to get in touch with him before she left. There was little more to that connection. It told him nothing.

He got his lawyers and briefly described his plight but not its origin. A car was to be sent for him after calling at his rooms to get his own Filipino, clothes, shaving materials, and money, supplied by the legal firm.

He waited for the car in a fever of impatience and dread. He was not sure why Fang Li had released him. There might be three reasons. First, Fang Li might have some feeling toward him because Foster had once saved his life. Not actual gratitude, as a white man would see it, but some Oriental equivalent of a "life for a life." Foster was none too sure of that. Again, it might be a case of bluff, visions raised that would stimulate Foster's imagination so that, thinking it over, he would consent to revealing the formula. The third possibility was that Fang Li had not held him for torture because he believed that Foster might prove stubborn, despite personal agony, but that he would break down if the girl were threatened with bodily harm. Fang Li was the type who liked to play cat and mouse. Foster's awakening in the empty house, his protracted efforts before he got clear, would have weakened his resistance.

He prepared for the worst and resolved upon two things. He would rescue Mary Callader and he would not relinquish his secret, the formula of the Omega Ray that might, in such hands as Fang Li's, destroy civilization, bring about a world chaos out of which the Saffron Shadow would rise supreme. That was what Fang Li was, a saffron shadow, casting the threatening umbra of a hybrid dragon upon all ordered existence.

FOSTER knew the friends to whom Mary had gone. They lived on the Massachusetts coast near Cape Ann in an old fashioned Cape Cod mansion now modernized, with beautiful grounds. They were wealthy and always entertaining friends with a lavish hospitality. He put in a call as soon as he reached his rooms. It would take some time for the connection. He had not said anything to the Calladers about his fears for their daughter's safety. Time enough when he knew facts.

While waiting, a letter came for him, registered and special delivery, asking for a personal signature. He knew well enough who had written and despatched it, without the dragon on the yellow wax that sealed the envelope. This time Fang Li had not bothered with a personal messenger. He might have deemed it more discreet not to use one.

Dear Foster:

I am not sure how soon you will get this. It depends a good deal upon your own ingenuity in freeing yourself from the situation in which I left you.

I had no intention of starving you to death nor to bring about your demise in any other fashion. You are much too valuable alive. Within twenty-four hours after this letter leaves me I shall send to have you released. There may be some difficulty about your personal appearance but no doubt you will overcome that. I do not underestimate your resources.

However, by the time you receive this letter your fiancée will have disappeared though she may not be immediately missed. Her own actions have simplified this move of mine in which, to quote chess terms, I feel I have taken your queen and threatened you with mate. You will remember that we played chess two or three times together at college. I believe I usually won but then the game originated with my ancestors.

It may not be altogether a surprise to you that Miss Callader has entered into this affair. You may have gleaned some inkling of that the other evening. You will remember the black cat?

It is within your power to immediately obtain the release and return of the lady on the terms that do not need repeating here. Mail a copy with working details of the formula to the Chinese Consulate, addressed to the Secretary, the papers to be in an enclosed and sealed envelope with my name upon it. I swear to you upon the honor of Fang Li that she shall be returned instantly to the friends with whom she has been staying.

Otherwise, I fear she may suffer—let us say, inconvenience.

To one as sapient as yourself, my dear Foster, I need not point out that any publicity, any attempt at police interference or the use of *force majeure* in any manner, will prove disastrous to Miss Callader. She is a hostage but in matters of this proportion the treatment of a hostage does not include immunity.

I shall receive your personal signature showing your receipt of this letter. I allow twenty-four hours on top of that. Failing your cooperation—may I again refer to the black cat?

Fang Li.

I shall be in constant touch with the consulate. I shall send you at the earliest opportunity a note in Miss Callader's own writing to assure you of her present welfare.

It was a devilish document. Foster did not doubt that Mary Callader was doomed to dreadful death if he failed to give out the formula. If he did the world was doomed to a frightful holocaust. The reference to the black cat was purely satanic.

He laid down the letter as the bell rang for his long distance connection. He had asked for Mary's hostess, Mrs. Adair, and she was talking. Now he asked directly for Mary and was instantly aware of a slight hesitation.

"She is out, Mr. Foster. I'm sorry. When she comes in—"

His wits tuned up by his fears, Foster caught the tension in her voice.

"When do you expect her?" he asked. He did not dare suggest that he suspected trouble. Mrs. Adair was kindly but she could never be discreet in the matter of news, and Foster knew that Fang Li's threats against interference or publicity were not idle.

"I'm not quite sure. She went riding this morning, by herself, as she usually does, on Twilight. You know, the big roan that will not travel in company. She said she might stay over to lunch with a friend of ours at Stafford. So—"

"I see," said Foster. "She's a fine horsewoman. I'm not worrying about her," he lied. "Tell her I shall call again later in the day."

There would be publicity, of course. That was unavoidable and Fang Li would recognize that fact. But he would resent any suggestion that he was connected with it. Foster was the only one who knew. The full responsibility rested upon him. And he knew she would not return from that ride on the roan horse. He remembered, with a groan, that the Adairs had a Chinese cook. He might or might not have anything to do with it. But Fang Li would surely possess a wide dominance. He had been plotting for over a decade. Someone had spied on Mary, known of her trip to Cape Ann, her daily lonely rides. She was gone.

He called up a flying field and got in touch with a pilot who was a friend of his, who had helped him with his secret experiments and demonstration of the Omega Ray, a fine flyer, absolutely to be depended upon.

"I'm in trouble, 'Red,'" Foster told him. "I want you and a ship. We've got to go to Cape Ann, right away. It is a discreet mission and it may be a dangerous one."

"That's the most interesting news I've heard in a coon's age," replied Red Taylor. "You've hired a flyer. It it's exciting enough I'll only charge you for gas

and oil. What do you want, the Sopwith or a gyro? I've got one of those now. Handy for short take-offs and quick landings. Shy on speed but it's not so far to Cape Ann. And bully flying weather."

Foster reflected for a moment then made up his mind. "We'll use the autogiro," he said, on a hunch. "I'll be leaving here in my car inside of half an hour. That should give you time to get set."

"About," said Taylor. "I'll do my best. Be seeing you."

FOSTER changed to suitable clothes and packed a small emergency bag. He took along a strong flashlight and a thirty-eight automatic. He did not consider himself a fighting man but he kept in good trim always and he had practised pistol shooting as a hobby that might some day be practical. He had always resented the ever increasing hold-ups and kidnapings and meant to qualify himself for resistance. Now that the emergency had thrust itself upon him he was grateful for his expertness.

He had not forgotten about the expected letter from Mary but it was not vital enough to detain him. He had to get to Cape Ann without delay and pick up what clues he could. It would not be easy, he assured himself. Fang Li was no ordinary opponent. With Oriental thoroughness he left all the ends of his ropes tucked in.

But the mail carrier arrived just as his roadster came from the garage. Foster glanced through the letter, then deliberately sat down to study it. It had been mailed in New York. Grand Central Station. He knew he could never trace it there.

Mary Callader was clever as well as beautiful. She knew a good deal about chemistry, though Foster had never let her know anything about the Omega Ray. It was too dangerous a secret for his sweetheart. But she was brilliant and he caught in the first glimpse of the letter more than a hint of some concealed attempt to make more direct contact with him than Fang Li would permit.

The wording was guarded. Fang Li would have edited it. Yet it was cryptic to Foster and he thanked God that the carrier had delivered it before he had driven off. He had been within two minutes of losing a most important clue.

> Dear Paul:
> I understand you know my present circumstances. This is to let you know that I have not been mistreated. They have, indeed, been very considerate. I had a severe headache, one of my regular ones, and they were kind enough to get aspirin for me.
> I am told my release can be effected on terms made known to you. I am not permitted to say any more except to beg you, for my sake, to keep proceedings secret.
> Lovingly,
> Mary.

Fang Li had passed that, hardly censored at all. But he could not know, as Foster did, that Mary had never had a headache in her life, had never used aspirin.

And she knew many of his laboratory tests. She had been especially interested in the function of the fluoroscope.

He lost no time in using the apparatus. The letter revealed nothing and he turned to the envelope, remembering how he had shown Mary a trick used during the war of writing a brief code message on stamps in a saturated solution of aspirin.

There, on the stamp glowing under the fluorescence from the tube, showed plainly, neatly penned, a capital Y, a little drawing like those found on cave walls and mana-stones of primitive men, an apostrophe'd "s" following; then a capital "I" and a period.

Foster studied it for a few moments

intently. Then he burned note and envelope. Fang Li would have supplied the paper, watched carefully while it was written and sealed and addressed. But he would not suspect when Mary brought a stamp from the little regulation book with waxed interleaves she always carried in her purse. She would have been clever enough to have written her message at some previous time before she tore out the stamp. It was all clear enough. The girl had outwitted the wily Manchu.

Foster got into his car and weaved skilfully in and out of traffic. He had luck with the lights and every moment counted. The autogiro was ready for flight when he arrived. Taylor was in flying togs and he had overall and helmet for Foster.

"All set to go," he said cheerily. He was a long, lean, windburned man with, fitly enough, the nose of a hawk and eyes that seemed made to search the deep distances of the sky.

"You know a place called Wyman's Island?" Foster asked him.

"Know the name. Island off the Maine Coast, unless I'm mistaken. Want to look it up? We've got charts."

Foster's blood tingled. "Good girl!" he muttered as Taylor led the way to the office and unrolled a chart. He spotted the islet with a forefinger. Wyman's!

Foster told him briefly what had happened. He could trust Red Taylor. There was no necessity to tell the exace that secrecy was paramount.

"I'll get me a gun," said Taylor briefly. "Then we'll go."

CHAPTER FOUR

Hell's Hideaway

WITHIN three hours they were hovering over the speck on the map, of which Taylor had made a swift tracing before they left. It was a rocky spot, sparsely covered with turf and grass and low huckleberry and barberry bush. Sheep were grazing there. There was a square, two-storied house with curling shingles and weathered, paintless clapboards. Its chimney was askew and crumbling. There were shutters on most of the windows but one or two were fallen from the rusted supports. A barn was tumbling, its roof ridge broken. Sheds were in the same condition, one blown flat. There was a well sweep, with the curb disarranged, the dry pole of the sweep split, the shaft a black pit without glint of water as they flew over it, circling on a survey before they settled down. No smoke, no sign of human life. Only the sheep, startled at first, now grazing again, scuttling rabbits, sea birds. The island was deserted apparently.

They lit close to the well. Foster's spirits had fallen, his face was grim. Taylor shrugged his shoulders slightly. It looked like a false lead.

"Any other island that sounds like Wyman?" asked Foster.

"There's Highland Point—not an island," suggested Taylor. "She might have just caught the words. Chinese accent?"

Foster shook his head. Fang Li had no accent.

"I'm going to look round on foot," he said. "Go through that house."

"O. K.," said Taylor. "If you want me, yell or shoot. I want to look over one of these cylinders. Missed a bit."

Foster walked away. He opened the top of his overall, pulling down the metal fastening so that his gun was handy. He was stubborn rather than hopeful. He still relied on Mary's cleverness. It seemed impossible that so promising a clue should fail.

The front door of the house was fastened but the back one had split and was sagging. Why anyone had built here was

a mystery. There was not a tree on the place and the soil was shallow, the surface uneven and rocky. It might have been a fisherman. Whatever the enterprise had been, it was abandoned. The sheep might be ownerless.

He entered the empty house, explored the lower floor and mounted the creaking stairs to the second story. He opened shutters and looked at the surrounding islands. There was a slight haze and it was hard to judge distances. But the nearest seemed two or three miles away, the mainland four or five times that. The place was absolutely remote. Surf chafed its eastern shore where the low cliffs had been eroded and wet reefs, weed-covered, lay at their base like great sea monsters basking in the shallows.

The cellarway was locked with a large, rusty padlock and he did not break it open. Disappointment and something close to despair gripped him.

He reclosed the shutters and descended moodily. There was so little time. Something moved in a dusty corner and his skin goosefleshed as he gripped the butt of his gun. Two green eyes shone at him, but they were low down. A half-plaintive, half-vicious wail followed, the *miaou* of a cat. It must have been left on the island, gone nearly wild, killing rabbits and nesting gulls and puffins.

He shoved the gun back in its holster and then shrank back as the cat sidled across the darkened room and showed plainly for a moment beneath a window. As Foster opened the door it darted out, almost between his feet, tail erect, back humped.

It was a black cat. The scene with the seething lime, the writhing beast in the flaying, searing caustic, flashed back on his memory. Cold sweat broke out on his forehead. If, within twenty-four hours, he did not find and rescue Mary . . . . . He would not think of it. There must be action. They would scour the air, survey the other islands, hover over Highland Point as a more or less forlorn hope.

The autogiro was in the air. It was well off the ground, rising in a stiff spiral, mounting fast.

Foster stood rooted to the spot, staring. Taylor might have gone up to test his cylinders. Foster was not a flyer but he did not think this credible. He ran forward, past the well curb, to where the plane had stood.

It continued to soar, then started north. On the way Foster had been vexed with its comparative lack of speed, now it seemed to fly like a pursuit ship. It diminished in size. The haze blurred it. It vanished. It was not coming back. Taylor had deserted him.

That seemed incredible. It was a stupendous, stunning blow. To think of Taylor's treachery was monstrous. He could not have become afraid of the job. There was no fear in him.

Then Foster saw a Stillson wrench on the ground. Like all Taylor's tools, its handle was painted a bright enamel red for identification. Taylor knew how tools disappeared round garages and hangars. And Foster had noticed it. Taylor was not the sort who ever leaves a tool behind after using. He was too thorough a mechanic.

Foster stooped to pick it up.

As he did so a shadow projected itself in front of him. A shadow that lay saffron-colored on the rock. At first he thought it was his own but it did not stop moving when he did. Part of it lengthened into an arm that moved as fast as a snake strikes.

Foster saw a burst of light that seemed at once inside his head and all about it. He felt the impact of a crushing blow that sapped the strength out of him as he twisted, still kneeling, caught hold of a man's legs, body, tried to drag himself up, blind from the blow, from blood that was stinging into his eyes.

The arm rose and fell again and Foster pitched forward, sprawled out on his face, utterly insensible.

FOSTER came back to consciousness lying on his back gazing up at a flat skylight. His neck was stiff and painful and he was conscious of dried blood on his face. He saw blank walls that seemed to be vaguely wavering while the chamber was filled with a greenish twilight. There were no shadows of any kind.

His arms were pinioned behind his back and they were numb from loss of circulation. His ankles were crossed and strapped with webbing. It was a very complete job. He was nauseated and his head throbbed. As he turned it, trying to size up his surroundings, he was aware of a large and painful lump above and back of his left ear.

Something flew, or floated above the transparent roof. It was more or less of a blur; it fitted in with the wavering walls and made him believe himself still partly blind, his eyes affected by the terrific blows he had sustained.

But he changed that opinion when a man, who had been seated out of his scope of vision, seemingly guarding him, waiting for him to move, rose and came toward him. Chinese faces are not easy to differentiate and remember. But he did not think he had seen this one before. This was a tall Manchu, almost a giant, with evil features scarred with an old slash. His eyes were hood-lidded, aslant and squinting. His blouse and pantaloons were wide, of dark indigo, his feet bare. He wore a leather sling over one shoulder and, attached to it, a shagreen scabbard in which was a curving knife, its handle also bound in sharkskin.

He looked down at Foster and grinned hideously. He had only the stump of a tongue. Foster remembered the torturers in his vision of Mary and the hollow brazen serpent filled with steam. The man was of that type, possibly a eunuch, a slave who obeyed implicitly, without thought about his orders, save when they gave him delight in the suffering he might cause.

He turned, went to a door curtained by dark green draperies brocaded in gold with a design of intertwining dragons, and spoke a few syllables. Then he kow-towed humbly as the figure of Fang Li appeared.

Fang Li still wore yellow, his adopted color as the future Ruler of the World. His outer garment was a long robe of shimmering silk, buttoned with topazes. A dagger was thrust into a sash and its hilt was topped by a flaming yellow stone. He wore no hat and his face was serene but it was the serenity of Satan.

"Ah, my friend Foster," he said, "it was good of you to come here. How you discovered the place is immaterial. I am not wasting curiosity on that."

He spoke impersonally but his eyes had clouded slightly. It was plain that the matter piqued him.

"Now I have you, your fiancée, and also your flyer under one roof. Rather a curious roof, Foster, is it not? Alto-gether a quite ingenious—shall we say—hideout? Not to be expected on a barren island. A residence, a fortress, a retreat; all in one. That is the Atlantic you see beyond the glass ceiling. Some ten fath-oms of it at this stage of the tide. Quite impossible to be seen, even from an auto-giro. I must thank you for having sup-plied me with an addition to my fleet," he added mockingly.

"No one will ever find me here, or you, unless you should carry out the infor-mation and I am afraid that may not be compassed. I shall have to withdraw my suggestions of immunity. You have for-feited them. It is true you do not know the way in nor will you ever know the way out, but you know too much. That, of course, applies equally to your fiancée

and to the flyer who, I gather, is a per-sonal friend of yours. You may be able to save them somewhat if you do not waste time yourself. Otherwise—"

He shrugged his shoulders. There was no mercy in the man. His blue eyes blazed with maniacal desire. He meant to have the formula and he meant also to glut his sadistic nature with the torment of his victims.

FOSTER looked again at the walls where the motion of the waves that rolled overhead cast the flickering shad-ows. He strove to think of some way in which he could best the madman and saw no hope. He was helpless.

His voice was hoarse when he spoke. "If you have any sense of justice, of equality, Fang Li," he said, "let me re-mind you that I once saved your life. You owe me something in return. You can take mine but spare those of a de-fenseless girl and a man who acted for me only out of friendship."

Fang Li chuckled. "Strict justice, from your standpoint," he answered, "would balance a life against a life. If you pos-sess the privilege of saving one, which shall it be. Your friend, or your sweet-heart?"

He did not wait for a reply but went on with manifest enjoyment.

"Friendship is like a pearl, says Con-fucius, but pearls are without value when one does not desire them. A defenseless girl, when she is beautiful, has many at-tractions. Bah! These matters count for nothing. They are less than grains in the hourglass of Time which even now is running out against your existence—and theirs. I may amuse myself with the woman. She may abhor me and that will greaten my pleasure. When I am through with her — providing you have not by then surrendered the formula—"

Foster strained at his bonds, rolled from the cushionless bench where they had placed him, striving to reach Fang Li, impotent though he was. Fang Li smiled at him, clapped his hands and the Manchu giant came back, lifting Foster as if he had been a child, setting him back at the commands of his lord.

"These things, Foster," said Fang Li, "were decreed on high. I must conquer. You, and all others who oppose me are as the dust beneath my shoe. Valueless after they serve their brief purpose. Once, and once only, I suffered a man to live after he had groveled before me and begged for the boon. I doubt if he so considers it now. I might spare yours after the same fashion."

He spoke to the Manchu who awaited dismissal. While Foster still writhed Fang Li surveyed him placidly, as curiously and impersonally as a vivisectionist might watch the jerking muscles of a subject strapped to the operating table.

The giant came back, shoving ahead of him something that had once been a man. He was white, almost bald save for a few gray straggling locks; dressed in worn, untidy clothes; thin to emaciation. There were scars on his arms, on his gaunt trunk. He was sightless and his right hand was curled like a withered leaf.

"Even if he could get out," said Fang Li, "he cannot see; the drums of his ears are broken and his tongue is a stump. Neither can he write. I have made sure he is not left-handed. Crippled as he is I doubt whether he could learn to use it. And he will not get out. But he lives. He was a coward.

"You have, of course, received my letter, also that of your fiancée who must have intimated to you, in some ingenious way, where to find her. I have not, as yet, got your personal receipt. It is doubtless on the way. You will remember that I gave you twenty-four hours. I shall reckon them from the moment of your arrival on this island. There are now some twenty-three hours left. At the

expiration of that period I shall keep my word. If you have not delivered the formula by then, voluntarily, I shall proceed to persuade you, by object lessons. This, in a way, is one of them," he added as he gestured with his head toward the frightful cripple. "He possessed a secret not as valuable as yours but, in a way, allied to it. A new explosive. You may have heard of it—N. R. T.?"

"You mean," said Foster, aghast, "that he is Norton Woodward?"

"He was. He hardly merits any individuality now. You will remember that he disappeared," said Fang Li. "Some said he was kidnaped. He was, though not for ransom. I gave him twenty-four hours, also. He held out for two hours after that. Now I have his secret."

"My formula is complicated," said Foster. "I cannot carry all of it in my mind." He was desperate, seeking for a reprieve of time though he did not see what he could do with it.

"I will do you the honor of assuming that you do not lie," said Fang Li, though it was plain he did not believe Foster spoke the truth. "I shall give you every opportunity of refreshing your memory. I have an excellent laboratory. I am sure even you will find it adequately equipped. There are others who have come close to the discovery to which you brought the requisite touch of genius. I trust you will be able not merely to hand me the chemical statement but give me a test of its efficiency. That will be quite necessary. It can take place out of doors. No one will take notice of a minor explosion on Wyman's Island, even if they should see or hear it. We will experiment with some of Woodward's N. R. T. I have plenty of it stored here, and also in other places. This is not my only hidden headquarters, you see. Now, I will have your bonds removed so that I may show you over the place. You can spare a little time out of your twenty-three. I do not think it will take you very long to prepare the formula, if you set your mind upon it," Fang Li ended, with sarcastic emphasis.

The Manchu guard thrust the unfortunate Woodward outside, where Foster heard him scraping along uncertainly. Then the webbing straps were loosened and, at a word from Fang Li, the giant chafed Foster's ankles and wrists to restore circulation. He sat up at last, saying nothing, his brain at work like a squirrel in a revolving cage, tremendously active but getting nowhere.

CHAPTER FIVE

Death by the Clock

TWENTY-THREE hours, less than that now. Flying, second by second, grain by grain through the hourglass of Time. A flash came to him of a picture he had seen as a boy in his grandfather's study. An engraving of a grinning skeleton seated beside a table that bore a big Book of the Doomed. Death's scythe hung on the back of his chair and there was an hourglass beside the book, with most of its sand run out.

Death, inevitable, for himself, for Taylor whom he had brought into the trap, for Mary. Worse than death, perhaps for her—torture of mind and body she could not long survive, unless she went mad. They would kill her then.

He could win an easy passing for the two of them if he capitulated and gave up his secret, played traitor to his country, to all the world.

The enormity of the situation, the immensity of it, swept over Foster and threatened to overwhelm him. His own life he might be content to sacrifice to keep the secret from this madman. But there was Mary, his love for her, hers for him; Taylor, trusty friend. What right had he to include them in such a bargain? Yet, in the cold light of logic, how could three be weighed against the countless thousands, millions perhaps, who would be enslaved and sacrificed by the frightful revel of blood and fire Fang Li was contemplating?

Then he realized that there was no question of a bargain. The three of them were already sentenced, whether Fang Li got the formula or not. Unless he could outwit him.

He could not fake the formula. Fang Li knew enough of chemistry to follow every phase of its production, would do so. The remotest fibers of Foster's being rose in revolt against this crafty, clever devil. He did not show it. He would appear submissive until the last hope was gone.

Then he recollected the day in the college laboratory. He had rescued Fang Li then. He could destroy him now. He could concoct some mixture under the pretense of its being part of the formula, something that would sear and scald and eat into flesh and bone even more than the quicklime had acted on the black cat. He would defy Fang Li, laugh at him, tell him he would not get the formula, then fling the acid compound in his face. After that, with Fang Li destroyed, there might be. . . . . .

Fang Li's voice, placid as a tiger's purr, and as menacing, broke in. "In case you are meditating a last minute attack on me, Foster, you will not find me unprepared. You are prodigal with your last hours. The sand sifts and the dark river flows swiftly to the sea of oblivion. For you foreign devils," he added with a bland contempt, "there is no Nirvana. Only the outermost, uttermost darkness. Come with me. I will show you my little domain; I will give you free access to your charming fiancée, and to Taylor. I would not spoil your final hours by being boorish."

He smiled and Foster sank teeth into his lower lip until the blood spurted in his effort to subdue himself. Fang Li was armed, he had men within call, yet for a second, as Foster regarded him, he throbbed with the desire to fling himself upon the other, fight him with his naked hands. It was absurd. Fang Li regarded him with eyes that clearly read his mood and jeered at it.

Foster glanced at his wrist watch. Less than twenty-three hours! Now twenty minutes after three. Afternoon, it must be, by the light filtered through the sea that set the wavering shadows on the wall.

THE place was marvellously built. There must have been a tunnel and, later, superb engineering to erect this place on the bottom of the sea. Foster wondered what poor wretch of an engineering genius had been forced into this service. There were rooms of smoothly coated stone or cement, tinted, plainly furnished, corridors that descended or ascended by ramps and stairs, their walls tiled. There was a sort of guard room where a dozen Chinese lounged about a table thrusting rice from bowls into their cheeks with chopsticks until their jowls bulged like those of apes. Arms here, in racks behind glass doors guarded with metal lattice. Bunks, benches, severity and discipline. All wore tunics with the ideograph of Fang Li upon their backs. All kowtowed before him. He was their lord and they were serfs, well trained, bound by superstition, linked to their master's flaming belief in his own supremacy.

Fang Li's own apartments were not spacious but palatial. Rugs, hangings, gods, teak and ivory furniture, divans, cushions, the scent of incense. Oleanders blooming in great vases, a Shama thrush singing in a golden cage. Flowering

plants made up of semiprecious stones in amazing accuracy of imitation.

Beyond this, the laboratory, precise as the operating room of a great hospital. Shining paraphernalia, modern apparatus. Spatulas, funnels, filters, test tubes, retorts, burners, stills, aspirators, dessicators and crucibles. U-tubes, pipettes, weighing bottles, burettes, scales, ovens, blowpipes, thermometers, and a score of special apparatus designed by experts for delicate processes. Carboys, glass-stoppered bottles, crystals, reagents, elements, materials of all kinds.

Nothing was missing; porcelain tables, tubs and drains with green-shaded, blue-bulbed electric lights over them. Fang Li pointed out the switches. There was ample power for fusing, for roasting and alloying, for electrolysis, catalysis and hydrolysis. At another time and place it would have made Foster's spirit yearn for such a workshop. Now it sank. Here was no excuse for failure. Somewhere a dynamo purred, back of a steel door that lacked lock or handle, that fitted into the wall like a plate in a ship's hull.

"We have our doors made waterproof in case of trouble," said Fang Li. "They close and open by hidden levers. Look over the place carefully, Foster. If there is anything you need I will see you get it well within the balance of your time. I have a cruising launch that can make forty knots and, by this time, the autogiro you so kindly brought here should have returned from its errand. I trust you have all the necessities, however. Make your inventory. I shall return presently."

"There is time enough for that," said Foster. "I want to see Miss Callader and Taylor. Until I assure myself they are being well treated I will not touch a vial."

Fang Li made his arrogant shrug. "They are, at present, quite comfortable," he said. "They will so continue until three o'clock tomorrow afternoon. Then we shall make the test and hold a conference as to the best—or the worst— manner of your shuffling off this mortal coil. If you wish to waste the time I will take you to them. You will not, I hope, be jealous of your fiancée's passing these, let us say imminent, hours in company with Taylor, fascinating as he is. It is not advisable to separate them. You may eat with them or have meals served here."

The basic chemical material for the production of the ray was common enough, found all over the world and extremely cheap. While Fang Li spoke Foster was looking at a most ample supply. But he had no idea of letting Fang Li realize how almost primitive the apparatus had to be. Schimkus, for Germany, had created a ray that exploded cartridges at thirty-five feet and, later, loose powder at five hundred. Germany had ignored him because the Versailles Treaty forbade it to make any use of rays. The British spent half a million in investigating death rays, about which silence was maintained. The Italian Navy had a disappointing experience with a man who claimed ability to set off submarine mines.

Foster had far outstripped all these. His energy could be sent from central stations to airplanes, ships and other motor apparatus from various points on land. It could be produced aboard mother vessels and it could annihilate munitions depots and artillery projectiles at long range. This he had proven and knew that certain refinements would produce further seeming miracles. He expected to ruin the motors of flying machines and bring them down, like ducks shot from a blind, to destroy the engines of war and merchant vessels.

He could create that energy in this laboratory, demonstrate it. But he showed no signs of certainty.

"I will go over it when I return," he said. "It will take time."

Time was what he wanted, though without true reason except, perhaps, the desire to live until the last moment, hoping against hope for reprieve, like a condemned man in the death house.

"Take all the time you like, up to twenty-two hours," said Fang Li. "You will follow me?"

Two hours gone, two precious hours, over eight per cent of the time to live that this incarnate devil granted them.

Fang motioned to a door which slid back as he rapped upon it. They went through the opening.

TAYLOR had a bandage about his head, put on by Mary Callader from the supplies a steward of Fang Li had produced. He smiled wryly at Foster as the latter entered.

"She's lying down," he said in a low tone after Fang Li had withdrawn. "Great girl! That earthborn Satan who just went out told her you were captured and told her, too, just what was in store for all of us. They had me bound like a mummy or I'd have taken a chance at strangling him when he hinted what her fate might be, the swine. I see they bumped you up a bit. There's a bathroom here. You'd better clean up. I've got iodine and bandages. I thought they'd cracked my cranium."

"All I need is a wash," said Foster. "I suppose they got you from behind, like they did me. I imagine they came up the dry well shaft. It's probably one entrance and there may be another camouflaged in the cellar of the old house. Fang Li says he has a fast cruiser and that your plane has only gone on an errand."

Taylor's eyes gleamed. "That should help, if we only get out of here," he said.

Foster nodded. "I've got a vague

plan," he said. "I may be able to start something if I can get Fang Li away. He has the ingenuity of a fiend. I wish I had some weapon—for Mary—in the last resort. I can't figure out much hope."

Taylor grinned. It was characteristic of the man. "When I was in France," he said, "there was a little motor mac' attached to the outfit who had been a tough egg. Served time, he told me. And he showed me a trick. 'If you ever have to go down back of the enemy lines,' he said, 'they'll frisk you good and plenty but here's one trick they'll overlook.'

"He showed me a long, thin blade of steel, flexible but workmanlike, that sheathed in the double leather of the back of his boots. It was a swell stunt and I copied it. He had an old pipe that stank to high heaven, with a cracked and burned bowl and a wide, flat stem to the wooden part of it. 'They'll never have the heart to swipe a pipe like that,' he said and then he showed how the blade fitted into the stem and the bowl made a handle for a mighty serviceable dagger. I've got mine on me, blade and pipe. I'll rig it and give it to Miss Callader. She may need it. We two can stand the gaff if we have to, old chap, but—"

Foster clapped him on the shoulder. "Good man," he said. "We're not licked yet. Let her sleep. I'm going back to stall in the laboratory. I suppose we'll eat around six or seven and we'll all do it together. I may have something to report and talk over. Fang Li has purposely given us these hours of leeway to prolong the agony. He'd like to break down our morale."

"He won't break it down," said Taylor. "Not yours or mine and, least of all, Miss Callader's. I don't know what you ever did to deserve a girl like that."

"I don't," replied Foster with a grim little smile. "Maybe I will if I get her out of here."

"I'm banking on your brains," said Taylor. "Me, I've got a good sense of balance but I'm better off the ground than on when it comes to strategy. I'll be seeing you, then, around six?"

It did Foster good to talk with the debonair flyer, to feel that Mary had a protector close at hand, a weapon with which to cheat Fate.

HE HAD many hours work ahead of him. Compared with Foster, Fang Li, as a chemist, was a mere amateur. Foster believed he could fool him unless the man happened to possess a special knowledge of gaseous irritants. That chance he had to take. And, despite the elaborate equipment, he had to make a special apparatus to obtain what he wanted. That on hand would have sufficed for the Omega Ray process but Foster had now to contrive special tubes filled with various copper oxides, to make a complicated set-up of burettes and pipettes, a day's ordinary work for two skilled laboratory men.

He had to get Fang Li out of the way lest he might recognize in the final assembly the purpose of the apparatus. It meant concentrated, unremitting and skillful labor, but the materials were there and it was the only possible—not positive—way to freedom and the retention of the secret ray.

Foster found Fang Li waiting for him in the laboratory. He had donned a crystal mask, an overall of heavy rubber with rubber gloves, the whole impervious to acids for at least several minutes. He took off the mask momentarily.

"You will find a similar outfit in that closet, if you need it," he said, indicating the place. "You don't mind me watching you for a while?"

Foster said nothing. Fang Li had forestalled a personal attack, his own diabolical instinct swift to be wary of danger. But Foster had looked beyond that. He commenced deliberately to select his tubes of glass and rubber, his water-jackets, his U tubes, materal for a mercury reservoir, sparking points, filters, graduates, capillaries and cocks. He deliberately juggled with them while preserving an attitude of extreme precision, hoping that Fang Li would be presently bewildered.

"I shall have to test the purity of some of your drugs," he said. "That I cannot do until later on. If they are adulterated or deteriorated, I cannot be responsible for failure."

"I am afraid I shall have to find you so," said Fang Li, silkily. "However, I shall personally do what I can to get you pure supplies if these prove deleterious. I am urgently interested in your success."

Foster's pulse went up. The tubing he handled trembled slightly. This was what he had prayed for, to get rid of Fang Li during the time he would be compounding certain chemicals. Fang Li could hardly trust his men to make the purchases. Neither could they be made before the supply houses—in Boston or New York—opened for business. That would be nine o'clock tomorrow—with six hours left. If Fang Li had not returned Foster held no doubt that he would have left instructions. He might even suspect he was sent on a fool's errand. He would be inexorable. The twenty-four hours was the actual limit. Fang Li might regret that he was not able to witness the execution of the two men but he would keep the girl's fate pending until he came back.

In Foster's desperate, half-formed plan, hours would not count so much as final moments.

And, while Fang Li watched his deliberate preparations, Foster strove to remember certain other formulas, born of the War. It seemed perversely as if his memory would fail him. He had several choices, having studied these matters.

Acute lung irritants, lachrymators, paralysants, vesicants and sensory irritants. The paralysant was simply H. C. N., hydrocyanic or prussic acid, immediately fatal. He had no sympathy for these serfs of Fang Li but he had to consider ways and means of liberating the gas he might find opportunity to use on them.

What he wanted was the diphenylcyanarsine that Germany used in 1918, her last contribution to a dying cause. It was a solid, melting at 46° centigrade which could be released from a fragile container as fine dust by means of a fulminator properly affixed, causing sneezing, intense pain of the nose and throat and instant nausea.

The figures escaped him though a hundred times he thought he had captured them. He plodded on with his assembly of apparatus, seemingly, and actually, absorbed.

The minutes passed, crystallizing into hours. Fang Li left him and he hardly noticed it.

It was close to six when he penciled down the formula, conned it over and made ash of it, sure of it now, imprinted indelibly on his brain. $(C_6H_5)_2 AsCN$. That was it, the virulent sternutator. It all came to him now.

CHAPTER SIX

Gas Trap

A GONG sounded. A steward, obsequious enough, asked him in pidgin English if he was ready to dine with his companions.

Foster arranged his work, washed his hands. Fang Li would come spying but he would not find anything. He followed the steward to where Mary Callader and Taylor awaited him. His eyes were bright, signals of his alert brain. His mien was confident.

Mary Callader was in her riding

clothes. She greeted him with a poise that made him proud while her glance showed her pride, her love and confidence in him.

"We'll talk French," said Foster in that language. Taylor spoke it fluently and Foster was fairly adept, as was Mary.

First, as the excellent meal was being served, she told him of her abduction.

It had been simple enough. They had spied on her, knew her usual route. She had come across a car which seemed to have broken a steering knuckle and was slued across the road. Her horse had shied and she had soothed it, finally dismounting to lead it around the car, with no one in sight. Then, suddenly, she had been seized, drugged and carried off. She had no memory of her passage until she came to in the undersea stronghold with Fang Li regarding her.

He had told her briefly of his own imperial status, the part she was to play in it.

"I do not think I gave him much satisfaction," she said. "I may even have got beneath his yellow skin. Then they brought in Mr. Taylor and said that you had landed and were in their power. Fang Li did not disguise his intentions toward me. Now, Paul, what have you contrived?"

FOSTER led Mary and Taylor to the laboratory where he explained his plan and showed them the apparatus which he had begun to set up.

"It will be a tremendous task to complete everything in time," he said. "And much depends on my being able to inveigle Fang Li into going himself after the chemicals I shall pretend to need. In case I fail completely and Fang Li refuses to leave, here is some cyanide which I managed to filch from the supply here in the laboratory." He paused and looked first at Taylor, then at Mary. "If worst comes to worst and that fiend starts his deviltries—well, it's a quick and certain way out!"

He showed them the deadly chemical that meant instant release.

"I'll take some of that," said Taylor. "Might come in handy. I wish I had a chance at Fang Li's food or drink."

Then Mary gave Foster a glimpse of the pliant blade, with its curious but efficient handle, which Taylor had described to him and which the flyer had given Mary as promised. She had slid it beneath the sport shirt she wore ready for instant action.

"I will take some of the cyanide," she said. "But first I hope to get a chance to use this."

Her eyes flashed. They were in a desperate situation but their spirits dominated it and that of Mary Callader's was not the least of the three.

But it was on Foster that the burden lay. He had work, to offset their travail of weary waiting, but he had always the spectre of possible failure at his elbow. Hours of delicate and precise work ahead, of frequent tests, of certain temporary failures.

At midnight he was scarcely halfway through with his task. He straightened up, his back aching, his body sweating from intense concentration. He was fighting Time, who was the twin of Death. Someone entered. It was Mary. She had brought him sandwiches and coffee. Then for a few precious moments Foster relaxed, gave himself up to what might possibly be his last moments of love.

"You will not fail," Mary told him just before they heard the soft shuffle of felt-shod feet. Then Fang Li appeared.

Her lips were still upon his own as

Fang Li's mocking accents made insincere apology.

"Life is short and love is fleeting," he paraphrased. "You must pardon me for introducing my own interests which, after all, if you look at it properly, are also your own."

His gaze traveled slowly, deliberately over the figure of the girl, appraising, anticipating. Foster gripped a phial of acid. Fang Li's eyes lifted and encountered the clear scorn in Mary Callader's eyes. He winced before it. And hated her the more with a hatred that would glut itself in a rich revenge, if he could compass it. He held no doubt of that. Through her love for Foster he would deal her exquisite torments. He would torture her soul and body. But he veiled his thoughts as the girl departed and devoted his attention to the half-assembled apparatus.

"It is elaborate," he said. "I fear I put you to much trouble but you have still fifteen—almost fifteen—hours ahead of you. May I ask you to explain the use of this apparatus, in terms I can understand?" he added, in false humility.

"I am creating a gas," said Foster. "It must be filtered carefully, checked over. Its base is a common mineral but unfortunately that mineral varies. In its usual commercial use it is not necessary to make the purifications my formula demands. A slight impurity will defeat success.

"Once I am assured my gas is perfected, either by analysis or through a spectrum—or both—I shall excite its radiations by electric discharge. It is essential that the potential of this discharge shall be at least equal to its voltage. I may have to call upon your dynamos for their utmost power. The Gamma Ray takes millions of volts, the X-ray sometimes a hundred thousand, sometimes a hundred, depending upon conditions. In my case it depends upon the purity of my basic chemical. My wave lengths for the Omega Ray are so determined."

"I understand that," said Fang Li, truthfully enough but not realizing that his understanding was limited. He was like a scholar who possesses a vocabulary of a foreign language but lacks any idea of the difficulties of its syntax. "When do you test the basic mineral?"

"When I have completed the apparatus. If it does not give me my ray with a fair voltage through this transformer of yours, I shall resort to inorganic and qualitative analysis."

Fang Li nodded. He knew the meaning of those terms though he had not mastered all the technique. And, despite his own aggrandizement, he had a grudging respect for Foster's skill. His attitude was not unlike that of the high chief of a savage tribe who admits the cleverness of his wizard.

"I shall see you again, after I have slept," he said. "I suppose that there will be little sleep for you tonight but, eventually, your slumbers will be lasting. What is it the poet says, one of your Occidental poets who so seldom see through the veil? 'Death is but a sleep—and a forgetting.' That is it. Foster, nothing may stand between me and my destiny. You serve me unwillingly but I think you serve me well. I cannot set you free, yet, if the test succeeds, you may ask a favor of me and I may grant it, even if I deny myself certain exhilarations."

"Thanks," said Foster curtly. "The biggest favor you can confer on me at present is to let me go ahead on this job."

MORNING found him infinitely weary but triumphant. He was ready for Fang Li. He had his weapons. He had yet to use them and win but much was achieved. The stress of that night had burned up vitality, had left him lined and hollow-eyed.

It was eight o'clock when Fang Li visited him again, once more carefully protected by mask and suit. With him were two guards who not only wore daggers but automatics. Things were closing in. Fang Li's geniality showed a certain strain.

"You have seven hours more," he said. "I trust that they will prove sufficient. I am not a patient man, Foster. And I keep my word. At the end of the period you perish, without benefit of any terms, if you are not ready for me."

"I am going to show you an experiment," said Foster. "You have made many such simple tests yourself. The basic mineral is too impure. I know of only two chemists—one in New York and one in Boston—where I can procure what I want. I will give you their names. Please watch me."

He took some of the mineral and placed it in a hollow made in a block of charcoal, then used his blowpipe. It was not an element and the various concomitants of its makeup glowed in the fierce heat. Foster moistened it with cobalt and the glow turned pink.

"There you are," he said to Fang Li. "Magnesia! It makes the stuff useless as muddy water. I must have purer material. It is up to you, Fang Li, to get it for me, if you want the formula, and swiftly. They lie in the balance, my life and the demonstration of the Omega Ray."

Fang Li eyed Foster with a look that sought to break down any tissue of trickery the American might have set up. He was almost convinced yet he knew he was pressing the other hard.

"I make you no promises," he said. "I give no pledge of lenience, of immunity."

"We will bargain later," said Foster scornfully. "Fang Li, despite all your lore of past generations, despite all your belief in your destiny, you may not be sure of it. But this one thing I promise you. If it is within my power, I shall prove to you the working of my Omega Ray. But, first, I must have fresh supplies of this. You can send for them, you can use the autogiro you took from Taylor. It will take but a few hours. Bring it to me with only half an hour to spare and I will make the demonstration."

He was bluffing magnificently while he waited to find out if Fang Li would react as he hoped. It would take hours to generate properly the gas for the Omega Ray, even as it would take hours for him to perfect the one on which he was working. If Fang Li would go . . . himself. He must.

"I shall go myself," he heard Fang Li saying. "Not with the plane. That would attract too much attention. The boat will be fast enough. I will bring you back a supply. I will wire both houses, demand a magnesia test, fetch the purer product. Then, Foster, we may learn more of our immediate destinies."

When he was gone, Foster joined the girl and Taylor at breakfast. He found they had got hold of Norton Woodward and made him understand that they were white, that they were friendly. There had been no interference. Aside from the menace of the time limit, they might have been honored guests.

After the meal, Foster worked feverishly once more. He had to generate his gas, though not the one from which the Omega Ray resolved. He had to watch its temperature as it changed.

At last, in the retort, crystals began to form, granules. He had achieved diphenylcyanarsine.

He held it imprisoned in a fragile receptacle, short of entire solidity, ready to break into noxious powder with the explosion of the fulminate he made and adjusted. The glass mask was no protection and he prepared wads of cotton saturated with filtration chemicals to place inside his nostrils, to bind across his mouth. The eyes would not be affected.

When all was ready at last, he glanced at his watch. It was twenty minutes after two. Fang Li had not returned. There must have been some unusual delay. Fang Li wanted the formula. Ordinary obstacles would not stop him.

CHAPTER SEVEN

The Omega Ray

THE Chinese steward who had served them their meals, a sort of majordomo, came to the laboratory and bowed.

"It is honor to inform you," he said in his clipped dialect, "that now forty minutes only remain. This my honorable master wished me to say."

Foster nodded almost cheerfully. A lot could happen in forty minutes.

"Your honorable master has not returned?" he asked. The man shook his head, bowed low once more and left.

Foster gave him a minute or so. Then he took his gas bomb and his saturated pads and found Taylor with Mary and Woodward.

"We'll tackle the guard room," he said. "This will put them out of commission. This soaked cotton will protect us. There are weapons there. The stuff is not cumulative but it will give us our chance. There are other men about, I imagine. Fang Li may return at any moment. We've got to find the way out but it's our only show. Mary, you can't be in on this. We'll take Woodward with us. The autogiro is somewhere above us. Ready, Red?"

The loungers in the guardroom seemed

to be more than Foster had expected. They had taken advantage of Fang Li's absence, perhaps. At any rate they were relaxed, playing fantan, absorbed in the game.

Foster stood in the doorway with Taylor. Their improvised masks roused the suspicion of the man who looked up.

"*Hola!*" he cried, in swift and brief alarm.

Foster tossed the bomb. There was an explosion, a cloud of fine dust. Instantly the men were seized with spasms of sneezing, choking convulsions, fierce attacks of faintness and vomiting. The two Americans made their way through the strangling mob and forced the doors of the armory closets. They found automatics and two modern, miniature Thompson guns, weighing less than ten pounds, but capable of throwing a thousand bullets a minute. There was ample ammunition and they loaded their weapons, leaving the writhing, gasping mass of humanity. The explosion had been sharp rather than loud, it did not seem as yet to have summoned aid.

Then they heard a woman's cry for help and bolted to where they had left Mary Callader. She was standing with her back against a carved screen. A Chinaman lay in front of her with the blade of Taylor's knife driven deep into his breast. The pipe-bowl hilt was in her hand as it had wrenched free as the man fell.

Woodward, blind cripple as he was, had closed with another Chinaman and his left hand was on the yellow throat in a death grip. Foster saw a knife rise and fall and he fired. The Chinaman dropped, shot through the head and Woodward swayed and toppled, his abdomen ripped by the deadly stroke, bathed in his own blood.

There was the clamor of a gong outside, shouts.

"We've got to get out of this," said Foster to the girl. "Got to find the way out. Come on. Here's an automatic. Don't forget to squeeze the grip as well as the trigger. Let's go."

Woodward was dying. There was no help for him, mercifully enough.

The one with the knife in him was the steward.

"Fang Li is coming," said the girl. "They had some sort of message from him, radio, I think. He said that Fang Li would be here on time, that there were only twenty minutes left and that I was to change to those robes."

Foster saw where garments of vivid scarlet lay on the floor. He knew their significance. So did Mary Callader, though more by instinct than actual knowledge. Robes of ignominy and shame for a white woman to attire herself in for a yellow man.

"I told him I would not," she said. "He laid hands on me and I lost control. I was keyed up. I snatched out the knife and struck. Woodward grappled with the other one as he tried to throw him aside. Then—you came."

THEY set the girl between them as they made their first adventure. Four Chinamen showed ahead in the passage, excited, alarmed, letting off their pistols. The bullets flew high and Foster turned loose with his Thompson, mowing them down. They passed them, riddled, the floor slippery with their blood. They reached the room where Foster had first come back to consciousness and pressed on. Two men fled before them. They might shut off exit in some secret manner. Foster made a sieve of one of them, the other bolted through heavy curtains, shrilling an alarm in Cantonese.

The curtains bulged. Foster thrust Mary back of both of them now. Here was counter attack on hand.

"Lie down," he ordered her as the curtains were swept aside and a charging horde made for them. They had knives and pistols; they yelled in high falsetto, jabbering, their slant-eyes glittering.

The room was riven with flame, fogged with smoke and made thunderous with the discharge of guns. From the floor the girl fired too.

Blood dripped from Foster's left sleeve. Taylor was hit in the left thigh. But the sub-machine guns had won. The place was a shambles.

The girl was unhurt. They barged past the lead-torn curtains into a passage, past doors to right and left and saw, at the end of the corridor, a faint circle of light.

There was blue sky above, a circle of it, infinitely blessed. They stood at the bottom of the well shaft. It was clear and there were hand and foot holds all the way up. Foster saw where a grating had been unlocked and thrust aside into a recess, doubtless in anticipation of Fang Li's arrival. The excited yellow men had neglected to close it.

Foster's watch showed five minutes to three. At any moment the men he had gassed, or rather powdered, might recover.

"Up the ladder!" he said. "You first, Mary. Then you, Red. Spot your plane. I'll be with you."

They clambered up the projecting holds of steel spiked into the bricking of the well and Foster stayed, to give them a start, to get Mary in the clear, give Taylor a chance at the plane. Blood throbbed out of him as he waited, listening to the scuffle of their climb, listening for sounds of fresh attack.

The latter came but it was a hesitant sortie. There were too many dead men in the way to inspire recklessness. A burst from the Thompson thoroughly demoralized them though Foster had some unpleasant moments as he made his way up the well shaft. They could have brought him down without danger to themselves, once he started.

He crawled over the well curb thankfully and saw Taylor looking over his engine. A Chinaman in aviator's overalls stood with his hands extended while Mary Callader held her gun on him. Then the motor sputtered into life, the propeller spun, revving up.

"All aboard!" cried Taylor. "Everything's O. K.!"

The noise of the engine almost drowned his voice. The Chinese flyer stood expectant of death, stoically. Foster tempered justice with mercy and knocked him out expertly with the muzzle of the gun he took from Mary. The man dropped like a length of chain.

They got into the none too capacious cockpit, he and Mary. His sleeve was crimson now and he began to feel weak from strain, from sleeplessness and loss of blood. He had leached energy for twenty-three hours. Blood was on the leather strap of his wrist watch but the dial was clear.

Three minutes of three!

Red Taylor pointed to where a boat came racing for the land, its bow lifting with the tremendous speed, foam all about her.

Out of the well shaft a yellow face looked and disappeared. The plane got grip of the air. They lifted, rising steadily. Mary was trying to get a tourniquet placed on Foster's arm as he gazed down to where Fang Li, knowing by the soaring plane that he had lost, stood staring upward. He was in American clothes. He had brought the unneeded chemical and he had been gulled. He stood motionless, his face a mask as the autogiro mounted, headed south.

"I'm coming back," said Foster. "I promised to give him a demonstration of the Omega Ray and I mean to. There can be nothing official about this. The machinery of the government creaks. That spawn must be wiped out. They are more dangerous than a brood of vipers. I only trust I get Fang Li with them. You're in with me, Taylor?"

"Through to the finish, Foster."

IT WAS almost thirty-six hours later when the autogiro hovered once more over Wyman's Island. The night was starlit and moonlit. The place seemed desolate and yet there showed a faint but distinct illumination of a patch of sea that was too confined to be seafire. It was the glow from Fang Li's underground fortress.

It might mean that he was there. Foster most devoutly hoped so. He had arrayed himself definitely against this monster—the term was not too strong—who was set upon the upheaval of the world for the gratification of his own ambitions. It should be a war to the bitter end, a private war, since it was too fantastic to be understood by ordinary men. It might be ended now.

Foster had shipped his generators up to the Maine Coast by truck. He had labored over them incessantly and now the autogiro was a supercharged instrument of destruction. The throw of a switch, the focussing of wave-lengths and the Omega Ray would be demonstrated.

Taylor came down almost vertically from two thousand feet to one, then to five hundred, to half that distance.

Foster was satisfied, bade him get elevation again, two thousand feet. Then he crouched, like a panther intent upon its prey.

He touched a key and a message leapt ashore and was answered. His assistants were ready now to release the voltage that would surge through his gas container, through the lenses, and discharge fearful, invisible force.

Nothing in the wildest dreams of Arabian romancers in their legends of afrits and djhins could equal this.

The unseen ray pierced disdainfully through the common atmosphere with almost the kinetic energy of a flaring sunspot, modified, subdued, harnessed, by the genius who controlled his discovery.

He sighted at the pale streak and shifted little cogs of brass.

Then the water directly offshore broke into a geyser that lifted high, spouting, bursting. There was a hint of flame, swiftly quenched, a roar that came to them above the engine's voice and made the autogiro tremble in midair. Then a Niagara, closing in, devastating, obliterating.

Woodward was avenged. His explosive, under the urge of the Omega Ray, had shouted his epitaph.

The autogiro winged its way to shore again. The two men landed, silently. They had been executioners, although perhaps saviors of the world.

"Flying back?" said Taylor finally. Foster shook his head.

"I've got to see about the transportation of this stuff," he said. "I don't expect any inquiry but it might be as well to offset it. You go ahead, Red. I'll see you later. I've got my car. I'll drive. My Filipino brought it here."

THE rules of traffic that prevail on the bridges spanning the two rivers that encircle Manhattan are rigidly enforced.

Therefore, Foster, driving south, sighting a face in the back of a costly sedan that was speeding north—a sedan he knew well, in which he had ridden not so long before upon a memorable journey —might not turn and follow. He had entered the bridge. Efficient, but hardly plastic, traffic officers would think him crazy if he pleaded that this was a question of the world's safety. They might arrest him for a crank; certainly have him detained if he tried to hold up the evening flood of vehicles.

There was not the remotest possibility of turning in the two set lanes of progress, with their signs and lamps, and white lines of control painted on the cement.

Therefore he swept on, helpless. He had destroyed the subsea fortress on Wyman's Island. He had damaged Fang Li's offensive but Fang Li had not been present when the Omega Ray blasted the hidden explosives.

His blue eyes in his high-cheeked countenance had glared at Foster at the entrance to the bridge. Glared implacably.

Foster had scotched the snake but he had not destroyed it.

The fate of the world still hung in the balance, with that mad genius at liberty, with all his millions, his insane egoism.

THE TORSO TRAP

by
John Lawrence

Author of "The Scarlet Comet," etc.

Beckett scrambled futilely as the big man crashed on him.

Five hundred thousand dollars in bonds—a jewelled cigarette lighter —and Maxton Le Marr's head! All three were missing when Beckett took the case. But missing bonds and headless corpses were that big dick's meat—and jewelled cigarette lighters are swell for illuminating the dark corners of a murder mystery.

CHAPTER ONE

Murder Mail

THE man who lived in the corner room on the third floor of the Carrolton Hotel couldn't sleep. For almost an hour, he claimed, before it happened, he had been leaning from his window. The room was in excellent position. Both a certain distance along Tenth and a certain distance down Fifth were visible from his windows.

At four minutes to four by the illuminated dial of his watch, the light mail collection truck swung around from Washington Square, stopped at the corner post box. The man in the seat with the driver stepped down on the far side of the truck, came round with a bag. He unlocked the bottom of the post box, held the bag under it till all the mail had run down, then relocked the box, walked round and climbed onto the truck again.

The truck moved up Fifth, came again to a halt at the box on the corner of Eighth.

The process was repeated in detail.

THE night was cold, clear; a high-riding winter moon supplemented the street lights. The man on the third floor could see what transpired, without effort. As the truck moved forward again, he ranged his eyes idly along, in quest of the next stop, realized that it would come directly under his window, at the Tenth Street box.

Half dully, he eyed the box. It stood in the splash of light from the street lamp directly above. Then something stirred very slightly, just below him, in the shadows of a niche of the building.

Still uncomprehending, he made out the slender form of the man in the peaked cap, huddled flatly against the wall.

The mail truck drew in abreast of the post box; the driver said something to the man who was descending with the bag. They both laughed. The postman started around to the box.

The street light, reflected from something metallic, flashed in the eyes of the man on the third floor. He caught sight of the man in the low-pulled fedora as he darted from the shadows across Fifth, scuttled, crouching low and out of the line of sight of both the driver and the man who was unlocking the box, across the street. He held something metallic in his hand.

In a perfectly timed movement, the man with the peaked cap stepped noiselessly from the shadows of his building, sprang to the side of the man who held the rapidly filling mail bag, as the man in the fedora circled, jumped on the running board of the truck.

Either one or both of them barked distinctly, "Stick 'em high!"

The postman gasped, dropped his bag and quickly elevated his hands. The driver of the truck was in heavy shadow, The man in the third-floor window could not tell what he was doing. The peaked-capped man dropped to his knees, began to sort through the letters on the top of the bag.

Almost immediately, he held one suddenly up to the light, ripped it open, and took out the enclosure. Bars of illumination fell across his face from the street light overhead. The postman blurted: "By God! Tom Durso!"

The peaked-capped man sprang to his feet with a curse, rattled something in a guttural voice toward the truck. There was a moment's silence, then the man on the running board of the truck barked something back. The peaked-capped man hastily stuffed the letter he had taken into an inside pocket, jerked up his hand.

A crashing spurt of orange flamed from the gun in his hand; the postman made a queer whinnying sound, staggered backward. The gun crashed a second time; the postman's head flew back, he stumbled, whirled around and crashed to the pavement. The driver suddenly roared for help Three stammering, roaring blasts flared from a gun in the hand of the man in the fedora; the driver screamed, coughed, there was the sound of a slumping fall, then silence.

The postman, writhing on the sidewalk with his hands at his throat made a sound like "*UH-uh-UH-uh*. . . . " for a little while, then was still.

The peaked-capped man and the man

in the fedora raced together, north on Fifth Avenue, disappeared around the corner of Eleventh Street, and as the man on the third floor of the Carrolton suddenly came out of his trance of horror, he heard the startled roar of an automobile exhaust, around the corner on Eleventh.

The man on the third floor raced for the telephone.

His call was registered at headquarters at exactly six minutes after four A. M.

The police gave all the information to the papers, except the identity and address of the eye-witness, and the fact that a name had been heard.

AT SIX minutes after two—ten hours later—Sam Beckett came down the hall of the tenth floor of the Universal Building, his big bony hands in the pockets of his Aquascutum topcoat, the shapeless gray hat pushed back on his stiff black hair. From one pocket protruded a folded Morning Sentinel. His hard blue eyes were veiled and his jaw was set. He pushed open the door marked "Beckett Private Inquiry Agency" and went in.

The slim, brown-eyed girl in the niche between switchboard and typewriter stopped tapping, swung around expectantly. "Morning, Sam."

"Hello." Beckett looked over at the mahogany bench against the wall—empty. He shook his head, pushed through the gate in the railing that surrounded switchboard, girl and typewriter, hesitated with one hand on the door marked "Private." "Call Barton Black at The Sentinel and get him over here."

"He's here."

"How?"

"He's been here for an hour. He's in your office."

Beckett grunted, went on through into the office, closed the door behind him. At the shabby oak desk a curly brown-haired youth was sitting with his feet up, smoking. He had the same copy of The Sentinel. "Hi, Sam, old boy, old boy."

Beckett unbuttoned his coat, scaled his hat at the costumer. "Well, I suppose I'm the talk of the town this morning, huh?" he said scathingly. "What with that splendid front-page spread on the Dalls case."

Black's face contorted painfully. "Am I God? Can I help it if two postmen get bumped off right at the deadline? Anyhow, I got it in the bulldog. Your name's in six times Sam and besides—"

Beckett hung his coat on the costumer, jerked The Sentinel from his pocket and slued it across the desk. It was folded open at page twelve. "Look at the damned thing! Right smack by a corset ad!"

Black lowered his feet, glanced down frowning at the item as though it were new to him. He shook his head. "Sure is too bad. Yep. However—"

"Get to hell out of that chair!"

Black flushed, slid out of the swivel chair. "Nuts!" he snapped bitterly. "You're worse than a damn prima donna!"

"Oh, I am, am I?"

"Damn right. I came up here with something hot—"

"Go right into the chorus. I know the verse. You've got a hot tip. I go out and risk my neck to turn somebody or something up. You trail along and get the inside story. If it works out and I crack the proposition, I get a swell publicity break—right on the first page. Only sometimes the first page jumps around and settles down beside a corset—"

"All right, wise guy, all right. You got a bum break this morning. I admit that, see? That don't mean it's my fault. I got information—red-hot information in the hollow of my lily-white hand—that'll more than make up for it. There's six grand in it, too—and a puff on every front page in town if you're a tenth as good as you think you are."

Beckett looked at him with a queer mixture of expression, leaned back in the swivel chair, put his hands behind his head. "Oh, yeah?"

"Yeah."

"What?"

"Nothing in the world but the name of the guy that put the heat on the postmen this A. M."

"So what?"

"So you can take fifteen minutes of your valuable time and run out and sneeze him."

Beckett's eyes got hard. "Listen, handsome, this office is run strictly for profit —and not the profit of your lousy sheet either. I'm very sorry about the postmen, but the feds'll handle that. And now— well, I'll be seeing you around, I suppose—"

"O. K., wisenhiemer. Watch The Sentinel to see who clips off the six-grand reward—"

"What six-grand reward?"

Black drew his shoulders up around his ears. "Oh, the six grand for the postmen killers. But I didn't think you were interested. And I know six grand doesn't mean anything to you—not any more than maybe your right eye. Well, I'll be seeing you ar—"

"You didn't say anything about any reward. Why the hell don't you learn to talk straight. How many killers are there?"

"Two."

"Well, all right."

"What do you mean, all right?"

"Go ahead. Who's this hood's name you're bursting with?"

"Tom Durso."

"Where'd you get it?"

Black shrugged. "The coppers know it. The eye-witness heard one of the postmen holler it out just before they bumped him off. He thinks they did it because the postmen did recognize Durso."

"Recognize him? How?"

"Sure. There's posters of the mug in every post office in the country. He's wanted for a mail-truck stick-up in Frisco."

"And I suppose you were chatting with the eye-witness and he told you this, eh?"

"Don't worry about that. My spies are everywhere."

Beckett sat straight in the chair, looked at the desk frowningly, slowly slid his hands into his trouser pockets. After a minute he said: "Tom Durso, eh?"

"Yep."

Beckett reached for the button on his desk, pushed it. When the girl came in, he said: "See if there's anything in the 'Rewards Offered' file on a bird named Tom Durso, Thalia."

She nodded went out. Beckett turned narrowed eyes on Black. "And you can keep that silly grin to yourself when Miss Morton's around, newshound, see?"

"Oh, is that so? Well, let me advise you that I and Miss Morton—"

The girl came back in with a poster. "There's two thousand dollars for his arrest and conviction. He committed a mail-truck—"

"Yes. Thank you."

THE girl went out. Beckett got up slowly, his eyes thoughtful, slid bony forefingers into the lower pockets of his shiny blue serge vest, wandered over to the window beside the costumer. After a minute, he half turned, eyed the reporter with distaste. "If this is a phony, Black—"

"No phony, Sam. This is hot," Black said with sudden seriousness.

Beckett reached down hat and coat, clapped the hat on, shouldered into the coat as he went through the door into the outer office, Black at his heels. To Thalia Morton he said: "Back some time today. You stick around, eh?"

"I'll be back, too." Black promised.

"Now that's a real thrill," she said sweetly.

They went out and down the hall toward the elevators. Black rubbed his hands, grinned. "Where to, now?"

"The P. O., you dope. They'll be hot-foot to find out what was taken from the mail bag. When they find that, the case will *be* a case."

"You got an in there?"

"I think so. I think I can work it out."

"Well, I know—"

Far down the hall behind them, the door of the Beckett Private Inquiry Agency flew open and Thalia Morton shot out into the hall. "Hey!"

They turned back.

"The demon headliner. The Sentinel is on the wire."

Black frowned. "Nuts. You wait here, huh?"

"Sure, sure. Make it snappy."

Black trotted off down the hall, his top-coat tails bellying out behind him. Beckett dug a crumpled pack of cigarettes from his pocket, lit one, stood smoking.

After about a minute Black burst out of the office like a whirlwind, his face alive with excitement, sprinted down the hall, came to a sliding stop with his hand on the elevator bell.

"There's been another one, Sam, so help me."

"Another what?"

"Killing. At the Carrolton Hotel. I've got to get over and cover it. I'll bet a week's salary it ties in with the other!"

"Who's killed?"

"Frank Hardy. The New York Stock Exchange firm—Hardy and Wilmerding. Big shots—and how!"

The elevator opened and they crowded in.

"Go on," Beckett said.

"That's all. The office just got the call. They don't know any more yet. Boy,

somebody has their nerve! Hardy's one of the governors of the Stock Exchange!"

The elevator reached the ground. Beckett spilled two people in front of him, pounded across the lobby, Black at his heels, and out. They jumped into a cab at the curb. "The Carrolton Hotel," Beckett snapped, "and forget the lights!"

CHAPTER TWO

The Corpse in the Vestibule

THE Carrolton Hotel boasts old-fashioned architecture. A short cement ribbon, bordered by iron wire fences, leads from the street to a door set flush with the sidewalk. Through that door is a vestibule. Three steps lead upward from the vestibule floor to a second pair of doors, which lead into the lobby proper.

The police lines were drawn at the street, excluding the milling, chattering crowd from the short cement walk. The taxi containing Beckett and Black stopped fifty yards above, braked into the curb. Beckett swung out, stood on the running board on tiptoe, took a quick bird's-eye view.

"Pay the cab, Black."

"Pay it yourself, you chiseller. What the hell?"

Beckett made a soft exclamation as he caught sight of a burly, red-faced man standing glaring importantly at the crowd, from a point just outside the door to the vestibule. "The stuffed shirt, by God!"

"Eh?"

"Sergeant Sloane, no less."

"Yeah? Well, this cab—"

Beckett stepped down, began shouldering his way into the crowd. Black cursed bitterly, dug out a bill and tossed it to the driver, plunged after him. He caught him as Beckett was showing his police card to the copper at the entrance to the walk. "You cheap muzzler," he snarled, "next time I—"

Beckett grinned crookedly. "Don't apologize, newshound."

Black ground his teeth, got out his own police card. They went up the cement together. Sergeant Sloane watched their approach with narrowed hostile eyes. As they came up, he stepped in front of them, barring their way.

"Well, Beckett, where the hell do you come in?"

"I represent Hardy's partner, Wilmerding," Beckett lied smoothly, "and I'm primed for trouble, some flatfoot tries to tie me up."

Sloane purpled, struggled with indecision a minute, stood aside. "You keep away from that corpse."

"Sure."

They went in. There were two plainclothesmen smoking cigarettes in the darkened vestibule, waiting for the morgue wagon. Sloane stood in the door behind them, said to the plainclothesmen: "Keep an eye on this guy. Don't let him touch that corpse."

They nodded. Sloane went outside again. Beckett took in the picture with quick shifting eyes.

Frank Hardy was lying at the bottom of the steps leading up to the lobby, very dead. The coconut matting under him was stained crimson in a spreading pool. Hardy was on his stomach, his head twisted sideways over his shoulder. His face was a powder-blackened mask of raw flesh, putty-colored. He had been shot in the head by a high-calibered gun at no more than a few inches range. His legs were drawn up, queerly twisted. One arm was stiffly outstretched; there was a small, pennant-shaped piece of brown cloth in the tightly clenched fingers.

The other hand was under his abdomen, vaguely distinguishable in the poor light. Beckett took a small flash from his pocket, knelt down, shot a quick beam along the floor. The hand was covered with drying blood, but it, too, was clenched, held brown cloth. And there was something that flashed metal between the back of the hand and the coconut matting.

Beckett shut off the light, got to his feet, caught Black's eye meaningly. "Nothing there, I guess."

Black nodded imperceptibly, turned, wandered carelessly over to the two detectives, pulling out his notebook. "Let me get your names and addresses, will you, boys?"

THEY brightened, took cigarettes out of their mouths, crowded around. Outside, a distance down the street, the melancholy clanging of the morgue-wagon bell became audible, drew nearer. Beckett edged nearer the dead man, watched from the corner of his eye as Black maneuvered the two coppers around. Slowly he bent his knees, then in a quick smooth motion, reached under the body, closed his fingers on something hard and irregular, snaked it out, stood up casually, slid his hands into his pockets.

Beckett coughed, leaned back against the wall. Black said: "Thanks, boys. I'll try to get it in."

Beckett said: "What do you make of that cloth, boys? In his fingers."

"Oh, I dunno."

"I'll tell you what I think. I think Hardy grabbed at the killer, caught his hands in the lower pockets of his vest; then when the guy tore himself away, the two pockets peeled down. What do you think?"

They looked judicial.

"If you'd just let me get close enough to take a better look—" Beckett hesitated.

"Sorry. You heard—"

The bell had stopped clanging outside, and now the door came open. Sloane stalked in, held the door open, flashed Beckett a quick look of suspicion, looked questioningly at the two coppers. They shook their heads. The morgue attendants came in with the grim wicker basket, set it down. Timmons, the medical examiner came right behind them, his bag in his hand. Beckett stepped around the corpse, sauntered to the door.

"See you around, Sloane."

"Wait a minute, Beckett."

"Sorry. I got no time." Beckett pushed through the door, let it swing to behind him. It opened again and Black came out, flushed of face. "Wait a minute, will you?"

"Come on, then."

"I can't. My story—"

"Nothing now."

"Oh, hell."

"Sorry. Nothing now."

Beckett turned, went down the walk, the curious eyes of the crowd on him. Like a swimmer, he breasted the crowd, wormed his way through to the curb, not daring to take his hand from the bit of metal in his pocket. He walked along the curbing, till he reached an opening between parked cars, stepped out, waved down a cab. He had the door open and a foot on the running board when someone said breathlessly behind him: "Beckett—Mr. Beckett!"

He turned, frowing at the delay. Just shaking free of the crowd, his hat askew, his face damp, was a man he had never seen before. He was well dressed, wore a fawn fedora, a dark Chesterfield overcoat, spats on black oxfords. In his tie gleamed a star-sapphire. His face was thin, red; anxious brown eyes were set close to a nose that was nothing in the world but a beak—thin, curving down, almost to the thin, white lips.

"What is it?" Beckett snapped. "I'm in a hurry."

"A picture! I've lost a most valuable

picture! Stolen. I've got to get it back. I want to retain you—"

"Call my office tomorrow," Beckett said. "I've got no time to discuss it now." He ducked his head, tried to step into the cab. The hawk-nosed one cried: "No, no. Wait!" and clutched wildly at Beckett's coat-tails, almost sent him sprawling as he yanked him backward to the road. "Listen—you must listen—I'll pay you well—pay you handsomely! I've got to get it—"

Beckett caught himself, turned on the excited man, his face flushed. "Listen, nitwit, one more play like that, and I'll hang one on your jaw. Now beat it!"

"No, no—listen. . . ." The man made another clutch at Beckett. Beckett put his hand out, straight-armed the hawk nose hard. The man yelped, staggered backward. Beckett jumped into the cab, snapped: "Shoot!"

BEFORE the hawk-nosed one could recover his balance, the cab shot away. Beckett called to the driver: "Uptown—the Universal Building!" and turned and looked back. The man was standing in the middle of the road, shaking his hands over his head.

"That guy must be nuts," the driver volunteered.

Beckett's forehead was furrowed. He did not answer, kept watching the man. He was glad he had. A long, dark sedan that he had not noticed, had pulled out from across the road, turned round rapidly. As it passed the hawk-nosed man, he waved viciously onward, pointed to the cab in which Beckett rode.

Beckett's eyes narrowed. He leaned forward. "Somebody's tailing us, buddy. See if you can shake that sedan."

"Huh? O. K."

They swung to the right at the next corner.

Beckett watched out the back with narrowed eyes. When the black sedan roared around the corner after them he could see two men in the car besides the driver. To his own driver he called: "Make for the Fourteenth Street subway station!"

"Aw, I can shake them babies—"

"You can play hell! Do what I tell you."

"Oh, O. K., O. K." He swung viciously north, pounded up Lexington.

"Circle a couple of blocks."

The driver cursed, slued wildly across Lexington without slackening speed, roared along Twelfth a block, then another. The sedan was just turning in behind them on Lexington.

"North now, then back across Fourteenth!"

The driver was good, if surly. He shot northward, made the left turn on Fourteenth, was blocked by a street car and the cars behind it, went out into the middle of the road, shot past the street car on the wrong side, cut back in and had a clear path to the corner. Beckett tossed a bill through the partition.

"You want to play some more tag, go over and wait for me on the other side of the street."

"O. K." The driver braked to a stop. Beckett burst out, ran to the subway steps, hurried down them, fishing for a nickel. He had to get change, then pushed through the turnstile.

Across the tracks, there was a downtown express standing in the station. Beckett was on the uptown side. He went to the edge of the platform, bent over, looked back along the tunnel. The head lamps of a roaring uptown car were just rounding a bend in a tunnel, twenty yards from the station. Beckett jumped down, stepped over the tracks, waited till the southbound car got into life and pulled away, then crossed those tracks and climbed up on the platform, made for the stairs.

The cab was waiting, right at the mouth of the kiosk. Beckett jumped in, and the driver shot away, followed the circle of Union Square, kept going straight north.

"Them guys in the sedan all went down in the subway just as you come up!" he bawled from the corner of his mouth. "I had to fix a copper for a fin. I figured you was good for it."

"Oh, yeah?"

"Sure; don't ya believe me?"

"All right. Get me up to the Universal Building."

"That was a smart dodge."

"What?"

"I say, that was a smart play, duckin' down—"

"Sure, sure. Get going, will you?"

IT TOOK him fifteen minutes to get uptown. Never once did he take his hand from the hard object in his pocket. nor did he risk taking it out to examine. There was a puzzled frown on his forehead and his eyes were listless as he pushed open the door of the Beckett Private Inquiry Agency.

Thalia Morton looked up. "Your boy friend's been on the wire for five minutes waiting for you."

"Who?"

"Barton."

"Oh, so you call him Barton, now, do you—"

"He's all excited. You'd better answer the call."

Beckett grunted, went through the gate, on into the office, picked up the phone. "Well?"

"That you, Sam?"

"Yeah."

"Listen, Sam! Wilmerding just arrived here. What do you think? Hardy was carrying five hundred government bonds—unregistered ones. He was going to deliver them to a client in the Carrolton."

"Who?"

"An old dame named Etta Wrongley. Rich as Croesus and twice as bugs. And listen—when Sloane found out you gave him a stall about being retained by Wilmerding he hit the ceiling. Watch out for him."

"Sure, sure. Listen—what are those bonds worth?"

"A bond is worth a thousand dollars, you chump."

"You mean he was carrying five hundred thousand bucks around?"

"Yeah, yeah. This Wrongley dame is a client of Hardy and Wilmerding. She has a big account. She ordered five hundred bonds from them, for a wedding present for a niece or something. The cops are up there now. I've been holding this damned wire open—"

"O. K. Listen—see if you can get this Wilmerding to lay something on the line in the way of a reward. Let me know."

"O. K., pal."

Beckett hung up, touched the button. The girl came in. "See if you can get a dame named Etta Wrongley on the wire at the Carrolton Hotel, fast!"

The girl nodded, ran out, dialed a number. Beckett followed as far as the door, stood with one hand on the jamb, waiting, his forehead wrinkled.

Thalia Morton said: "Miss Etta Wrongley, please. . . ." and waited. Slowly a puzzled look came over her face. "Say what are you trying to hand me? I . . . Eh? . . . No kidding? She must be batty. Wait a minute." She looked up at Beckett. "The girl says the old dame hasn't had a telephone in her room for twenty years. She thinks they're sinful or something."

"All right. I expected no better. Come in here a minute."

He turned back toward his desk. For the first time he took the hard object from his pocket—and almost tripped over his feet. He stood rooted, staring at the thing. The girl came in behind him, rattling on: "If you'd quit master-minding and maybe tell me. . . ." then caught sight of the object in his hand. "Oh, my Lord!"

CHAPTER THREE

Headless Horror

IT WAS a cigarette lighter, of white gold or platinum, small in size, even undersize. Set in the case, in profusion, were diamonds. In the centre was one tremendous, blue-white stone. Parallel rows of smaller diamonds crowded the casing of the lighter. Almost reverently, Beckett moved over, laid the device on the green blotter on his desk, stood back, fascinated, Multicolored light scintillated in the office, flashed rainbow hues from the gems in the lighter. Thalia said almost in a whisper: "How beautiful!"

Beckett said with a weak attempt at a grin: "That's somethin', eh?"

"It must be worth a thousand dollars, Sam."

"Ten thousand, about, to us, sweetness." Beckett took a long breath, shook off the spell of the flashing stones. "Look—Frank Hardy was shot to death a while ago. He struggled with the man that killed him, and ripped out the lower pockets of the killer's vest. This lighter was evidently in one of those pockets. I found it under Hardy's body. There aren't four stores in town that would handle stuff like this, and it ought to be a cinch to find out who bought it. You get your coat on and go find out. Make it snappy!"

"You mean—"

"I mean that when you get me that name—and description, we'll knock off the sweetest little piece of reward money it's been my pleasure to handle. Now get going. I'll—"

The door came open, and the beefy figure and furious face of Sergeant Sloane was framed in the opening, one hand bulging his jacket pocket. "Oh, is that so?" he snarled. "Well, how would you like a stretch for grand larceny, Beckett, you wise—"

Beckett's eyes veiled. "What do you want?" He reached over cooly, swept the lighter into his pocket.

"A lot of things—put that back!"

"Grow up, fathead. Even you can't walk in and pinch a man's private property."

Sloane's eyes narrowed till they were mere lines in his fleshy face. He walked over stiff-legged, faced Beckett across the desk. "Try one more of your fancy stalls on me, Beckett, and I'll jug you. Right now, I dunno fer sure whether I'd rather sock you one, or have the lighter. You better not make up my mind fer me. And don't try to play me for a patsy—I heard every bloody word you said. But I'm givin' ya a break, see?"

"Yeah?"

Sloane nodded slowly, his eyes on Beckett's. "Yeah. I'm takin' that lighter. I'll give you one more minute to hand it over, then I'll call two men I've got out in the hall and pinch you. And I can manage to hold you till we find out where that lighter ties in with the kill. I don't figure you'd care to explain to a judge just how you happened to glom onto it, now, wise guy, would you?" He held out his fleshy hand, wiggled his first two fingers. "Put it right there, now—or face a judge."

Beckett said nothing. His face was a mask, his eyes burning coals. For the space of a minute he stood rigid; then his hand went slowly into his pocket. "All right, fatty," he said, "you win." The lighter skidded across the desk.

Sloane pounced on it, eager-eyed, held it up, then off at arm's length. The diamonds flashed fire. Sloane dropped it into his pocket. "See you around, Beckett," he said grinning, flicked his hat and walked out, banging the door behind him.

BECKETT slid his hands into the hip pockets of his trousers, walked slowly over and stood staring out the window. The vein on his forehead stood out, throbbing. Outside, the telephone buzzer began to sound. Thalia stood without moving, watching him, with hurt eyes. "Aw, gee, Sam," she blurted, "that's tough."

Beckett nodded absently. "Yeah."

There was a long silence.

Thalia started forward. "Sam—"

"Answer the phone, beautiful. I'm not in, except to the newshound."

The girl hesitated, finally turned and went outside, sat down at the desk, plugged in. Beckett stared out into the darkening winter afternoon. The phone on the desk gave a tinkle. He swung half round angrily. "I'm not in, I told you."

"Snap out of it," came through the door. "This is a customer."

Beckett compressed his lips, strode over and picked up the phone grimly. "Well, hello," he snapped.

"Mr. Beckett?" The tones were excited. "Mr. Sam Beckett?"

"Yeah, yeah."

"My name is Le Marr—Maxton Le Marr, Mr. Beckett. I . . . I have been referred to you. . . . I want your services . . . need your services, and quickly. The fact . . . the fact of the matter is, I . . . well, I feel that an attack may be made upon me. . . ."

"My fees," Beckett cut in grimly, "are a hundred dollars a day, right now, with a five hundred dollar retainer. If you're prepared. . . ."

"Surely, surely. We will not quarrel

on that point. My address is One Fourteen and a Half Waverly Place. I must have . . . can you come right away . . . this instant?"

"What's your trouble?"

"I am afraid. . . . I have serious reason to believe. . . . Well, a business deal, Mr. Beckett . . . . trouble has developed . . . . really serious. I don't like to talk over the phone."

"All right," Beckett said, "I'll come down. You'll have that retainer ready, eh?"

"Yes, yes. You'll come right away?"

"Right away."

He hung up the receiver, stood glaring at the desk a minute, set the instrument down, then went slowly over to the door, and out.

"If Black calls up, tell him what happened, Thalia. Tell him I've got another case—one with a fee in it, and to hell with the postmen and Hardy and Wilmerding and The Morning Sentinel. Where's Waverly Place?"

"Same street as Washington Square North. And, after all, this isn't the end of the world. You look as though you'd lost your last friend."

Beckett glared at her, jammed his hands in his pockets. "Listen, sweetness—ten thousand berries just went out of here in that jackass's pocket. What am I supposed to do? Send up a rocket?"

"Aw, Sam—"

He kicked the gate open, went through the outer door into the hall, slammed it behind him and smashed the glass. He opened it, put his head back in, ground out: "Get this damn thing fixed," closed it and walked on down the hall.

HE RODE south on the subway to Sheridan Square, crossed to Waverly Place, plodded east, his hands sunk in coat pockets, the hat jammed down on his head. The sky was black now. A fine sifting fall of snow was coming down, turning to water as it touched the sidewalk. Cursing, Beckett walked stiff-legged, planting his feet wide apart to avoid slipping on the treacherous asphalt.

He followed the bend of Waverly, went on toward Sixth Avenue, watching the street numbers half absently. One Fourteen and a Half appeared to be the other side of Sixth.

As he approached Sixth, he dug around in his pocket for a cigarette, got the battered package out, explored with a bony forefinger. One cigarette. He dug it out. It was broken in half. He smashed it against the curb, almost lost his balance with the effort, cursed bluely, checked himself with a hand on the corner lamp post, swung abruptly back toward the entrance to the drug store, set back a little from the corner.

Twenty yards behind him, a slender, rat-faced youth, wearing a peaked cap, tried suddenly to halt; his feet shot from under him, he made a raucous noise in his throat, clawed the air wildly, and came down on the pavement like a thousand of brick. There was a clank of metal as he hit.

Beckett's eyes widened. A nickeled revolver skidded across the pavement into the gutter. He frowned, started quickly —too quickly, toward the youth. One of his own feet missed fire. The youth was up in a second, cursing furiously. He made a dive for the gun, snatched it up, shot between two parked cars and ran across and along Gay Street.

Beckett stood looking after him a minute, his eyes puzzled. Then he shrugged, turned back and went in and got his cigarettes.

When he came out, he paused, took a long look up and down Waverly Place, but if there were anything suspicious in sight, he could not locate it. He went on, more alert; crossed Sixth.

One Fourteen and a Half was just a few houses beyond. It was a former residence, remodeled more extensively than most of its neighbors, into a small apartment house. Iron railings fanned out on the sides of the three stone steps that led to the tiny vestibule. Beckett came up casually, hooked one arm around the railing, turned his back on the house, looked once more along the street.

There were several pedestrians in his line of sight, but they seemed strictly concerned with their own affairs. East, toward Washington Square, he could see nobody. After a minute, he tossed away the butt of his cigarette, turned and went up the three steps.

Evidently there were just three apartments in the building. The top name on the row of bells was Maxton Le Marr. He pressed the buzzer, stood watching the street behind him.

There was no answering click to the door; nor was there the usual telephone arrangement.

After a few seconds he frowned, stepped back, ran a finger down the three buttons.

THE door clicked violently. He went in. The narrow, carpeted hall contained a flight of carpeted steps. On the curve of the landing above he could see a floor lamp set in a niche. A door to his right opened and a bald-headed man with a newspaper in his hand looked out inquiringly.

"Sorry," Beckett said. "I guess I pressed the wrong bell. Looking for Mr. Le Marr."

"Next floor," the bald-headed man said, and closed the door.

Beckett went on up the stairs, was in a hall, the duplicate of that below. Three doors confronted him. On one near the front was a card. When he was close to

it, it spelled "Le Marr." He knocked, waited, listening.

After a half minute, he knocked again, hard. The door swung open under his impact.

Beckett frowned, pushed it open the rest of the way, hesitated on the threshold. The room before him was a living room. The walls were cream-colored, the woodwork black. A Chinese desk was in one corner, a table with a pot-bellied red lamp in the other. Before a cheerful fire burning in the grate, a huge, wing-backed chair was drawn close. From the depths of the chair, a pair of blue-trousered legs stretched out, ended in crossed ankles on the fender. Over the side of the chair, an arm, cased in the sleeve of a dressing gown, was hanging. There was a pipe in the hand. Smoke ascended slowly in a thin spiral from the bowl.

Beckett coughed, knocked again on the open door, but the man in the chair made no indication of hearing. Beckett frowned, cleared his throat loudly. "Mr. Le Marr!"

There was no answer. Beckett walked in, and around the chair. No wonder. The man's head was missing. His trunk ended in a horrible, blood-stained stump!

On the floor, almost under the blood-soaked chair, the firelight reflecting purple stains from its blade, was an antique blue-steel sabre. On the wall, to the right of the mantel, hung a scarred leather scabbard, empty.

Beckett gazed, sombre-eyed, registered details on his brain. His eyes narrowed slowly as he became aware of something familiar. The blue-trousered legs ended in spats on black oxfords. Beckett stepped more to the right, peered at the V of the blue dressing gown. In the tie, stained though it was, the star-sapphire still gleamed.

Beckett scratched his chin, roved his eyes around, noted a costumer in the shadows at the end of the room, went over. A black Chesterfield overcoat and a fawn-colored fedora hung carelessly from the costumer.

Maxton Le Marr and the man who had attempted to stop him outside the Carrolton Hotel, were one and the same person!

CHAPTER FOUR

10 X L

BECKETT took a gun from his shoulder holster, turned toward the rear of the apartment. Sliding doors made one wall of the living room. They were open. He walked through, alert, found a dining room, a bedroom, and a kitchen, conventionally arranged. They were all empty, richly furnished. He went back to the living room, found a switch to an overhead light, supplemented the glow of the table lamps with the chandelier in the ceiling.

Items of interest began to crop up.

Behind the spot that the door would cover when open, tight against the wall, was a crumpled, dirty handkerchief. Beckett's eyes widened. He went over and picked it up, made a wry face, held it by one corner, located the laundry mark. It was 10 X L.

He retraced his steps through to the bedroom at the rear, opened a drawer in the bureau, pawed through it, located a pile of clean sport shirts. They all had the same laundry mark, but it did not correspond with that on the handkerchief. The shirts were marked 23 B.

Back in the living room, he finally found the telephone, on top of the Chinese desk, dialed a number. After a minute, he said in quiet tones: "Sam, Thalia. Take this down: 10 X L. Got it? . . . . Right. It's a laundry mark. Find out who it belongs to. . . . Eh? . . . No, find

the laundry company first, then they can probably tell you who the customer is. Work hard. I'll call you later."

He hung up, stuffed the handkerchief gingerly into his hip pocket, resumed looking around. On the table under the pot-bellied red lamp was a rack of books. He went over, ran an eye over the titles. Best-selling novels, a treatise on the growing of roses, and—a yellow, paperbacked book the size and shape of a bar of laundry soap. Printed in bold type in black, across the top of the cover was "Investor's Pocket Manual." Below, in even larger letters was "Hardy and Wilmerding, Stocks, Bonds, and Other Securities; Members of—" here followed a list of the exchanges to which the firm belonged—"Forty-Nine Wall Street, New York City." And the telephone numbers.

For a minute, Beckett stared in frowning astonishment at the booklet, then whirled round, almost tripped over the rug, and strode to the phone again. From the front of the book, he took the phone number, dialed.

As the monotonous sound of ringing began, he glanced hastily at his watch. Twelve minutes to five. Chances were that . . .

"Hello."

"This is Police Headquarters." Beckett made his voice gruff. "I want to speak to whoever is in charge there. Any of the partners in?"

"No . . . no, sir, Mr. Fenton, the cashier, is, though. Will. . . ."

"Put him on."

After a few seconds, a dry, quavering voice said: "Yes, sir This is Fenton."

"Take a paper and pencil," Beckett said, "and take this down. I want to know the following: first, did you have an account or any business dealings with a man named Maxton Le Marr?"

"Why, yes, we. . . ."

"Get it all down, first. Then answer as quick as you can," Beckett said with growing intensity. "I want to know all you can tell me about this Le Marr. Was he a friend of Mr. Hardy, or of anyone else down there. What kind of business did he do. How long has he had dealings there?"

"Just . . . just a moment, sir. I'll have to take a look at his ledger sheet. . . ."

"Make it fast, then."

"I will, sir."

Beckett wiped the dew of perspiration from his face, waited. When the old man came on the wire, he said: "Mr. Le Marr has had an account here for about five months, sir. He traded a great deal, sir, but on modest margin. The account was closed out by check three days ago. Mr. James J. Corcoran, one of our customers' men handled the account. No one that's here now seems to have seen Mr. Le Marr. I think he did most of his trading over the telephone, sir."

"Tell me about this Corcoran."

"Eh? Why, I . . . I don't just know what you mean. . . ."

"How long has he been with the firm? How old is he? Give me a full description. Also how long was he there before Le Marr started trading with him."

There was another wait, shorter this time, then: "Why, oddly enough, sir, Mr. Corcoran joined the firm just about six months ago. I have his application here. He had had no Wall Street experience, previously. . . ."

"That's plenty," Beckett said grimly. "What does he look like?"

"Why . . . why, he's a very big fellow . . . . it says here he's twenty-eight, quite dark . . . dark eyes at any rate. I really don't . . . you know we have so many . . . . Oh! he has black hair . . . . a slight bald spot." The cashier hesitated. "I . . . I'm afraid . . . is that sufficient?"

"O. K. Where does he live?"

"The Granby Hotel on West. . . ."

"Thanks." Beckett hung up, held the receiver down a minute, lifted it again, put his finger down to dial, cursed, hung up, hunted a phone directory, located his number, dialed quickly.

"The Granby Hotel," a pleasant voice sang. "Good afternoon."

"Mr. Corcoran please—James J. Corcoran."

"Just a minute, please."

Again a wait, then: "I'm sorry. Mr. Corcoran checked out last night, sir."

"Forwarding address?" Beckett asked.

"No. No forwarding address."

Beckett hung up, cursed, stared at the floor, rasped a hand across his chin. He went back and looked at the dead man again, without seeing him, took another look through the rooms. He found nothing more.

Once again in the living room, he holstered the gun under his shoulder, went over and stood looking down at the Investor's Manual, finally left it where it lay. Turning his coat collar up once more, he walked quickly to the door, turned back with his hand on the knob for one final searching survey, shook his head, opened the door—and stopped dead with his foot halfway across the threshold.

A heavy, beefy face was illuminated by the glow from the standing lamp in the hall. A huge, service Colt was trained on Beckett's middle. Sergeant Sloane's hoarse voice rasped hastily: "Up, Le Marr! Up fast—or I'll. . . ." Then the uncertain light fell on Beckett's face as he moved to elevate his hands.

BECKETT said quietly: "If you'll put that howitzer back in the garage, I can put my hands down, copper."

Sloane's mouth closed with a click of teeth. There was fury in his eyes, bewilderment also. "You again, eh?"

"Oh, sure. I get around."

There was a moment's silence. Beckett put his hands down slowly, hooked thumbs on his pockets. "Well, sorry I can't stay, Sloane, but—"

"Where's Le Marr, Beckett?"

Beckett's eyes narrowed. "Why do you want him?"

"Never mind the patter. Where is he? Did you get him?"

"No. I didn't get him. And don't get wise, copper—tell me why you want him and maybe I'll give you a break."

Sloane put his hands on hips. "Say, what is this? Are you trying to stall me you don't know this is Le Marr's?" He opened one big hand suddenly. On his sweaty palm lay the glittering, diamond-encrusted lighter.

Beckett blinked, caught himself. "I see," he said vaguely. "Well, I'll tell you —Le Marr seems to have had some trouble, Sloane."

"Eh?"

"Matter of fact, somebody's killed him."

Sloane took a minute to get it. Then his face suffused with blood. He swung round, called loudly: "One of you stay there and don't let nobody down—including this guy. The other come on with me."

A plainclothesman detached himself from the shadows at the head of the stairs, stalked up the hall.

"All right, Beckett," Sloane said grimly. "Back inside."

Beckett shrugged, turned and shouldered through the door once more, went back in and stood off to one side. Sloane plowed in after him. The other copper stood in the doorway with drawn gun.

Beckett waved a hand wearily. "In the chair, flatfoot, in the chair."

Sloane shot him a black look, eyed the chair, walked around it, stopped suddenly,

exclaimed something under his breath, stared.

"Cripes! Phone the M. E., Tully!" he said, awed.

"Where's the phone?"

"On the desk," Beckett volunteered and fished a cigarette from his pocket.

Sloane suddenly snapped his glance back to Beckett. "You seem to know everything—where's the rest of this guy?"

Beckett shrugged. "I'm afraid I couldn't tell you."

"Well, what could you tell me?"

"Nothing."

Sloane's free hand balled into a fist. He took a quick step toward Beckett, fury in his face. "So help me, Beckett, you start talking—fast—or you'll rot in the Tombs for a month. I've got you tight this time, and you know it. Found on the scene! I'd like to see that wise lip of yours wiggle you out of this!"

"You will," Beckett said, "and you'll see that wise lip of mine make trouble for you, too, fatty. Where's the head? Find that and you'll have a Chinaman's chance of holding me. It's not in this apartment. I looked. And that puts me out in the clear, see?"

"Oh, yeah? Well, I guess I'll let you tell that to the lieutenant on duty, just the same, Beckett. Stand over there. Long time I guess since you took a ride in the joy wagon. Too long."

BECKETT'S eyes narrowed. He started to speak, stopped, eyed Sloane with tight lips. "Take me down—or hold me here more than three minutes Sloane, and it's a pinch. I'll sue you for ten times everything your fat carcass is worth. Cut out this comedy and I'll give you what I've found out here. But—I walk out in three minutes."

"I'll make you no promises, Beckett. I'm willing to listen, and if you seem to be in the clear—"

"Horsefeathers. You know I'm in the clear. Where's the head? Whoever killed Le Marr took the head with him. I haven't got it and it isn't here. That lets me out. I'll play ball with you—on my terms. Otherwise you can stew in your own juice. Now make up what passes for your mind fast—I'm not waiting till the M. E. arrives."

Sloane stood red-faced, shot a sidelong glance toward the other plainclothesman, who had finished phoning.

"Oh, I guess you're all right, Beckett," he said judicially. "I won't hold you. Let me hear what you have to say."

Beckett smiled faintly. "Over there." He pointed, stepped around Sloane, went back to the table, picked up the Investor's Manual. "This is a book put out as you can see, by Hardy and Wilmerding. I called them. Le Marr was a trader in their office—an active trader. A customers' man named Corcoran handled his business. Three days ago, Le Marr closed out his account. Yesterday Corcoran—James J. is the full—checked out of his hotel, leaving no forwarding address. You can probably get his description from the Granby Hotel. I think Corcoran and Le Marr had some business together. Corcoran went to work for H. and W. at the same time Le Marr opened his account there.

"This afternoon, just after you left my office, Le Marr called me on the phone, told me he was in danger over a business deal and wanted me to protect him against an expected attack on his life. I came down, got here too late. I've been poking around for about twenty minutes. That's all."

Sloane eyed him anxiously. "Sure you're not holding anything out, Beckett?" he said.

Beckett took one of his buttons, flicked it against his fingernail. "Listen, Sloane—I think you're about the dumbest guy in the world. So I'm going to tell you exactly what I think. This is straight—and it's my honest opinion. If you can find Corcoran and make him talk, you'll have this case and two others, all sewed up. But—I don't think you're smart enough to beat me to it. So long."

Beckett walked to the door. The copper barred his way, looked anxiously at Sloane. Sloane said: "All right," and Beckett turned down the hall. The copper behind him called to the one at the head of the stairs: "O. K., Schwartz, leave him by," and Beckett went down the stairs.

CHAPTER FIVE

Death Spot

A LITTLE knot of three people, including the bald-headed man, were clustered around the bottom of the stairs. With the easy freedom of old acquaintance the bald-headed man inquired: "What's the matter up there?"

Beckett shrugged. "Mr. Le Marr is very sick." Then he stopped suddenly, looked at his wrist-watch, stepped up close to the bald-headed man. "I'll just use your phone, if you don't mind," he said and flashed his badge.

The bald-headed man's eyes widened. "Sure, sure," he said hastily. "Martha—show the gentleman the phone."

Beckett went into the apartment, preceded by a trim-looking girl in a wrapper, with honey-colored hair and a very plain face. She led him to the rear of the apartment, indicated a room that corresponded to the bedroom above. Beckett closed the door, dialed his office.

Thalia Morton answered wearily: "Beckett Private . . ."

"Sam, baby. Find out yet?"

"Oh—not yet. But listen—I tried to tell you before, but you hung up. Barton called and said to tell you that the old lady at the Carrolton—Etta Wrongley—claims she never ordered any bonds from her brokers. They were sending downtown then for the letter she is supposed to have sent them. I don't know yet how it came out. He hasn't called back since."

"O. K. Keep after the laundry mark hard. It means a lot if we get it. I'll be in shortly, I guess—or I'll phone again in a few minutes. 'By."

He hung up, went back out. In the living room, the bald-headed man and the girl were waiting with an older woman. Their eyes followed him in curious question. At the door Beckett paused, bowed. "Thanks very much. If you ever have any trouble just ask for Sergeant Sloane."

The bald-headed man beamed. "That's all right, sergeant. Hell—"

Beckett noded gravely, went out, went through the two doors of the house, stopped on the stone stoop once more, pulled his coat tighter, stood looking carefully around for a minute.

The police roadster was parked, empty, before the house.

The sky was pitch black now. Street lights gleamed fitfully through the snowfall as the white flakes dropped with ghostly silence, giving the street a queer, hushed feeling. It also made the visibility terrible.

Beckett started down the steps, hard blue eyes trying to pierce the darkness. He stopped halfway down, worked the gun from under his left armpit into his coat pocket, kept a hand on the butt, went toward Sixth.

One Fourteen and a Half stands exactly in the centre of the block between Sixth and Washington Square. The Sixth Avenue corner—the south corner—formerly housed three apartment buildings and a block of stores fronting on Sixth. Some obscure plan, evidently abandoned since the depression had set in, had removed all those buildings, left the corner a broken, pitted clay bog. Between Beckett and the lot lay a solid block of maybe ten houses, all of more than average height. They seemed almost to close over the narrow street. The heavy, falling pall of snow, and the inky blackness overhead made the short canyon ahead of him an ideal spot for any lurking trouble.

And furthermore, Beckett was expecting trouble—soon.

He took the outside of the sidewalk, cat-footed along, one hand tight on the gun in his pocket, sharp eyes raking the shadows of the buildings as he came abreast each one, stalked slowly past.

Nothing happened.

IT WAS almost with a feeling of bewilderment that he found he was past the last house and in the radius of the glow, feeble though it was, of the Sixth Avenue street lights. He stopped, turned back, looked along the street behind him, finally shrugged, went on toward Sixth.

With a tremendous, high-pitched roar, a motor suddenly accelerated in the road behind him. Beckett spun round, tugging at the gun in his pocket. It stuck. A huge, black monster of a car, lightless, seemed to leap in the air toward him. Beckett cursed wildly, tried to dive aside.

His foot treadmilled on the slippery walk; the front tires of the car hit the sidewalk; the driver spun the wheel. A front mudguard slammed Beckett's buttock, seemed literally to mashie him from his feet. The terrific force flung him fully fifteen feet through the air. He was flipped completely over; landed with a thump that knocked the breath from his body. He skidded, slipped, rolled head over heels on the slimy clay, pitched head foremost into a shallow pool of water.

The icy water helped. Gasping, coughing dirt, he kicked himself over to the right, landed on his back. His head was spinning; and he was ill at his stomach.

Mostly, he was furious. He fought the giddiness, strove for breath. His eyes cleared. The picture behind him was suddenly visible. The car had come to a stop. It's lights were on. The rear door was swinging open. A huge, gorilla-like man was racing toward Beckett. Fifteen feet behind came another, smaller man. Both were slithering, sliding. Beckett put all his strength into an effort to rise, found himself hopelessly mired. The big man reached him, raised his arm. Beckett saw the blackjack as the man dived at him . . .

Crashing orange flame spurted from Beckett's hand. Three staccato yammering reports split the night. No one was more surprised than Beckett. He had forgotten the gun. The big man was blasted back by the force of the shots, seemed to hang in the air a split second. Beckett scrambled wildly, futilely; the heavy man crashed on top of him, screeching, clawing at his chest, but the blackjack had fallen from his hand.

Beckett fought like a wildcat to shake free, managed to get his hand around the man, pumped crashing lead in the direction of the car. There was a yelp of pain, then footsteps receding. Beckett heaved mightily, slid the big man off his chest; the little man was racing, ducking low, one hand holding his elbow, back toward the big sedan. Beckett steadied himself on one knee, looked along his sights, jerked the trigger.

The gun clicked futilely. Cursing, he threw it down, dug to his other armpit holster as he leaped to his feet, stumbled in pursuit. The little man reached the car, dived head foremost into the open tonneau. With a clashing of gears, the car seemed to leap forward. Beckett threw down, aimed for the driver, let a full clip of cartridges roar and stammer from his hand, before he realized the glass in the car was bullet proof. The

car shot across Sixth, speeding with incredible swiftness, swung across Gay and disappeared.

A block away a police whistle was bleating. Scattered pedestrians were running toward the vacant lot from all directions. Beckett turned back, hurried to the side of the groaning hood, dropped to one knee beside him, ripped open the man's topcoat.

His shirt and suitcoat were warm, sticky. Beckett located the two bullet wounds in his left breast. The man was as good as dead.

FOOTSTEPS were clattering on the sidewalk; blurred figures were visible through the falling snow. Beckett shot a quick glance over his shoulder. There was no one yet within fifty yards of him. With practised fingers he made a lightning search of the gorilla's pockets. There were two letters in his inside pocket. They went into Beckett's.

A flashlight stabbed through the gloom. Beckett straightened, took the man by the shoulders, shook him. The man groaned, opened his eyes, spoke through twisted lips. "Gemme a doc, fer—God's—sake—I'm dyin'—"

"You'll die here," Beckett clipped ominously, "if you don't talk fast. Why did you jump me? Who sent you for me?"

"Oh, God, gemme a doc—"

"What'd you jump me for?"

"The lighter, fer God's sake," the man groaned, "the lighter ya took—" A sudden spasm of coughing shook his frame. The beam of the flashlight struck suddenly into Beckett's face.

"Put yer hands up, you!" A harsh voice barked from behind the light. A gun gleamed. Beckett stood up, raised his hands.

"Holy hell! Murder!"

"Not at all, not at all," Beckett said

stonily, but the copper was on one knee beside the wounded thug. "Stand still, you!" he shot at Beckett, kept the gun trained on him, holding both him and the thug in the beam. The man on the ground suddenly stopped coughing; blood was streaming from his mouth. His eyes took on a glassy stare, and his jaw sagged open.

Beckett said: "All right, Moynihan, he's dead. How's for me wiping some of this real estate off the face?"

The copper looked up sharply. "Who's that? Beckett?"

"Yeah."

"What happened, Beckett?"

Beckett drew a coat sleeve across his mouth, with a net gain of nothing, spat, cursed. "This bird and another drove up in a car and knocked me over. Then they came after me with a sap. It's around somewhere. I plugged this one and winged the other but he managed to make the car and get away."

"Who are they?"

"Ask me."

FROM different directions, more coppers arrived breathless. More lamps came into play. The arrivals shot hurried questions at Moynihan.

Beckett said: "You know, I'd just as soon go now, Moynihan."

The copper looked worried. "Hell, Beckett—you can't walk out on this!"

"Don't be like that," Beckett said reproachfully. "I've got places to go. You can always get me when you want me. Where you going to take the stiff? Precinct?"

"No. Headquarters'll probably take it over. But, honest to Gawd, Beckett— I'll get hell—"

"Why?"

"Well, Cripes—you're the only witness, and—"

"I can't give you any description, Moy-

nihan—hell, it was pitch dark, as you can see. There's nothing I can add to what I just told you. I'm not going to take it on the loop. Tell you what—I'll give you my word to show up at H. Q. within an hour and a half. Great Scott, man—you going to let me catch pneumonia? I'm soaked through!"

"Well, look—why not come along to—"

"I'd like to—but I can't do it, pal. I'm on a hot trail. After all, they don't hand out private licenses for nothing. You're strictly sanitary if you let me go home to change my clothes."

The copper shoved his hat back on his head, bewildered. "Well, gosh—"

"Thanks, Moynihan. I won't forget this." Beckett stepped quickly around the body, and strode toward Sixth Avenue, the target of astonished stares from the crowd.

He hit the pavement, walked half a block north, flagged down a cab. When the driver swung in and caught a look at the condition of Beckett's clothes, he hastily reached back and barred the door. "*Unh-uh*—not in my cab, buddy!" he said and would have moved on.

"Ten bucks," Beckett said wearily.

"To where?"

"The Universal Building."

"Leave us see that ten."

Beckett dug it out gingerly, handed it to him. The driver examined it carefully, pocketed it. "Get in, brother."

Beckett got in, fumbled for the switch to the drop light, as they moved away from the curb. When they were two blocks north, he got out the letters he had filched from the dead hood.

Both were in a woman's handwriting. Both were addressed to Jake Fitch in care of M. Le Marr, 114½ Waverly Pl. N. Y. C., which was a disappointment. Beckett took them out and read them. A girl named Peg had evidently been a very intimate friend of the addressee. She called him "Jakey dear." The envelopes were postmarked Santa Barbara, Cal.

CHAPTER SIX

Smith

WHEN Beckett pushed open the door of his office, Thalia Morton was saying in a weary voice: "Well, for Pete's sake, he said he'd be in or phone me—that's all I know. No, I don't think—"

The broad-shouldered young man facing her swung around as the door opened. "Ha!" he said.

"Hello, newshound."

Thalia Morton half rose. "Oh, Sam—your clothes!"

"Yeah. Bad, eh? Any luck on the mark?"

The girl's face was pale and drawn. "Not yet. Lord, there's an awful bunch of laundries in this town, Sam."

"Stick to it, baby. It means a lot." He pushed on through into the private office. "Come on, scribbler. I'll catch you up."

Black followed him in, closed the door behind him. "The note to Hardy and Wilmerding asking for the bonds was a forgery, Sam, but what a forgery!"

"You hear anything about what just happened down in the Village?"

"No. What?"

Beckett shucked his mud-caked coat, went over to a cupboard in the corner and got another coat, practically the same, but seam-worn and rusty. "Get your pencil out. Ready?

"All right. What I pinched from the corpse at the Carrolton was a diamond-inlaid cigarette lighter. A hawk-nosed gent tried to get me to come to his place, just as I was leaving the Carrolton. When I turned him down, he had me followed in a big car. I gave the mugs that were following me the slip in a subway sta-tion, and came on up here. I no sooner got to looking over the lighter than Brother Sloane busted in and glommed it away from me. While I was busy tearing my hair, I got a phone call, supposed to come from Maxton Le Marr, down on Waverly. He offered big money for a bodyguard, so I went down there. There was a little hood following me—at least he was following me when I was getting close to the house. When I went into Le Marr's apartment, there was a corpse without any head, sitting in front of the fire. From the clothes, it was obviously the same gent that had tried to waylay me at the Carrolton.

"I poked around the apartment. Some-body had dropped a handkerchief with a laundry mark on it, that didn't belong to Le Marr. I'm tracing that now. There was also a little handbook of stocks on the table with 'Hardy and Wilmerding,' plastered all over it. I phoned their of-fice, found out that Le Marr had had an account there—a big one—and recently closed it out. Big traders don't usually close out accounts so abruptly unless they've had trouble with the firm, Bart. The customer's man that handled Le Marr's account is named Corcoran. I tried the hotel he lived at, but he'd checked out two days ago.

"Just when I was leaving the apart-ment, in walked the stuffed shirt again—Sloane. Get an earful of this: that fancy cigarette lighter belonged to Maxton Le Marr. Well, Sloane tried to monkey round and make me some trouble. I pointed out that he couldn't do anything till he found that head—"

"What head?"

"The corpse's head."

"Where is it?"

Beckett grunted disgustedly. "Probably in some incinerator by now. I don't know, and I don't care."

"Why do you suppose it was cut off?"

Beckett shrugged. "Perhaps revenge—or maybe there was something around Le Marr's neck they couldn't get off. How the hell should I know? That angle will work itself out in time. Anyhow, I tipped Sloane off about this customer's man—Corcoran. He's probably broadcasted the description, and they'll be on the lookout for him everywhere. Nevertheless, I'm convinced that Corcoran is only a minor part of the proposition. He probably had a clear record, and this gang of thugs got hold of him some way and got him into Hardy and Wilmerding as an inside man. There's at least three others—Durso, a bird named Fitch, and—well, I don't know who else."

Black looked puzzled. "Fitch? How'd you—"

"Don't rush me. When I left Le Marr's apartment, a car came up over the sidewalk at me, and knocked me kicking into a vacant lot. Two hoods were on the running board and they came after me with a blackjack. I killed one of them, and I think, winged the other one. The one I killed was named Fitch. Then—"

"Give me the details of the fight, Sam. That's good for a puff."

Beckett did.

"Great," Black said enthusiastically. "Let me phone."

"Horsefeathers," Beckett said. "This stuff isn't for publication yet. Wait a couple of hours and I'll give you the go-ahead, and also a finish to it—one way or another. Tell me about that note."

"Note? I did tell you. It was a forgery."

"Yeah. Well, that opens it up. This mob burgled the letter box to get something with Etta Wrongley's signature on it, then forged another letter to the brokers asking for delivery of those bonds. They waited till Hardy showed up with them and then robbed him."

"And killed him."

"And killed him. They seem pretty loose with their trigger fingers. I guess they must all be pretty badly wanted. Well, I don't just see where Le Marr fits in yet, but I will. Meantime—"

The door flew open. Thalia Morton, flashing-eyed, stood in the doorway. "Sam! I've—Come out a minute."

Beckett nodded at the desk. "Go ahead and phone, Barton—but just the story of the fight, mind." He went out, closed the door behind him. "Plug in a line for the newshound," he directed.

"I've got it, Sam!" the girl announced breathlessly, jamming in the plug. "I've got it! It's a man named Smith at Sixty-four Morton Street."

"What is?"

"The mark! The laundry mark!"

"Oh, the laundry mark."

For one minute Beckett stood with his hands in his pockets frowning, then hatless, walked out.

MORTON Street is a street of many angles, and twinings, narrow; the buildings are high. At night, few windows seem to be lighted—at least at seven-thirty at night. Beckett got out of the taxicab at the corner of Seventh Avenue. His guns, holding fresh clips, were in the pockets of the fresh coat.

Quietly, yet at a quick walk, he slipped up the silent street, limping a little from the bruise on his hip. A young woman, hatless, her hair like a boy's, wearing flat-heeled shoes, hurried past him, eyed him antagonistically. Far ahead of him, the Ninth Avenue elevated rumbled by.

He walked by Number Sixty-four without stopping. It was a musty, narrow, ancient house. A flight of brownstone steps led up to a porch. Brass letter boxes gleamed inside a vestibule off the porch. Inside the hall a single incandescent globe hung from the ceiling, vaguely visible through the cheap curtain on the front door.

Four houses down, he swung casually and came back, stood in the shadow of the steps a minute, inspected the front windows of the house. On the ground floor, over his head, was a sign "Adele Richard—Hemstitching." There was no light in the window. The only lighted windows in the front of the house were one on the second floor, one at the very top. The third and fourth floors were dark. The second-floor window had the blind drawn.

Beckett went up the steps, looked over the bells. Adele Richard's was the first one. He read them all, found no one by the name of Smith. But the third bell in line had a vacant name plate.

Beckett peered through the glass panel of the front door. The house was narrow. There were evidently two apartments on the first floor. He looked back at the bell plates speculatively, went back to the stoop, looked up at the lighted window in the second story, then gave the bell at the extreme opposite end from Adele Richard a short push.

After a minute, the door clicked. He opened it silently, slipped inside, eased it closed, stood waiting.

Far above, a door opened. High heels clattered on the floor boards, ceased. A shrill feminine voice called: "For Miss Barclay?"

Beckett said nothing. There was another moment's wait, then the heels went back across the floor. A door closed.

Beckett started up the stairs, avoiding what creaks he could. When he reached the second landing, he took both guns from his pockets, hefted them in his big hands, hesitated.

The hall was narrow, small. The staircase up which he had come bounded it on one side. The doors of the two apartments on the floor opened toward the front and rear of the building respectively, not into the side wall. A single, dim bulb burned in a wall bracket in the center of the side wall.

A greasy card, thumb-tacked to the panel of the door at the rear said: "Peters." There was no card on the other door.

Keeping close to the wall, his rubber-soled shoes deadening sound, Beckett moved forward. When he reached the light, he unscrewed the bulb, plunged the hall into semi-darkness. A tiny sliver of light shone through the keyhole of the door before him.

He went up and put his ear close to the door.

MUTTERED voices and the sounds of movement came from within. Something heavy was slued across the floor. Someone spoke in short syllables, but the words were indistinguishable. Beckett bent down, put his ear to the keyhole, just in time to hear a key grate in the lock. He straightened quickly, dropped one gun hastily into his pocket, stepped aside. The door opened.

A hand carrying a suitcase emerged, set the suitcase on the floor. A voice said: "—hell with it. I'm going."

Beckett grabbed the hand. In one fast motion, he jerked the hand down, twisted hard. The owner screamed with pain, fell forward. Beckett jerked the arm up, spun him round, gave him a knee heavily, let go. The little man plunged headfirst across the room, took a nose dive onto the cheap carpet. Beckett stepped right into the room after him, his gun trained on the heavy-featured man whirling from over a second suitcase with one hand diving to his waist band.

"Hold it!" Beckett snapped. "Hands away from you!"

For a split second the other hesitated, and Beckett's finger tightened, then he complied. His hands came out. The little man was scrambling to his feet. "Lie still!" Beckett barked, "And keep your hands stretched out over your head!"

The little man was still, lay face downward. Beckett came on in, heeled the door shut behind him.

"I suppose your name's Smith," he said to the heavy-featured one.

"Yeah. And whoever you are, you're going to get—"

"I can remember," Beckett said, "when it was Tom Durso."

Silence.

Durso cleared his throat. "You've made a mistake, mister—"

The little man on the floor had edged his head around. "Beckett!" he bleated and subsided once more. Durso's eyes gleamed, and he snapped his lips closed.

Beckett nodded. "Good memory for faces, wart, eh? Well so have I. Get your hands higher, Durso, and turn around."

Durso raised his hands instinctively, then flushed. "I suppose you're talking to me."

Beckett shrugged. "Play your little games if you must, Tommy—but watch the muzzle of this cannon. I feel nervous. Turn around."

Durso turned. Beckett held the gun against his neck with one hand, ran the other over Durso's person. There was a hammerless revolver in his waistband and a pair of knucks in his hip pocket. Beckett threw them over by the door on the floor.

"Over in the corner, Tommy. Hands high and the face to the wall." Beckett said. "You on the floor—get up, and don't let those hands wander around. I might think you were trying something funny and I don't fool around when the case is murder."

Durso walked toward the corner. "You

must be screwy, Beckett. Murder. Hell, we—"

"When it's your turn to speak, I'll let you know," Beckett said, and reached down and grabbed the little man by the slack of the coat, helped him to his feet. With quick fingers he frisked him also, reaped a small-caliber automatic, added it to the pile.

"Now you in that corner, Moses," Beckett said. As the little man walked to the second corner, Beckett shot a quick glance into the next room. Beyond it the bathroom door stood open. It was a small bathroom, and all visible through the door. It was empty, as was the bedroom.

Beckett asked in a matter-of-fact voice: "Where's Corcoran?"

No answer.

"All right, then. Where are the bonds?"

Durso said to the wall: "What's your proposition, Beckett?"

"None to you, sweetheart. You're worth cash on the hoof—among other things. The rat over here might get himself a break if he's not in too deep. You hear me, squirt?"

Durso said in a harsh voice, "You keep your trap shut, Ike. This guy's four-flushing."

BECKETT stepped over and slashed Durso hard across the ear with the gun barrel. Durso cursed, whirled. The blood ran down the side of his face. Beckett put the muzzle of the gun in his face and he stood glaring impotently. "You dirty—!" Durso burst out. "You'll get yours."

"You'll get yours in about one second, greaseball!" Beckett snapped. "The next time you open that face, to be exact. I'm getting tired of treating you nice. Turn around. Hurry, or .... Now stay there."

He dug in his hip pocket for a pair of cuffs, had them half out when he caught sight of a coil of insulated light-extension wire by the floorboards. He decided to save the cuffs, use the wire. There was none too much of it. He shackled Durso's hands behind him economically. Durso said nothing.

He walked over to the corner where the little Jew was standing, examined the raised hands with interest. They were slender, white, almost feminine.

"The penman, eh?" Beckett said in a surprised tone. "I was wondering where you came in. Hold your hands together!"

When he had twisted the last of the wire around the Jew's hands, Beckett swung him round. "Now, brother—you talk. Don't bother to lie, because I know most of the story. If you do try a fast one, I'll pistol whip you within an inch of your life. And answer fast. What's your name?"

"Cohn. I—Ike Cohn."

"You're the penman in this mob that forged the letter to Hardy and Wilmerding. You copied the signature from the letter that Durso and his pal glommed from the letter box. Right?"

Cohn swallowed, licked his lips, said nothing.

"Where are the bonds?"

"I swear I dunno, Beckett! I swear it!"

"They're in this room somewhere, eh?"

"No! I mean—I don't know—No, they ain't here."

Beckett hefted the gun in his hand. "I suppose your big shot's got them."

Cohn shot a worried look at Durso, nodded his head quickly.

"Where is Corcoran?"

"Out. He—he ain't been here since this morning."

"You expecting him back?"

"No."

"What!" Beckett roared.

"No. I—that is, I don't think so.

Geez, Beckett, don't jump on me like—"

Beckett compressed his lips, glared down into the shifting, beady eyes. "Save that stuff. Where were you heading for with those bags?"

Sweat rolled down Cohn's face. He opened his mouth, closed it, cleared his throat.

"Come on, come on," Beckett said impatiently. "I—"

A voice from the bedroom said mechanically: "Attention all cars—all cars attention!"

CHAPTER SEVEN

Two Birds and a Bullet

BECKETT whirled toward the sound, eyes narrowed. For a moment, he had forgotten the radio in the next room. Then, as the police broadcast continued, he relaxed, stood listening.

"Wanted for murder—James J. Corcoran. Age 34. Height five ten to six feet. Eyes brown. Hair brown. Figure slender. Slightly stooped. Wears horn-rimmed glasses. Last seen wearing dark blue topcoat and black felt hat. Is armed and dangerous. Officers will not hesitate to shoot this man on sight. That is all."

Beckett grunted, swung back to Cohn. "That's who you're waiting for, Cohn, isn't it?" he rapped out. "Don't lie. I heard you talking when I came in. You were waiting for Corcoran—the brains of this outfit, weren't you? Weren't you, damn it?"

"Y—yeah, but—"

"But what?"

Durso coughed. Cohn said: "Well, yeah."

Beckett took the second gun from his pocket, reversed it as he strode toward Durso. His voice was harsh, quiet. "I told you to keep quiet, Durso. Now by God I'll show—"

Outside in the hall something scraped

against leather. Beckett stopped dead in his tracks. The two hoods looked round slowly, curiously. Beckett's lips tightened. He tiptoed across, slowly, noiselessly, to the door, listened.

The sound of breathing was audible on the other side of the door.

Durso suddenly shouted at the top of his voice: "Scram chief! It's Beckett!"

If Beckett had locked the door; if he he had thought to bring the suitcase inside when he entered the apartment, or possibly if Durso hadn't chosen to shout a warning, the man outside might have escaped. As it was, he didn't have a chance. Beckett cursed in his throat, snapped into split-second action before the first syllable was well out of Durso's throat.

He yanked the door open; a dark figure in felt hat and top-coat was crouched over the keyhole; in his hand was a blued-steel revolver. Beckett swung hard with the automatic, crashed down on the hat; he clamped the man's gun wrist in one bony hand, jerked him across the threshold. The listener tried to shout; Beckett hit him again, on the side of the head. The blued-steel gun skidded across the room; the intruder dived heavily to the floor, slid a foot or so, and then lay still.

Beckett stood looking down at him a minute, then satisfied he wasn't shamming, gave the door a shove too. It hit the prone man's shoes, checked. Beckett stooped down to lift them out of the way, but his eyes were on Durso and they were cruel, hard. "Now I'll attend to you, wise guy!" he rapped out—and stood stock-still staring at the shoes in his hands. He blurted softly: "Holy Judas H. Priest!" dropped the feet hastily, stepped up and turned the man over, ripping off the felt hat.

It was the newshound, Barton Black!

For just a moment, Beckett stood purple-faced with exasperation and disappointment. Then his lips clamped together and he whirled toward Durso, his eyes flaming.

Durso was watching him, trying to edge along the wall. Beckett clubbed one gun, trained the other on Durso's abdomen. "Freeze, Durso! Or I'll give it to you way down low!"

Durso's face went pale as he read Beckett's eyes. For a moment, they stood facing each other across ten feet of carpet. Then Beckett started toward him.

A cold voice clipped from the doorway: "Stand right there, Beckett—and drop those guns!"

AT twenty-one, Beckett joined the cops. At twenty-nine, he held a first-grade rating and a sweet record. For seven years since, he had operated the agency with important success. In short, he was a good cop. Morally, it's true he rated no medals. Physically, he was nothing to write home about. But he had that peculiar quirk of mind that leaps instantly from a premise to a conclusion, eschewing the clumsy process of reason. Hunches, intuitions, whatever you call them—Beckett had learned to lean on them. Now, in the fraction of a second that he hesitated, no one could possibly run over the pros and cons of the moment. Behind him stood a cold-blooded killer with four corpses on his back trail. That Beckett was designed for the fifth seemed obvious. Surrender now meant death later at the whim of the man behind him. If he forced the man to shoot, it would arouse immediate pursuit—maybe. Unless the man were a dead shot, there was a chance that Beckett might close the case right here and now with his own thirty-eights. That the man would get the first shot was inevitable, but. . . .

Almost at the invitation to drop his guns, Beckett flung himself to one side, dropping to his knees, twisted. . . .

Crashing orange flame spurted from the gun in the man's hand. A pillar of red-hot, searing fire slammed down from the skies on Beckett's head, knocked him wildly over backward. Vaguely he felt his guns drop from his hands; there was a sudden scream behind him. Then blackness, as of a tremendous storm, seemed to race toward Beckett.

Miles away, someone said: "Dead." Then a scurrying. Then the slam of a door.

Three quarters stunned, blind with shock, fire leaping and raging in his brain; a buzzing, flashing, roaring pounding at his ear drums, Beckett lay entirely unable to move hand or foot. His senses seemed to no longer have connection with their organs of use. Yet even in the instant the bullet hit him, he was waging a terrific fight to retain consciousness.

Something—maybe the thickness of his skull, maybe the force of an ascetic-like will power—kept him from lapsing into complete insensibility. Beckett was no pigeon. The hard-faced agent had taken it before. Even so, the bullet that had plowed a furrow across his scalp should, by all standards, have laid him on the ice for most of an hour. Yet it didn't. The room rocked, spun crazily round under him. Wave after wave of nausea swept up from his stomach, yet he fought them grimly down, fought down too the temptation to relax.

How long he fought, he had no idea. It seemed like all eternity, before he finally gained control of his body once more.

EVENTUALLY he opened his eyes. The room floated giddily before him. He groaned, moved a little, put his hands to his throbbing temples. There was blood on his face, caked. He got one palm on the floor, struggled to rise to a sitting position. The effort nearly wrung a cry from his lips, as a piledriver came down inside his head. But his almost lost vitality was surging back into his veins. He gritted his teeth, struggled, staggered to his feet.

The room was in semidarkness. Only one bridge lamp was burning in the corner under a black-fringed shade. He tried to take a step, almost lost his balance, stumbled dizzily across the room, brought up against the wall.

The consciousness he had fought for returned. He felt the light switch directly under his hand, turned it on, flooded the room with light, fumbled across to a window, managed to get it open. For a few seconds he let the shock of the icy night strike against his face, drew in deep lungfuls of the chilled air, felt infinitely better. Then he turned and looked at the room.

Barton Black still lay just inside the door. Two chairs were overturned. The bag still stood open on the couch. On the floor in the corner where Cohn had stood was the slashed wire that had bound him. In the corner where Durso had stood. . . .

Beckett's head was suddenly clear as a bell. He stared incredulously, wiped the particles of dried blood from his eyes, looked again. There was no mistake.

Stretched out on the floor, his hands still tied behind him, a great pool of blood staining the carpet under his head, lay Tom Durso, shot through the throat.

Uncomprehending, Beckett strode hastily across the room, a bewildered look on his hard face.

Durso was quite dead. His eyes were wide open, staring. The bullet had evidently severed his jugular, probably snapping his spine as well.

Then sudden illumination burst like a rocket in Beckett's brain. He swung round, looked at the door, identified his own position when the shot had creased his skull. The grisly, ironic suspicion became a certainty.

He had been directly between Durso and the man who had shot him. The same bullet that had knocked Beckett down, had killed Tom Durso!

He dropped to one knee by the dead hood, but was barely down before he was up again, cursing his own stupidity. The blood had not yet dried on Durso's wound. Barton Black still lay unconscious from a not too severe blow. Centuries though it had seemed, no more than two or three minutes had actually, could actually, have elapsed since Durso was shot!

Cursing, he whirled toward the window, clambered out onto the fire escape, glanced hastily up and down.

Half a block away, racing toward Eighth, were two shadowy figures—one short and small, hatless—the other tall, carrying a flapping brief case in one hand.

Beckett made a queer noise in his throat, took one step downward, cursed wildly, ran back and into the room. He scooped his two guns from the floor, then leaped out again, and raced down the iron stairs.

Strangely, the shot seemed to have attracted little attention. Two people were standing outside the house gazing up curiously as Beckett dropped the last few feet to the cement. They meant little in his life. He lit running, winced as his head gave a throb, pounded on along Morton.

THE bend in the center of the long block of Morton between Seventh and Eighth hid the fugitives. Beckett put his head down, clenched his teeth, and ran, coat-tails bellying behind him, hatless.

He hit the bend, saw them, a hundred yards ahead of him and not ten feet from the corner. He threw up his right-hand gun.

Bang! The echoes caromed in the narrow street. Cohn stumbled, clutched at the tall man's arm, almost threw him off balance.

Bang! Beckett's gun roared again. The tall man was shaking Cohn off. Beckett's second bullet sent the little Jew crashing forward on his face. He did a queer half-somersault and tumbled into the gutter. The tall man swung round; his face was a dim blur in the darkness. Beckett snapped two quick shots at him. Three long spurts of violet belched from the tall man's hand. Beckett heard the snick of a bullet past his ear, ducked out into the road, and then the tall man was gone around the corner. Beckett sped on.

He raced past the little man, shot him a hurried glance. The street light shone down on the contorted face. It was Cohn, all right. When he reached the corner, swung wide, the tall man was diving into a taxicab eighty yards away. Beckett looked down the sights of his gun, jerked the trigger. Two shots blasted out before he loosened his finger. They rang metallically against the body of the cab. Beckett cursed. The cab snorted, shot away, raced up the street.

Beckett jumped to the middle of the road, waved his arms wildly. A touring car almost ran him down. Beckett sent a shot into the air, danced till the man was almost on him, forced him to a screeching stop. He jumped away just in time, then was back in an instant. He leaped onto the running board, poked the gun through the open window.

"After that blue taxi, buddy," he snapped, "and fast, or—"

The scared motorist let in the clutch suddenly, almost jerking Beckett from his perch. They stammered forward, then speeded up, roared northward.

Inch by inch, they gained on the taxi.

Beckett dug awkwardly in his pocket for a spare clip of shells, crouched low, the wind whipping through his hair, flapping his coat-tails. At Eleventh, there was suddenly a clear path between them. Beckett aimed low for a tire, jammed the trigger home, and kept it there.

Six stammering, racking reports boomed out. The sound of the bullets against the cab was distinctly audible. Beckett's startled driver swerved suddenly, almost ran over the curb, jerked back onto the road. Beckett cursed silently. The only score was the shattering of the red lamp on the tail-light of the taxi. An oddly angled shot must have shattered the ruby glass. The tail-light now gleamed white.

Traffic was light, but getting heavier. The driver's swerve to the curb had cost them distance. The taxi had increased it's lead.

Beckett roared into the car: "Faster, you mug!" The driver did his best.

Cross traffic was getting heavier. Beckett warned loudly: "Don't stop for any red light!"

The driver nodded hastily, his face white. They pounded on.

CHAPTER EIGHT

Sloane Slams a Door

HUDSON Street merges with Eighth at Abingdon Square. The bobbing white tail-light suddenly swerved, disappeared to the left. Beckett shouted wildly: "Left! Left on Bank! They're headed for West Street."

The driver said nothing, ducked to the left-hand side of the street, made the sharp twist into Bank on two wheels. Beckett heard him gasp a prayer as the car rocked over the curbing. Then they were straight again, shooting down Bank.

The turn at West was easier. They shot out under the shadow of the elevated runway; the tires screamed on the rough paving.

Fifty yards ahead was the taxi. Even as Beckett looked, they ducked across, ran on the wrong side of the street. The Gansevoort wharves loomed only a short distance ahead. Beckett roared once more at the driver: "They're trying for the docks. Block them in! Swing wide!"

The driver obeyed, swung to the right, ducked a pillar of the elevated.

The taxi whirled out of sight, to the left, behind the Cunard warehouse.

"Stop!" Beckett barked, and the driver tried to slow down, made it jerky, almost broke Beckett's neck, finally checked the hurtling speed of the car. He was scarcely at rest before Beckett was off the car. He swung across to the left, raced toward the piers.

The white tail-light of the taxi was still visible, at the side of the last warehouse fronting the dock. Beckett ducked into the shadow of the overhanging lip of the sheds, ran, suddenly emerged onto the wooden planks of the dock.

Far at the end of the pier, the brief case still flapping in his hand, ran the tall figure. There were two or three piles of bales on the dock. The fugitive raced, ducking low for them, dashed to the shelter of the first pile.

Beckett sprinted after him, caution lost in the furious intensity of the pursuit.

Two vicious red flashes, and the bark of the tall man's gun roared out; something hot and heavy slammed Beckett in the shoulder, spun him round, he lost his balance, fell scuttling on the dock. He twisted, got to his feet in a flash.

Two new clips were in his automatics now. He ran toward the bales, the two guns spouting flame in his hand. He let four bullets from each gun stream into the pile of bales, stopped.

From behind the flimsy wooden structure came a choking groan, then the sound of a crashing fall.

Beckett's lips twisted into an ugly smile. He walked toward the pile of bales quickly, shot a hasty glance over his shoulder. The dock police had not yet been aroused, apparently. The pier and the dock sheds in sight all seemed to be deserted.

He approached the pile of bales cautiously, stopped, listened.

Labored, painful breathing, almost a wheeze, came from behind. Beckett suddenly ducked down low, dived from the shelter of the bales in one long leap that carried him almost across the pier.

One single crimson flash roared almost in his face, but his move had saved him. In the same instant, his own right-hand gun blazed furiously, almost automatically, raked flaming shots into the kneeling, dark figure behind the bales. The man gave a queer shriek, was blasted clean from the dock, tumbled wildly over backward. His gun skidded from his fingers; he hit the boards with a crash, lay still.

Beckett waited, half crouched, breathing heavily, one finger fooling with the safety catch on his left-hand gun.

There was no motion.

He approached, knelt down, put his hand inside the man's coat. The clothes were warm and sticky. His heart was not beating.

Beckett's head was throbbing again, furiously. For a moment, he bent it down, bit his lip to clear it. It let up a little. He fumbled for a match, turned the dead man over full on his back.

In the glare of the tiny illumination, he looked down at the unmistakable, thin, still slightly red face and narrow, curving, hawk nose of—

Maxton Le Marr!

Beckett grunted, dropped the match.

He put his hand into Le Marr's breast pocket, took out a leather wallet. Without inspection, he jammed it into his inside coat pocket, got up, looked back along the pier, searched around, located the brief case and Le Marr's gun. The gun went into his hip pocket. The brief case was ripped open; Beckett's hand plunged inside, felt the crisp crackle of official paper, pulled some part way out. Even in the fitful light from the dock lamps far off, he could see that he held bonds in his hands.

He snapped it shut, turned and ran back down the dock.

When he rounded the corner of the warehouse, the taxi was still standing where he had last seen it. His own car had vanished. Beckett frowned, ran toward the taxi, gun ready, sprang onto the running board, barked: "All right, but—" and stopped.

The taxi was empty. Beckett blinked, got down, looked around, down the alley up which they had come, found nobody in sight. He looked at the tires of the car.

The rear left was flat as a pancake.

Far away, in the direction from which the chase had begun, came the screaming of two police sirens.

Beckett's forehead creased. He ran around, looked at the dashboard. The ignition keys were still in the lock. He jumped in, flung the brief case in beside him, trod on the starter.

The cab came into life. He hastily backed, turned round, shot out to the street, the flat tire *bump-bumping* on the rough cobblestones. He swung south on West Street, speeded up to a moderate thirty, rattled on.

Two blocks ahead of him a police cruiser suddenly whirled round the corner, came toward him, a giant searchlight flashing from side to side. The beam caught him full in the face for a moment, held him, then passed on.

Beckett grinned faintly, speeded up.

THEY had taken Cohn to the morgue. When Beckett pulled the thumping taxi in to the curb before Sixty-four Morton again, all the cops in the world seemed to have congregated there. A half dozen newspaper reporters were circulating around. A huge crowd had gathered.

As he braked to a stop, two harness cops turned toward him angrily. One of them snapped: "Get to hell out of—"

Beckett climbed out. "At ease, boys. It's me—Beckett. I did most of the shooting around here lately," and strode across the walk. They let him go. Somebody repeated his name in the crowd and the newspapermen heard it. They were all over him in a minute, shouting questions, but he shook them off, went right on in.

Two more cops were in the lower hall. Beckett flicked a hand in greeting. "Hello, Humphries. Hello, Kramer," and would have passed up the stairs.

Kramer said quickly: "You can't go up, Beckett. The sergeant said no one was to come up."

"Sergeant? Who?"

"Sergeant Sloane."

Beckett grunted. "All right. Go tell him I'm here. With Hardy and Wilmerding's bonds." He waved the brief case. The patrolmen's eyes stuck out. "Yeah?" He started up hastily. "Just a minute."

He came down, said it was all right, and Beckett went up.

In the front apartment, Barton Black, a wet towel around his head was sitting with his back to the wall, on the floor, looking green. He held the telephone in his hand, was obviously debating whether to use it. Two more uniformed men were standing around the room. The body of Durso was covered with a coat. Sergeant Sloane, his hands behind his back, was rocking to and fro on his feet, a pleased grin on his face.

As Beckett came in, Sloane waved. "Well, Beckett!" he said patronizingly, "I hear you got the bonds."

Beckett closed the door behind him. "Yeah, I got them."

"Good work, Beckett. Too bad you couldn't have been here to see me get Durso."

Beckett stopped, eyed Sloane narrowly. "You got him?"

Sloane waved a hand at the body. "There he lies," he said as though that removed the last shadow of doubt.

Black said nothing, but his eyes were questioning Beckett's face. Beckett turned round to him. "You phoned in that story yet?"

"No," Black said. "I was hoping you'd come back. I've given them everything you gave me up till now. They're holding the press for the rest of it. Let's go, eh?"

Beckett nodded. Sloane frowned, started across the room, "Now, look here—"

"Shut up," Beckett clipped harshly. "You listen in, dumbness, and maybe you'll find out what this case is all about."

HE SQUATTED down on the edge of a chair, spoke in quick tones, with gestures. Black set the phone beside him, took out a notebook hastily.

"Here's the whole story," Beckett said. "Use what I gave you before to fill in.

"This mob, consisting of Maxton Le Marr—don't interrupt—James J. Corcoran, a bird named Jake Fitch, Tom Durso and the little forger Ike Cohn that you picked up off the street, were working to snatch this half million in bonds. Corcoran, who was an employee of Hardy and Wilmerding, was their tip-off. How they contacted him is just one of those things—could have been done in a hundred ways. He tipped them off that this dame Etta Wrongley never used the phone. In other words, she wrote all her orders to the brokers.

"They waited around the Carrolton Hotel till they saw her mail a letter. The Carrolton has no letter box of its own, so she had to use the corner box. Then they waited for the mail collection truck, tried to hold it up. A postman recognized

Durso, so they gave both him and the driver the works.

"They took the letter, and this Ike Cohn copied the handwriting, sent a letter to Hardy and Wilmerding asking for this delivery of bonds. They picked their time and spot, and when Hardy showed up with the securities, they were waiting for him. However, he put up more of a fight than they anticipated, and during the fight, that cigarette lighter fell out of Maxton Le Marr's pocket. Evidently he was present himself at the stick-up. You know about the lighter and you know about my trip down to Le Marr's. Also the fight I had, when I killed Fitch.

"Now, this is my guess—I don't think you'll find it wrong. First of all, the stiff we found in Le Marr's apartment, was not Le Marr. It was Corcoran. I figure that Corcoran hadn't expected to be mixed up in murder. When he found he was, he got scared and I guess they thought he might squeal. They killed him, dressed him in Le Marr's clothes, left a book with Hardy and Wilmerding on it, knowing that someone would find it and check up that end. Obviously, it looked like Corcoran had killed Le Marr. The alarm was sent out for Corcoran, but none for Le Marr. All Le Marr wanted was twenty-four hours to make his escape from the country with the bonds. They cut off Corcoran's head, made that phony call to me, partly to try and get back the cigarette lighter which I had given the sergeant here, partly so that I would get the alarm out for Corcoran.

"However, you know about that. I came over here after I got the line on the handkerchief. When I arrived, Durso and Cohn were all packed up, waiting for someone. I got in tied them up. Then you knocked on the door. I thought it was their big shot—Corcoran—or Le Marr as it turned out. So did Durso. He shouted a warning and I whipped open the door and bopped you on the nut."

Black jerked his head up. "You?" he said incredulously, "Jesus—"

Beckett spread his hands. "I'm sorry, Barton, but hell, I didn't know it was you. As a matter of fact, Le Marr was right behind you. He got the drop on me, but I chose to shoot it out. In the shooting, they creased my skull, dropped me for a couple of minutes—and Durso was killed —get that, Durso was killed!"

Sloane said belligerently, "Now listen here, Beck—"

"Shut up," Beckett snapped angrily, "before you get yourself into a mess you can't get out of, Sloane!"

The copper subsided, his mouth open, his throat working. Beckett went on.

"I came to, chased after Cohn and Le Marr. I dropped Cohn at the corner here. I chased Le Marr to the Gansevoort piers and dropped him there. He had the bonds with him. I grabbed his taxi and drove it back here. I get the reward for the bonds, if any. I get the reward for the killers of Hardy, if any, and by God, I get the reward for Tom Durso, of which there is some!"

Sloane purpled. "You do like hell! I get—"

Beckett sprang out of the chair, tugged the gun he had picked up from beside Le Marr at the pier, from his pocket, shook it under the copper's nose. "There's the gun that killed Tom Durso, wise guy! Why don't you grow a brain? I shot Durso, and I shot him with this gun. You can play hell trying to get away from that. I've got proof!"

Sloane tried to say something, choked, turned his back and strode out into the hall, banged the door behind him.

One of the coppers said hesitantly, awkwardly: "You—you shot him down with his hands tied, Beckett?"

Beckett stopped stock still in the center of the room, eyed the copper evenly for a long minute.

"Yeah," he said. "What about it?"

MANY HAPPY RETURNS!

WHEN this issue of the magazine appears on the stands DIME DETECTIVE will be exactly a year old. And that is why we append the conventional birthday salutation at the top of this page. The phrase is a peculiarly apt one to use in relation to our own anniversary for "Many Happy Returns" expresses almost literally the results of the magazine's first twelve months' existence, both from our own standpoint and—if enthusiastic letters from readers may be taken as an indication—from the point of view of all you people who have found DIME DETECTIVE MAGAZINE a continuing source of pleasure and diversion.

More than a lot of water had flowed under the proverbial bridge since the day last November when "The Shadow of the Vulture" threw its eery spell of mystery and horror over detective-story fans all over the country. Since that time the magazine has increased steadily in circulation and popularity until, finally, it has reached a point where it no longer has to take its hat off to its elders. The youngster has—in the short space of one year—become a man. And what a man!

Here's a prediction. With more and more of the same and richer sort of thrill fare with which we have been stuffing it —that's a promise!—by this time next year the man will have become a giant and—but that's enough of that. We've tooted our own horn a good deal in the pages of this department during the past year and now we're going to give you elbow room to tune up and play.

For example—here's D. E. Thompson of Syracuse, N. Y., who says, "I always thought I had to pay 20 or 25 cents to get quality but when I tried DIME DETECTIVE the first time, believe me, I got 25 cent quality for a thin dime—"

And Jack Darrow, who writes in from Chicago, and has been a reader of the magazine from the first issue. He states, "Reusswig has done the best covers I have ever seen on any detective magazine. I hope that DIME DETECTIVE will soon be published twice every month—"

And Mrs. O. H. Bernhard of Omaha, Neb., who writes, "I am very disappointed this month—" (Oh—oh! That doesn't look very propitious.) "—because you left out the Cardigan story. That's the first story I always look for. Of course the author could die, but I hope not—" Well, the rest of the letter makes everything all right. No, Mr. Nebel is far from dead, or Cardigan either. And for the benefit of all his fans we want to say right here that during the next year that big dick from the Cosmos Agency is going to be with us regularly.

And Harry L. Coppola of Watervliet, N. Y., who says, "Your magazine is getting better and better by the issue and I hope you keep it up. You sure have first-rank authors and I don't mean—"

And F. M. Finley of Oakland, Calif., who writes, "I feel as though I had gotten in on the ground floor of a good proposition when I picked up the first copy of your great little (?) magazine—"

And Verle R. Hillman of Bellaire, Kansas, whose regular letters of criticism and comment almost every month have been much appreciated—

And—and—and—

We wish that there were room to include all of the loyal boosters. Maybe we'll have to issue a supplement to the magazine some time just for that purpose. But then anything the size of a mail-order-house catalogue would be a fairly bulky proposition. At any rate we want you all to know that we do appreciate your interest and trouble in letting us know what's what about the magazine.

Call again. We're going to be right here for a long time to come!

123

www.ingramcontent.com/pod-product-compliance
Lightning Source LLC
Chambersburg PA
CBHW080911020726
47502CB00008B/2421